JUSTICE COMES DUE

JUSTICE COMES DUE

BIRTH OF HEAVY METAL™ BOOK 7

MICHAEL TODD

MICHAEL ANDERLE

DISRUPTIVE IMAGINATION

LMBPN Publishing
PMB 196, 2540 South Maryland Pkwy
Las Vegas, NV 89109

First US edition, August 2019
Version 1.04, December 2025
eBook ISBN: 978-1-64202-426-5
Print ISBN: 978-1-64971-675-0

JUSTICE COMES DUE TEAM

JIT Readers

John Ashmore
Jeff Goode
Dave Hicks
Kelly O'Donnell
Jeff Eaton
Dorothy Lloyd
Deb Mader
Peter Manis

Editor
Skyhunter Editing Team

DEDICATION

To Family, Friends and
Those Who Love
to Read.
May We All Enjoy Grace
to Live the Life We Are
Called.

CHAPTER ONE

I need this finished so I can move on to the next phase. Dammit. Why does it always come down to having to wait for things to fall into place? I'm a mover and a shaker, not a sitter and a quaker.

There was a time when she would have enjoyed sunbathing surrounded by people who professed to love and adore her as their benefactor. Today, however, she separated herself from the sycophants—such an ugly word but so true, she thought acidly—and devoted herself to the challenges she faced.

Sitting out in the sun, enjoying the view, was still a pleasurable experience. Her house in Ibiza was on the water and looked over one of the highest-end beaches in the area. It regularly saw celebrity DJs and musicians perform for the young or newly rich who came to enjoy their winter vacations to a wide variety of upscale music.

But today, she barely spared a glance for her surroundings. Worry nagged insistently at the back of her mind and demanded her focused attention. It had been there ever since she had talked to Salinger Jacobs and he had shared his thoughts on their chances of surviving their foolishness.

Or was it greed? Either one is possible. Except the scientist seemed to have a set of values that outstripped hers, so perhaps the former was more appropriate for him. Or he simply wanted the glory and rewards of scientific discovery?

Whatever his original motives might have been, "royally fucked" had been his exact words. She traced a finger along her veins with a scowl and studied the vibrant blue that spread so insidiously. With a mild flutter of panic that seemed to creep in more often lately, she couldn't help but feel he was right.

I may be royally fucked but I will not give up. There has to be a way—something I can do to overcome this and turn it to my advantage.

Molina wasn't the type of woman to go quietly into the night. She would continue to fight and try to find what she was looking for until she died or...whenever the journey she was on reached its end. It was a tough way to live but it was the life she had chosen.

Despite the inherent anxiety, the situation also provided a challenge she enjoyed. That was why she persisted in her search through the details he had retrieved from the lab and left for her in exchange for her life.

So, instead of watching the beautiful people outside tanning, swimming, and drinking, she chose to dig through the information that could save her life.

And what better time to do it than now while I wait for that chapter of my life to close and a new one to open?

An abundance of technical shit had been collected by the specialists she'd hired to examine the data and she scanned the laptop with some attempt at eagerness. She had the assurance that they didn't mind keeping everything they looked at confidential, irrespective of what they found and whether it was simply groundbreaking or utterly horrifying.

She knew for a fact that they would find a plethora of both in the files that had been transferred.

They kept her updated regularly on their findings, and since she couldn't share precise details of the problem she needed to solve, she had to sift through the mountains of data they sent her on almost a daily basis.

At first, she had thought that it would be easier to find what she was looking for—some kind of cure for the changes she could feel and see overtaking her body and spreading like a weed. Most of what she read—couched in scientific jargon that, quite frankly, bored her overactive mind—simply went over the top of her head but she persisted. Perhaps if she waded through it enough times, something would stand out.

If Sal wants to think he is royally fucked, let him. I will not be beaten so easily.

One of her usual staff members stepped out of the house with a tray that didn't have a drink on it and she sighed with relief. She knew what he brought, given that she had left her phone in her room to help her focus a little more on the work she did outside. *Not that I found anything of note.*

Admittedly, there were ideas discovered in the lab that would jump her pharmaceutical stocks ahead by at least three or four years of research. People hated the moral problems that came from human testing, but the fact remained that it worked, whether they liked it or not.

The call on the buzzing phone carried to where she was seated at the pool was a solution rather than a problem.

Perfect timing. She glanced at her watch and smiled, relishing the simple truth that the long wait was over.

"A phone call for you, ma'am," the man said in English with a soft Latin accent. He was the type she generally fell for, but Molina was feeling something for someone else at the moment. Besides that, she was too busy with everything else to care about her love life.

"Thank you, Jorge," she replied and stroked his wrist gently as he turned away. While she wasn't interested now, it didn't mean she wouldn't be in the future. She would consider it an investment.

He smiled at her before he returned to the house. She picked the phone up and glanced at the number to confirm it wouldn't be traceable. It met her expectations, mainly because she had invested a great deal of money into making sure that was the case. She had insisted that she receive this call since the pilots tended to be a little paranoid about who listened in on their operation and had balked when she made it a non-negotiable condition.

"It's very simple, gentlemen," she'd told them. "Aside from the fact that I intend to be a part of this, albeit from a distance, there is no way in hell I would trust a complete stranger with critical information. You will have to call me to obtain the code that will enable you to fulfill the mission and be paid."

The hundred thousand Euros that had arrived in their bank accounts made them more amenable to her stipulations—and, hopefully, capable of following her directives without argument.

After all the uncertainty that had surrounded her since this whole debacle had started, it now appeared it would finally reach the logical conclusion. She wanted to be sure it happened.

In all honesty, if the pilots selected for the mission had been problematic, she could have simply made sure someone a little more receptive to her purposes would replace them after they faced some kind of injury or death in the family. People in that corner of the world had languished under oppressive and corrupt puppet regimes for decades, which meant corruption was a way of life that seeped into almost every element of their daily existence.

It truly was weird how communism inspired this kind of pure capitalism, she thought with a small smirk.

Molina always got what she wanted. Except, of course, for finding a cure for possibly poisoning herself with alien blue goop. But that was still a work in progress. She anticipated success, even if it wasn't clear at the moment.

"Are you connected to my comms, ma'am?" the pilot asked over the deafening roar of the helicopter's rotors in the background. Chatter from a few people was muted but barely audible. She assumed the man had a copilot and perhaps a gunner or two added to the mix, given where they would fly into.

"I have audio," she replied and leaned back in her seat.

"Unfortunately, there will be no video coverage of the operation, so you'll have to settle for listening in while we operate," he said crisply like he talked while he worked. It would be difficult to access the biodome, so she would have preferred to know his focus was on the objective rather than talking to her.

"The biodome hatch is now open," the pilot reported, perhaps to ensure that his crew was advised of the status rather than simply Molina herself. She assumed the men would remain vigilant. They were under no impression that this would be a milk run. It could be but given what they knew about the Zoo and what had been reported to be inside the dome, they would undoubtedly be as careful as possible.

"I see movement on the sensors. Do you see anything?" the man asked his gunners, and from the sudden thunder of massive machine guns, the men behind those guns had chosen to shoot first and ask questions later. From what she'd heard and read of Heavy Metal's team and their experiences while inside the fucking dome, the team in the chopper were certainly wise for taking that approach. While the plan was for the helo to remain airborne and not land, they could never predict if or when the alien creatures would finally develop wings—at which time they would be in the shit.

She couldn't question the decision to simply annihilate the mutants on sight. They intended to wipe the place off the map anyway, so a few monsters having an early taste of what was to come was irrelevant.

"There's far more movement coming from the biodome," she heard through his headset.

"Maintain fire. You know the drill," he responded and displayed an impressive amount of cool-headedness as he worked to both keep the chopper in the air as well as connect the UI of his aircraft to the servers. They had decided this would be a more effective method to activate the failsafe that had been built into the lab and the dome to allow anyone inside to destroy the entire facility if something went wrong.

"Server connection established. Connecting to the failsafe sequence now," he confirmed calmly.

Originally, she'd thought to simply use the remote activation device she'd been assured would work. Until, of course, someone had pointed out that the Zoo had a habit of scrambling signals. Based on the fact that the Heavy Metal team had lost contact with their hacker during their mission, they had to assume that communication into and out of the dome wasn't possible.

It seemed entirely stupid to take the chance with something that would most likely not work and miss the opportunity to obliterate it before it became even more of a problem. Thank God, someone had thought to create the failsafe in the first place or, in Sal's words, they'd be "royally fucked" in more ways than one.

It begged the question, though, of exactly how bad things had become for the people who were in there that none of them could see the real danger and take the necessary steps to end it. They'd either waited too long and been overwhelmed or it had happened too quickly and suddenly for them to react. They had been scientists, not soldiers. All of them had been thoroughly briefed on the dangers of anything getting out of control inside that dome. Regrettably, they would always have that moment of uncertainty, a lack of commitment to their duty that most soldiers had in spades and so could usually be counted on to do what had to be done, no matter the consequences for them or others. That small difference had allowed everything to go to shit.

If she ever decided to attempt something like this again, she would make sure the failsafe button was in the hands of someone who wouldn't consider the morality of blowing themselves and their coworkers the hell up. Personally, if she had to.

"I have successfully accessed the failsafe protocol," the pilot said over the steady drone of gunfire in the background. "Setting the timer for sixty seconds. Please advise override code." She spoke clearly and concisely, and he repeated it as he entered it into the system. "Failsafe activated. T-minus sixty seconds to detonation. Pulling out of the biodome now."

More gunfire erupted and Molina's heart thudded in her chest. Honestly, she would have triggered the explosion even if there were anyone inside. Some people would say that was heartless and the unnecessary deaths would be a detriment to morale, but it had been that kind of thinking that had caused all the problems there in the first place.

"Clear of the biodome. Sealing the hatch," the pilot said and still sounded calm and in control, although she could hear a hint of tension in his voice. Once they were clear and the hatch was sealed, the explosion would be contained within the dome itself to cleanse all the mutant beasts from the earth.

It's a real pity the same can't be done with the monsters in the Zoo, Molina thought and no longer paid much attention to the phone call. She would have preferred to see—or someone else see and confirm—that the explosion did happen. Given the magnitude expected based on the enormous quantity of ordnance used to create the failsafe, no pilot in his right mind wanted to hang around longer than he had to. She would simply have to accept that the disaster would be completely obliterated and move on.

"Hatch closed," the pilot said and now allowed himself a soft sigh of relief. "Moving out before detonation. Mission accomplished."

"Good work," she said and cut the connection. That was one problem solved, at least, she thought and scowled when the sight of the blue veins in her arms suddenly brought her mind back to the problem with such an elusive solution. She would need to keep working on that.

For now, though, she had other plans to put into motion.

"Jorge?" she called, pushed slowly from her seat, and stretched languidly before she turned to see the man already there, waiting for her instruction.

"Could you get the car ready for me?" she asked. "I have an appointment I need to attend to."

"Of course, ma'am," he said quickly and hurried away to alert her driver that she was ready to head to the private airstrip. Heavy Metal remained a problem, but for now, all she could do was stick as close to them as she could. *And I have an idea of how to do that.*

Unfortunately, it required her to travel to Philadelphia in the middle of winter. The thought alone made her shudder.

It wasn't that he didn't appreciate being home. Despite his current predicament, there were more than enough reasons to celebrate. Getting out of an area that was considered one of the most dangerous on the planet alive—and in reasonably good health—was always a plus. Being able to see his family in Russia was good too. The fact that most of his finances had been transferred to the kinds of countries that would keep the additions to his accounts away from the grasp of the corrupt Russian tax collection agencies was even better.

Remember, Gregor, you don't have that much to complain about. You could still be in the Zoo.

He reminded himself of this more than once and glowered at his manacles where he sat an uncomfortable wooden chair. It looked like it had been bolted to the floor since the Stalin era. For now, he waited for a military tribunal to have a chat with him about what had happened in the Zoo while he'd been there.

His present situation did contain a few severe negatives, but he constantly compared these to his escape from the snapping jaws of massive monsters that evolved from the DNA of creatures that were found on earth and were twisted into nightmarish horror stories by alien goop.

Yes. When you look at things from that perspective, why be afraid of the bureaucratic nonsense a military tribunal can throw at you? Even a firing squad is not so bad. It is much better to be shot close to home than eaten and shat out of an alien panther or another monster.

He was in Moscow, about fifty kilometers from the hospital he'd been born in, and he couldn't feel bad about that despite his circumstances.

A group of bailiffs stepped out of the courtroom and strolled to where he was secured in the abandoned hallway. It had been a while since he'd been to one of these trials, and he'd never attended as the person accused. The few times when he had been called ended with him having to testify for or against a couple of his senior officers. He smiled inwardly when he recalled that he'd told the truth about them maybe half the time.

It was all a political show anyway and it wasn't like they would give him the benefit of a fair trial. They already knew what they wanted to do with him, and everything that transpired there was to make sure it was all in the books and completely sanctioned by the powers-that-be.

The bailiffs released Gregor from the chair but cuffed his hands in front of him before they pushed him silently toward the doors of the courtroom.

"Quickly now," one of the men said and shoved him again. "With luck, this will take only a few minutes and we can get the hell out of here."

"I shall do my best to not delay your smoke break," he responded sarcastically. "It is merely my life, after all."

"Well, maybe you'll get lucky and you won't end up like that one."

It appeared he had been called immediately after another sentencing, as a man was led off in chains by a team in uniform. He frowned and bit back a retort as he realized that didn't bode well for his case. Then again, he had long since given up on even the hope of reprieve. It was inevitable that he would go to prison.

"Regarding the case of Lieutenant Gregor Popov," the judge said as he leafed through the case file like he already knew what he would find in there. "Taking a mission from the FSB and including a foreign entity, thus risking our national security."

It wasn't like he'd had a choice in taking the mission. Besides, the operation as a whole had been a success. All they were looking for was someone to throw under the bus over the death of their pet project since apparently, no one wanted to touch Jacobs, Kennedy, and Monroe. Then again, he didn't want them to get into trouble because they had helped him, which was why he had left individual names out of his report. It was a professional courtesy that had not been extended by the scientists the Heavy Metal team had put their lives on the line to rescue.

Perhaps some thanks were in order. He hadn't been given access to the specialists' reports, but him saving their lives might have been enough to keep him away from a firing squad.

The witnesses came forward. They'd neglected to call any of the members of the team he had assembled and only brought in a handful of the scientists. Of those who were present, he recognized one of them as the man who had been the most incensed when their test subject was killed by Sal, and he was the only one whose statement felt sincere. The others looked like they had been ordered to deliver their statements or face a similar fate as Gregor did. He didn't blame them. They had careers ahead of them that would be brought to a standstill if they were put in one of the military prisons.

The judge looked up from his desk, which had concealed what looked like a phone as the last witness finished her statement. The man looked rather bored but that only confirmed the suspicion that his fate was already decided.

"Does the defendant wish to plead guilty to the charges?" the judge asked and leaned forward as he waited for Gregor to answer.

Wait, plead guilty? You ask that now after all the evidence against me is already presented? Maybe this was how military judgments were delivered, but he hadn't been provided with legal counsel either. It was like they had gone out of their way to make sure he knew there was no way out of this.

"I...plead guilty?" It felt better to frame it as a question —less like an admission of guilt he hadn't earned and instinct rebelled against. He glanced at the group of high-ranking officers, which he guessed included many people who wanted this to go in a very particular way.

"If you were to deny yourself the right to appeal this hearing, this court would be willing to offer you five years of detainment in a minimum-security facility in Volgograd," the judge continued and made no effort to look up from the files—or phone—on his desk. Gregor couldn't be sure which. He startled when one of the bailiffs placed a paper in front of him and shoved a felt-tipped pen into his hand. Inanely, he wondered if that was because most other pens could be used as weapons by the more violent prisoners.

The paperwork was a declaration to confirm that he would not be prosecuted further and the matter would be considered resolved as long as he made no appeals to the verdict handed down by the judge in his hearing. His sentence would constitute a five-year detainment period in the minimum-security prison in Volgograd, where most of the lesser offenders of military backgrounds were sent. He was even presented with the option of being released on parole after he had served two years.

It was a generous offer and a very clear sign that some people very high up on the food chain wanted this matter resolved with all the loose ends tied and no possibility of the press—national or international—catching a whiff of it. He wondered if it had anything to do with the elections that were coming up.

Gregor sighed, knowing full well that this would be the best offer he would ever get. Honestly, if he tried to fight it, he would probably end up in one of those pre-trial facilities that were known for inmates spontaneously committing suicide.

He signed his name hastily at the bottom of the sheet, which was collected and passed to the judge.

This way, he could possibly get out on parole in the allotted two years due to the prisons being a little overcrowded. His family would be able to visit in the meantime, and maybe once he was out, he could ask Sal, Courtney, and Madigan for a job since his time with the military was indisputably at an end.

The judge looked at the paper that had been signed,

added his scrawl quickly at the bottom, and pounded his gavel briskly.

"Lieutenant Gregor Popov, I hereby dishonorably discharge you from your position as lieutenant and remand you to the custody of the Ministry of Internal Affairs to serve out your sentence, which shall begin once you are delivered to the Volgograd Minimum Security Detainment Facility," the man said in a quick and practiced speech. He motioned for the bailiffs to take him away. "This court is adjourned."

The other high-ranked military officials in attendance stood and had already begun to march toward the exit when an aide stepped into the room. He rushed to where the judge was currently in the process of leaving the room for a lunch break. The official paused as the younger man whispered something in his ear and gave him a file and a phone. He narrowed his eyes and raised his hand to stop the bailiffs from escorting Gregor away. The former lieutenant narrowed his eyes and wondered what the delay could be.

At the judge's instruction, he was brought back to his seat while the gathered officials whispered amongst themselves.

"Lieutenant Gregor Popov, due to extreme circumstances that require your expertise, the Ministry of Defense has determined that you will not be remanded into the custody of the Ministry of Internal Affairs and that you be reinstated to your original rank," the judge said quickly but looked annoyed at this highly irregular turn of events. "As such, you will be returned to your post in the Sahara Desert. Your new orders will be provided to you en route. Do you have any comments that you would like to add to the record?"

They were returning him to the Zoo. Fuck. "Honestly, I would prefer to carry my sentence out here if it's all the same to you."

"Your comments have been noted," the man stated. "Dismissed."

They began to move away again, and the judge ordered the bailiffs to uncuff him as a couple of uniformed members of the military police arrived to take custody of him.

"Lieutenant," one of the men said, waiting until the other officers had left the room. "We are here to escort you to the Kubinka Airbase where you will receive your new orders and ship out tomorrow at first light. If you will come with us?"

Gregor shrugged. It wasn't like he had any choice in the matter, right? "Can you tell me why my circumstances have been changed so drastically?"

As he predicted, though, neither man answered him and instead, made their way smoothly to the door, expecting him to follow. It was for the best anyway, he supposed. Neither of these men was likely to have been read in on the topic and if they had, they probably weren't in any place to discuss it with him lest they end up in a very similar trial as the one he had just experienced. Although, he thought with sardonic amusement, it would probably have a very different outcome.

Some people would consider themselves lucky that they had avoided prison. For himself, though, he couldn't help a sinking feeling that told him he was exchanging a comparatively short punishment for a death sentence. "Death by Zoo" was what some of his comrades had called it back in the day—back when they still had veterans running the base.

He was escorted outside where two vehicles with black military plates waited for them. Once they climbed aboard, both of the armored light utility vehicles eased away from the sidewalk where they'd been parked and set off to the airbase where he had landed about a week before.

CHAPTER TWO

Damn, this view is utterly spectacular.

Sal grinned, stretched lazily, and leaned back to enjoy the massage provided by the jets. The jacuzzi was perfectly positioned to make the most of the sweeping vista. Some people said money couldn't buy happiness and while he might have agreed with them at one time, these days, he was more of the opinion that they simply didn't try hard enough. That was a little materialistic of him, of course, when he soaked in a warmed jacuzzi the hotel-slash-casino had somehow fit on their penthouse terrace, he didn't much care.

An appealing sense of decadence surrounded the tub, prompted by the sweeping view of the city below and the ocean beyond—or, to be accurate, the Mediterranean Sea.

Without a doubt, this seriously kicks the ass of every other vacation I've ever taken.

The bar was set low, admittedly—he hadn't lived the high life before—but that didn't mean he couldn't enjoy their time there. They were away from the Zoo and had left Davis to take care of the compound. Anderson handled the business end of Pegasus while Savage and Terry shuffled papers and did what admin tasks they could while they recovered.

Things were a little hectic with the shares on the market but not the kind of hectic that had them shooting and being shot at, which allowed them a little downtime too. Everything else essentially ran on autopilot, and there weren't any issues that needed personal attention from any of the three of them. While Anja finished her vacation and returned to the compound before the Russians tried to take a crack at her again, they would have some them time.

Madigan soaked in the jacuzzi with him and wore her sunglasses in the way he had come to recognize as her taking a nap. He had never seen her this relaxed before. *It's a little scary when I think about it. What if she doesn't want to go back to being the hard-ass who keeps us all in line for our safety?*

As if she could read his thoughts, she tilted her sunglasses up and met his stare with a raised eyebrow.

"Are you enjoying the view?" she asked.

"No," Sal replied quickly. "I mean, yes, of course. Always. But that wasn't what I was thinking about."

"Pray tell, what were you thinking about, Dr. Jacobs?" she asked as she let her sunglasses drop into place and leaned against her cushioned seat.

He knew it shouldn't, but a thrill traced down his spine every time someone called him Doctor. It wasn't necessarily the same chill that came when Madigan said it since that was reserved for her and Courtney, but it was nice to know that all his work had some tangible results.

"I simply thought that I don't think I've ever seen you this relaxed before." Sal chuckled and stretched forward to squeeze her shoulder. "It's a good look on you. I'd recommend you wear it more often."

"I won't lie, I've needed time away from the Zoo—and the compound," Madigan said. She smiled and lowered her head to place a kiss on the back of his hand. "That said, I joined your little Heavy Metal venture for the work and not the perks. About three more days of this relaxing and hanging around in the room, fucking and ordering room service, and I'll be itching for real action. A few more days of that, and I'll get into drunken bar fights down there in the casino. Somehow, I don't think the Monaco authorities appreciate visitors throwing punches at the millionaires who come here to gamble all their hard-earned money away."

"That's a good point," Sal admitted and leaned back as well. He sighed contentedly when the jets activated again to massage his back in slow, circular motions and decided he was reasonably sure he could get used to this kind of lifestyle. Although he probably still needed to work, even with the ten million that Molina had paid them for their trip into the Chernobyl lab burning a hole in his pocket. But he was lazy at heart, and while there was nothing quite like the rush he felt when he pushed his body to its limits in the Zoo, he was well aware of the cost of that now, and maybe it was time to start scaling back.

No, it felt ridiculous to even think about it. Eventually, he would get antsy for those combat-produced endorphins and he would charge in there with Madigan and Courtney. He merely wondered what his life could be like if he went back to being only a researcher, working in a lab and getting his data. While he would probably be called in to work a few late shifts, he would spend most nights at home, wherever that was.

He was well aware that he wouldn't think like this if it hadn't been for what they'd run into in Chernobyl, though. It was possible he might be experiencing post-traumatic stress, and maybe what he needed to do was talk to a professional about it. He probably would, eventually, but he needed to come to terms with what happened in there first and he doubted that he would manage that by talking about it to Courtney and Madigan. One would tell him to suck it up, probably, and the other would be overly concerned for his well-being and tell him to give up going into the Zoo or getting into combat situations entirely until he felt better. Oddly enough, he still wasn't sure which woman would take which approach.

"So, what do you think we'll do next, Sal?" Madigan asked and surprised him because he'd assumed she'd returned to napping. She placed her hand over his, which lingered on her shoulder, and squeezed it. "After our vacation time is done and we need to acquire more cash to stuff our coffers with?"

Sal shrugged. "I'm not sure. We could always keep going into the Zoo, taking samples, selling whitepapers, and collecting pita flowers and the like. Still, I can't help but feel we're simply reacting to everything the jungle has to throw at us. We know those tentacle monsters have been in there for a while but we didn't realize the implications at the time. It means there's still too much that we don't know about the place."

"Wait, we've known about those ugly bastards?" Madigan asked, suddenly a little tenser.

"Yeah, remember the tentacles that came down from the trees when we were dealing with Andressa Covington?" he reminded her. "I think it's rather safe to say that the creatures are one and the same, although we are waiting for second opinions to come in. Honestly, many of the experts have simply dismissed our findings in Chernobyl as crazy since there is no official record of any of the goop being used outside of the Sahara. So we're a little stuck there, unfortunately."

"Eh, I'll take your word for it over theirs any day of the week," she asserted. "That said, I don't think having only me believe you will be enough for you, so how do you think we can go about proving the doubters wrong?"

"First of all, you and Courtney believing and trusting in me are all the belief and trust I need," Sal said in an attempt at flattery. He was fairly sure it worked but restrained himself from a smirk. "Secondly...yeah, proving that we found Zoo-like shit in Chernobyl with the Russian and Ukrainian government swearing up and down that there was no secret lab there will be difficult. We'll need to find a way to prove our hypothesis another way. Maybe we could try to find one of the monsters in the Zoo and take some samples and get video. People already know something alive and with tentacles is in there. We merely need to prove what it is."

"Not to be a wet blanket or anything, but I'd put considerable money on those creatures being guarded by the biggest and the baddest the Zoo has to offer." Madigan grunted and looked like she did want to get some sleep in this time. "If we intend to do something like that, we need to pull it off with serious planning and prep time under our belts. Maybe a larger team? We could bring in a few friends and allies from around the different bases to provide help. Do you think Gregor would be down for a mission like that?"

"I doubt it," he replied and looked up when he heard Courtney raise her voice inside the suite. Despite the fact that almost everything ran on autopilot in Philly, they still needed to work with her and at least keep her in the loop on the company's decisions. Now that the stock sales were in progress, there was a considerable number of issues to keep her in the loop on. "He called us in when he was forced to go on an immediate run into the Zoo on the FSB's orders. If we asked, he'd probably say yes, but you don't want to force someone into a situation like that, you know?"

She nodded. "There's also the small point of him heading to Russia to face the music for asking us for help."

"Who told you that?" he asked.

"Anja said she was trying to help him by making sure some of the incriminating records disappeared," she explained. "I remember that specifically since she told me that if she disappeared randomly in the middle of the night and didn't come back, that would be the reason. Apparently, it was possible that the sharper trackers in the FSB might be able to find her based on what she did."

"Huh. Fair enough. Is there anyone else we might be able to call in for a job like this?"

She held off on answering and looked up as the glass door of the terrace opened. Courtney wore a deep-purple bikini draped with a long, elegant, and almost transparent sarong that was blue with yellow floral patterns. Her hair was done up like she anticipated some enjoyment of the day, but she looked stressed as she spoke into the phone.

"Yes." She growled and put Anderson on speakerphone to allow her companions to listen to the conversation as well. "I'm well aware of the fact that most of the stock purchases were made by me, but the rest of the board doesn't know that."

"They suspect it," Anderson replied. "Hey, Sal, Kennedy."

Madigan raised a hand in greeting and Sal nodded as their teammate joined them. The former colonel had pulled his weight as part of Courtney's team over the past few months, and while they had started on opposing sides, the man had more than proven that he was there to help.

"Suspecting isn't the same as knowing, Anderson," Courtney continued, sat on the edge of the jacuzzi beside Sal, and rubbed his shoulder gently. "As long as they don't know for a fact, they can suspect all they want."

"Okay," he conceded. "I'll try to play it off innocently but I'm not sure if I'm built for all this politicking."

"Don't sell yourself short, James," she encouraged him. "You're better at this than you think. Besides, people don't like to question the word of a military veteran."

"It's truly fantastic to hear that I can take advantage of my time in the military to pass as an honest man," he commented dryly. "And what about the...other matter we discussed?"

"You know I had nothing to do with that," she grumbled defensively. "It was resolved before I could help with it, and there's nothing I can do without pissing the board off more than I already have. Let Savage know about his role in this, and I guarantee he'll be more than happy to help."

"And if he isn't?" Anderson asked. "Knowing the man like I do, I think I can predict that he'll be a little... difficult."

"I think he'll go for this anyway," Courtney insisted. "If he doesn't... Well, we'll simply have to find a way around it. I don't think we should push him too hard since he's supposed to be recovering from his injuries. If he doesn't agree to it, we'll think of something else."

He sighed and nodded. "I'll see what I can do to get him on board."

"I appreciate it, James." She smiled. "Stay in touch."

She hung up and placed the phone and her sarong on a nearby table before she slid into the hot tub next to Sal and leaned her head on his shoulder.

"Problems?" he asked and raised an eyebrow.

"None that are close enough for me to care about," she replied and kissed his cheek tenderly. "And as nice as this hot tub is, I think I'm in the mood for a proper swim. What say the two of you that we head to the pools after lunch?"

Sal shrugged and looked at Madigan.

"I'm up for that," she said with a chuckle. "I've been meaning to give the bar they have up there a try anyway. It would be nice to have some company."

"Sal?" Courtney asked.

"Yeah, like I'd let the two of you run around this place without a chaperone." He laughed. "I'm in."

"How long do you think you and Bev will stick around here?" Savage asked and looked up from tinkering with his pistol to the woman seated across from him. She was fairly attractive in her tough Latina kind of way, but he was well aware that he wasn't her type.

After that conversation had occurred fairly early in their relationship, things were quick to develop into something similar to what he shared with Sam—not quite a brother-sister bond but one based on similar interests and shared experiences. Amanda Gutierrez was a woman to be reckoned with in the field as well as being a bona fide genius in combat engineering.

Ever since she'd arrived in Philly, she had spent considerable time in Savage's team's warehouse to examine and test the veritable arsenal of weaponry they had at their disposal. The fact that many weapons had gone missing from various laboratory facilities during Monroe's takeover meant it had been his job to retrieve those missing pieces. The insurance companies Pegasus had hired to secure their products began to pay out, and Courtney realized that if some of the equipment simply remained missing, they might come away with a profit as well as being able to arm and equip him and his team without having to pay for it—in dollars, anyway.

It left them with an arsenal that needed to be organized if they wanted to determine how it would be useful in the field. He could improvise as well as the next guy, but he was mostly old-school in his knowledge. While he could strip, clean, and put any weapon back together quicker than anyone else, when it came to finding out exactly how the more tech-based weaponry was supposed to work, he needed help. With Anja taking a little time off, he needed different help and Amanda had stepped into the role.

She appeared to relish it almost more than the vacation she was supposed to be on. He enjoyed watching her work and helped her in any way that he could. With the sale of the stocks, there wasn't much for someone in his particular role to do, which gave him the time to simply do what he loved—select and play with new weapons and watch sports.

Savage was a Seahawks fan and Amanda was, for some strange reason, not. Even worse, she was a Forty-niners fan. No one was perfect, he reminded himself.

"You've tuned me out for about fifteen minutes, haven't you?"

He looked up from the magnetic coil he was priming, blinked, and settled his attention on her. Amanda grinned like she'd caught him with his hand in a cookie jar or a pot stash. He wouldn't be able to bullshit his way out of this one.

"Yeah, sorry about that," he confessed and shook his head. "I've been focused on getting this stuff done right. There's no need for it to suddenly go wrong because the fine-tuning was off by a couple of millimeters, right?"

"Well, given that you're doing a better job of it than you did yesterday, I'll give you a pass on listening to what I said," Amanda replied, took the coil out of his hands, and replaced it with another one.

"What did you say?" he asked as he returned to his work with real enthusiasm. A small amount of pleasure came when he worked with his hands like this, although it would take a great deal of washing to get all the grease off.

"You asked me how Bev was handling being here in the States and doing all the touristy crap while I'm stuck in the warehouse with you," she said.

"Well, yeah, I remember that, obviously." He chuckled.

"Of course you do." She smirked. "And I replied by saying that while Bev is more than happy to run around the city in the dead of fucking winter and work her tourist yayas out, I feel far more comfortable in a nice, warm environment, working with my hands and teaching you how to not completely suck at this job."

"You're paraphrasing, right?"

"A cookie for the attack dog."

"Kennedy told you to say that, didn't she?" he snarked and the armorer laughed.

"Guilty," she replied.

"Well, not to be all sentimental or anything, but I'm enjoying my time spent around you too," Savage replied. "Even if you are a Joe Montana fangirl."

"How can one not be a fangirl of the greatest quarterback to ever play the position?" she quipped in response.

"Well, one couldn't," he admitted. "Which is why I wonder why you're a Montana fangirl."

She responded with a one-fingered salute before she focused on her work.

"Anyway, the point I tried to make was that while you're here, having the time of your...well, year, what is Bev up to?" he asked, changing the subject quickly. He didn't want to piss off the woman who had one of his magnetic pistols in her hand and knew how to use it.

"Well, I tricked Anderson's wife and kid into exploring the city with her," she replied. "She's a huge Rocky fan, so

MICHAEL TODD & MICHAEL ANDERLE

they spent most of yesterday going through the sights from the movie if her Facebook feed is anything to go by. As long as I show up for lunch and dinner in a slutty dress, Bev appears to be fine with it."

"Have you asked her about her feelings?" he persisted, finished the second coil, and pulled up the boot it was supposed to go into.

"Who died and made you Dr. Phil?" Amanda demanded.

"Well, I assume Dr. Phil would have to die for me to be Dr. Phil, but that's not the point," he replied with a smirk. "I'm only saying that while you're enjoying yourself here, I think Bev might have come over to spend time with you, engaging in both your interest in weapons engineering as well as her love of boxing films starring short Italian actors."

She looked up from her work. "And you would know this how?"

"I never claimed any knowledge," he replied and tried to shrug without letting it interrupt what he was doing with his hands. "But being outside a relationship—or most relationships—gives a guy perspective, you know?"

Amanda nodded. "Well, I guess I could spend more time with her while we're here. I'll talk to her about it at dinner later tonight."

"Which means I'm probably uninvited from dinner tonight," he added.

"Social convention dictates that I protest weakly," she pointed out and changed her voice to a slightly higher pitch. "Oh, no, there's no need for you to not come to dinner with us. I'll be able to have an intimate conversation with my girlfriend with you around."

30

"And social convention on my part dictates that I come up with a bullshit excuse to get out of your weak re-invitation." He altered his tone to deeper and more accommodating, but with a trace of humor. "Forget about it. I have a thing to do at that allotted time in the evening anyway. You two kids have fun."

She grinned. "Thanks, Savage."

"No problem. Besides, it's not much of a bullshit excuse anyway. I do have to be at the airport to pick Sam up. She's gotten far enough in her recovery that the doctors cleared her to travel, which means she'll leave sunny Monte Carlo and return to wintry Philly. Lucky bastard."

The armorer narrowed her eyes at him, connected the last piece of his combat suit, and motioned for him to pass her the boot he was working on. "So, when you decided to talk to me about how my relationship with Bev was going, you knew you would have to cancel dinner anyway and you started that whole line of questioning to get us on that topic?"

Savage handed her the boot. "I don't know what social convention dictates in this situation. I'll merely gloat over how genius my plan was and how well it worked while I puff an imaginary cigar."

"It was ingenious," Amanda replied with a chuckle. "And you managed to help my love life while you were at it. Maybe you are Dr. Phil."

He grimaced. "I'll pass on the job of having to track the craziest of basket cases to therapize because it makes good television, thank you very much."

"Fair enough," she conceded and finished the last

touches on the suit. "Are you ready to take this baby out for a spin?"

As it was mounted on a dummy, it didn't look like much. Amanda had explained that most of the power going into a combat suit was streamed through a single line of moving parts that powered all the suit's other functions. This meant, hypothetically, that if you were willing to sacrifice most of the armor, you could use most of the power functions of it with a quarter of the weight and even less of the conspicuousness of wearing the full combat suit.

Besides, with his particular model, there was more to be gained from having the power functions of the suit. The reactor on the back would power the pistols he had grown accustomed to carrying. While the selection of ammo would be a little more limited, he could still count on the weapon being considerably more powerful and versatile than the single pistol he'd previously used—in theory, anyway.

"Let's do this." He stood, rolled his neck, and began to strap the pieces of the suit on over his clothes. The gauntlets would need to be included, as they were what transferred the power from the reactor to the pistols in his hands. The boots would also need to be taken from the suit as they contained the coils necessary to allow him to walk and move in the added weight of the half-suit, which was still significant compared to no suit at all.

Once it was on, Savage immediately felt that it was a little bulky, but after a few minutes of jogging around the room, he was able to adjust to the strangeness and the unfamiliar demands. He let it carry him through most of the motions until he was ready to test it in practice combat situations.

The first Amanda wanted to try was two cinderblocks they'd picked up from one of the abandoned warehouses in the area. As tough as they were, they would provide the perfect testing ground for the physical capabilities of what he carried around.

He took a running start and picked up speed more rapidly than he thought he would, hurdled a few obstacles, and allowed the rudimentary software in the suit to guide him until he reached the first block. Slowing slightly, he ducked under an imaginary punch or shot and swung his fist at the block. The hand moved almost too fast and twisted his shoulder a little, but the result made it worth it when he watched the target shatter into a hundred small pieces.

"Huh." Amanda grinned. "That was awesome. Do it again."

He agreed with her on the awesomeness of the abilities and rushed to the second one, feeling a little more comfortable with the movements and capabilities of the suit as he reached it and punched with his left hand this time. The action brought the same result. He grinned and looked at her.

"Don't rest on your laurels yet, Robocop. We still need to try the weapons," she reminded him and he nodded and walked to the shooting range. Moving slower was a little more awkward. The suit was built for speed and agility, not simply walking around. He drew the pistol from his right holster and aimed it downrange at the dummy they used for target practice. They'd gone through their fair share of them, and after the fifth replacement, it didn't make sense to name them anymore. You merely got attached to the expressionless bastards that way.

He pulled the trigger and felt the whine of power that flowed into the pistol. The hint of lag lasted only a few milliseconds before the needles the weapon fired hurtled downrange. He wasn't too accurate at first since he was used to compensating for a kick that didn't materialize with these weapons. After a few attempts, he delivered six in a tight ring in the head and seven more in the chest.

"Why don't you use both pistols?" Amanda asked. "You have to admit it would look cool if you're into that...ugh, cowboy crap."

"It would be cool but in a combat situation, the eye can't track two firing lines at once," Savage pointed out. He checked the weapons and the power situation of the suit before he moved back. "When I'm in the full suit, I can let the software control the left hand. It takes care of aiming and I simply pull the trigger, but without an HUD, I can't do that."

"Good point." She grunted and rubbed her chin, deep in thought. "Maybe we can find some kind of smart glasses to plug into your suit that'll give you a rudimentary HUD to work with?"

"That's a possibility," he agreed and holstered the weapon. "And with a trench coat or something, I can cover the bulk of the suit until I'm in a combat situation."

"Yeah, people will definitely call shenanigans when you're suddenly able to jump over walls and punch through cinderblocks," she agreed.

"Screw cinderblocks, I'll be able to punch through

ribcages." He grinned. "I'm kind of looking forward to that. But unfortunately, this is the part of the afternoon where social convention dictates I tell you I have to head to the airport to pick Sam up. Do you want me to give you a ride?"

"Yeah, you could get me back to my hotel for a quick shower before Bev swings past to pick me up for dinner," she replied. "I noticed some fine-tuning issues in the suit that I don't think I need your help with tomorrow. If you could set it up on the dummy over there, that would be great."

"Will do." He began to place the pieces of his suit on the figure they'd kept it on while they'd worked on it before he locked the warehouse and they started back into town.

CHAPTER THREE

As it turned out, Bev was already waiting for Amanda at the hotel, which meant Savage needed to beat an even hastier retreat than he'd planned. Apparently, the sight of her woman covered in grease and sweat from when she was working got Bev hot under the collar. The two of them headed rather hastily to the room and left him with nothing to do but set out to pick Sam up.

He was happy their relationship was so healthy, he decided as he drew out of the parking lot of the hotel. The first stage of his journey took him to the nearby apartment building complex Terry had called home since he'd moved there more or less permanently from his house out in the middle of nowhere. He owned the whole area back home, the sniper had told him once while they'd been drinking, and he'd been looking into renting or selling. Courtney had, of course, made an offer on the land—more than what anyone else in the area was willing to pay for it—but since she would probably use it to build another one of her research labs, he wanted to think about it for a little while longer.

Savage sent the man a message on his phone to let him know that his ride to the airport was there. Terry had been the first to suggest that they pick Sam up when she arrived, which made him feel a little badly about his friendship with the woman. They'd decided they would pick her up together and would even throw her a little welcome-home party.

And that was about as far as they'd gone with the planning. Neither of them knew much about what Sam was interested in. She was big on guns, fighting, and weapons—and drinking and being promiscuous as a strong, confident woman who didn't need a man to make the first move. But other than that, they were a little lost.

They could always simply take her out drinking, of course, but given that she was coming out of recovery from serious injuries, Savage doubted that taking her out drinking while she was on what they could safely assume was a shit-ton of different medications was in good taste. Or safe, for that matter.

"Have you given the coming-home party any more thought?" he asked his companion as they pulled away from his apartment building.

"I have." Terry nodded.

"Do you have any ideas?" he persisted when nothing else was forthcoming.

"Not a one," the man grumbled and shook his head. "Come on, it's not like she knows we planned to throw anything for her. We can simply come up with something safe and secure. How long a drive is it to Disneyland?"

"On the other side of the country?" he asked incredulously. "I think you mean Disney World, in Florida, which...is also on the other side of the country but heading south. Besides, how old do you think Sam is?"

"Well, she's British, so I assume she never went there as a kid and she might want to go there now as an adult." He shrugged.

"Right, and after all the time you've known Samantha Davis, do you think she needs to get in touch with her inner child?" he asked sarcastically. "The one who wants to go out in the humid heat of Orlando, Florida, and deal with a horde of crying, screaming kids and adults who are either bored or dressed as cartoon characters. Not the one who likes to see things go boom."

Terry scowled at him. "That is a good point, but I don't hear you coming up with a better idea."

Savage made a face. "You make a good point too. But we can't take her to any theme parks. I don't think the first thing Sam needs when she gets back Stateside is the reminder that she has to have a sense of humor while dealing with the two of us."

"So, what ideas do you have stirring in that brain of yours?" the other man asked after they'd driven in silence for a few minutes.

"I'm still stuck on getting her to that new karaoke place on fourth," Savage ventured. "You remember how we had to drag her away from the karaoke section of the casino. That seems like the kind of inner child we could probably safely wake up inside her."

The sniper chuckled. "Yeah. Unfortunately, that place has a two-drink minimum, so unless we can somehow get her to pretend she's pregnant, I don't think we'll be able to sneak her in."

"How do you know it has a two-drink minimum?" he asked as they reached the edge of the city limits and began to wind into the hills beyond where the private airstrip Pegasus tended to use was located and where Sam would land in a half-hour or so.

"Well, she's not the only one with an inner child in need of awakening," Terry replied. "I happen to like singing, and when a friend of mine invited me for her birthday, I couldn't say no. You should hear me singing 'Journey.'"

"I fucking should." Savage laughed. "And would this friend of yours happen to be a girlfriend of yours?"

"We're not labeling it for the moment," he replied and sounded evasive. "But yeah, I spent the night at her place last night, so I think we might label it soon."

"Don't get too clingy too soon," he advised him. "Otherwise, the label you'll get is 'broken up.'"

"What the hell do you know, anyway?" his companion demanded. "You've bounced from one-night stand to one-night stand, all crazy women who obviously can't do any better."

"There's no need to be hurtful," he protested and veered onto the two-lane road leading to the airstrip. "I'm away from the whole romanticizing of relationships, so I think that gives me a little perspective on the whole thing. I'm not quite disillusioned by it yet, which means I'm not biased. My advice, therefore—should you choose to take it —is to be a good enough boyfriend to keep her coming back but don't be too pushy about establishing bound-aries. A rule of thumb is that if the girl likes you to be jealous, she's one of the crazies and you should leave her to me."

Terry couldn't help a laugh. "I'm sorry, I didn't mean to be hurtful. And honestly, that does sound like good advice."

"Well, thanks." He chuckled. "Besides, you forget that I used to be married myself, so I'm well aware of the pitfalls that could get you in trouble and have probably fallen into at least half of them, which gives me valuable insight."

Terry eyed him with a slightly chagrined expression. "Yeah, I forgot about that. Sorry."

"Don't apologize, man." He smirked. "I'm only saying that a wise man learns from his mistakes and a wiser man learns from the mistakes of others. That's all I'm saying, promise."

The sniper nodded and leaned back in his seat. Monroe and Anderson had arranged for Savage to have a new company car along with the new apartment, and he had to say he liked the new wheels. It was a brand-new sedan straight out of the Chevy factories, with all the nice and new accouterments one could expect with a modern car these days. It was a company car, though, and therefore ridiculously easy for Pegasus to track—and basically anyone if they had a mind to do it—but for a vehicle to drive while he waited for something to do, it wasn't terrible.

If it turned out that he needed to move off the grid, he could simply pick up one of the three used cars he'd bought off the Internet and parked around the city. He had a couple of weapons stashes waiting for him in the area as well, with cash and IDs that he might need in a pinch. It had dug into his cash flow quite substantially, but given that he didn't have to pay for utilities or even gas for the car, it wasn't like there was anywhere else his money could go.

He had prepared for the worst-case scenarios they might face through the years. Savage had money stockpiled should he need it and more sat in a savings account that would go to his daughter should he bite the dust, but other than that, he had a reasonable amount of disposable income.

"So…" he rumbled as they pulled into the designated parking area a few hundred yards away from the landing strip that would welcome Sam back to the US of A. "The suggestions to beat are Disneyland, Disney World, and a karaoke bar that requires our friend to drink while she's on medication. Are we the best of friends or what?"

"Or what is right." Terry smirked. "Hey, if worse comes to worst and we can't think of anything, we simply tell her that what we planned was to do anything she wants to do and let her lead the way while being credited for being great friends."

"That's…actually the best idea we've thought of all week," Savage admitted. "How come we didn't mention it sooner?"

"Well, our first instinct is to plan like we do for an operation with everything ranging from A to G, and maybe even T. We automatically tried to make sure we had all the variables accounted for while planning a welcome-home bash."

"Yeah, I don't think we're cut out for this shit." Savage grunted his annoyance. "We should have cut our losses and planned something quiet and calm for her recovery at my place. Did you know they got me an apartment with three bedrooms? Three? How many people did they expect would live there?"

The other man shrugged. "What would we have done there?"

"I don't know." He sighed. "There's an MMA event tonight, and I think I remember Sam talking about how she was a fan—something about liking to see men in tight shorts wrestling with each other and how it's hot but still interesting to watch. We could have bought a couple of six-packs, ordered pizza or Chinese, and stayed in."

"Honestly, that sounds like a great night to me," Terry acknowledged. "Which, interestingly enough, is a solid indicator that Sam would ditch us like she did high school."

They paused in their conversation when a small jet began its descent from the clouds. It settled smoothly onto the landing strip and taxied gently to where they waited. Savage wasn't sure how Monroe had managed this many private plane rides for the two teams.

Maybe she justified it as business expenses to the board and that way, she would be able to wangle tax breaks from it or something. But what the hell did he know? If the woman wasn't able to afford it, she would have told them so. The fact that she still revealed that ability meant now was not the time to question what the hell she was doing.

The plane came to a halt and the two men stepped out of the car. The door lowered and a staircase unfolded to allow the passengers to disembark. Savage narrowed his eyes at the soft whine of a machine as Sam appeared, seated in a wheelchair.

One of the attendants stood behind her and pushed her

toward the stairs, which worked as an escalator and allowed her to descend. The teammates shared a concerned look as they walked to where she made slow progress, wrapped in a blanket while she leaned back in the chair.

Once she was down, the attendant continued to push her to the men who were there to greet her. The concern mounted in Savage's mind. All he'd heard from Monroe was that her recovery had been thorough, which was the only reason why her doctors in Monte Carlo were willing to let her travel across the Atlantic. Had stories of her recovery been exaggerated or had something happened during the flight?

Sam looked like she was dozing off, but she woke and blinked slowly when she saw Terry and Savage approach her.

"Oh...hey guys," she whispered hoarsely. "I...didn't know you were coming to pick me up here. You shouldn't have."

"We— Of course we'd pick you up, Sam," Terry said and kept his voice soft as he moved closer and tried not to frown while he tried to determine what was happening.

"No, I mean, you really shouldn't have," she said, her voice still weak. "That...sedan there doesn't look like it's wheelchair accessible. Besides, Courtney said they'd send an ambulance to pick me up and take me to the hospital here."

"She didn't tell us any of that," Savage said and narrowed his eyes. Something wasn't quite right but he couldn't put his finger on it.

"Didn't she?" she asked, looking around. "Oh, well. I

guess the two of you aren't high enough on the social ladder to be filled in on details like that. Don't take it personally. I guess I'm simply a bigger deal than you two now."

Terry started to smell something was up too and kept his distance as he tilted his head suspiciously. Sam stared at them a few moments before she realized the jig was up and uttered a clear peal of laughter as she pushed herself from the wheelchair.

"Damn, I hoped to be able to keep you lads going for a few more minutes, but I guess I pushed my luck there a little." She chuckled, drew a few bills from her pocket, and handed them to the attendant who had helped her down. He tipped his hat before he took the blanket and wheelchair to the plane. Sam wrapped Terry in a tight, warm hug first, then she turned to give Savage similar treatment.

"It seems like you missed us." The sniper laughed when she stepped beside him and draped her arm over his shoulder, and they began to walk to the car.

"You're damn right I missed you, and not only because I was stuck in a fucking hospital bed, eating food that... Well, I want to call it crap hospital food, but at the private facility where Courtney put me, they had a chef and everything," she said. "Three-course meals, a menu, plus snacks and video games whenever I wanted, all from the comfort of a bed that's more comfortable than what I have at home. Are you fucking kidding me? That place has to be expensive."

"Yeah, Dr. Monroe does like to flaunt her money," Terry agreed and ducked when she flipped her long, brunette hair free of the bun she'd worn it in.

"Yeah, but after three weeks of that bullshit, I was ready to get home, spend time with my boys, and get back to work." She grinned and ruffled Savage's hair until he moved away to prevent it.

"We're not your…boys," he protested. "Your men, at the very least."

Sam grinned in response. "So, what kind of work have you been up to lately?"

"Mostly handling paperwork and pretending to be actual security consultants," the sniper replied. "Boring desk-job shit. Nothing you would have been interested in."

"Ugh, thank goodness I missed out on that." She laughed.

"Well, we were still walking off some of the injuries from the mini-Zoo," Savage said. "They wanted us to keep working, but there wasn't much we could do."

"Some of us recovered a little faster than others," Terry pointed out with a glance in Savage's direction.

"What's that supposed to mean?" he asked.

"At least I didn't sleep with my nurse to get me discharged early," the man pointed out. "And that's all I'll say about it."

"You're gross," he complained. "I think I liked you better when you told everyone to watch their gosh-darned language."

Terry grinned at him as they reached the car. "We're all glad you're back, Sam. It hasn't been the same without you."

"I should hope not," she replied saucily and slid into the back seat. Savage took the driver's seat and the other man rode shotgun. "So, what do you boys have planned for my grand return to business here?"

The two men exchanged another worried look.

"Well...we were thinking..." Terry started to say but fumbled and his teammate came to his rescue.

"We're here to do whatever the hell it is you want to do on your return stateside," he said quickly and nodded at her when he looked into the rearview mirror. She didn't look like she was buying it but she didn't seem to care whether they were lying or not.

"Well, that's great!" she exclaimed and placed a hand on each of their shoulders. "Because there's this new karaoke place I've been dying to try. It said online that it's a two-drink minimum, so we'll have to immediately get sloshed once we arrive. That's a win-win if I've ever seen one."

"You're the boss." Savage chuckled, put the car into gear, and eased away from the airstrip.

It is impossible to get any sleep on these aircraft. Gregor grumbled and muttered as the whole plane shuddered from another section of turbulence and jarred him awake. The massive, herculean beast of a plane was supposed to get them from Moscow to the Zoo on a single tank without needing to land anywhere to refuel, but that didn't make it a luxury airliner. It was designed to cram as much as possible into as small a space as possible.

Logically, it meant they were lucky to have any seats at all for the duration of the flight. Gregor had seen some of the flights others took that had relied almost solely on the talent and ability of the crew to remain on their feet for ten-plus hours.

Honestly, he had hoped for retirement by now and to be able to spend time with his family. It had been a while since he'd been home, but he'd been shipped out too soon. While it would have started with him spending time in jail, at least his family would have been able to see him. Not only that, the biggest monsters he would have to deal with would be guards who didn't want him to have an extra scoop of gravy with his potatoes in the food line.

No such fucking luck. They think freedom is preferred, even freedom in the bowels of hell. That questionable liberty meant orders to go out into the middle of fucking nowhere to die in a place that had started to haunt his nightmares.

Which is no freedom at all. What the hell can I do out there that they aren't already doing? The Zoo is still the Zoo, and I am still the fool that goes in there on the orders of those who hide safely behind their desks.

Nothing had been shared with him about the situation that had replaced incarceration with an unexpected return to the alien jungle. They hadn't even told him how long he was expected to stay there or if they would lock him up again once it was resolved. He'd been reinstated but the judge had said nothing about the charges. It wasn't paranoia to assume their continued existence. The only difference would likely be that others would be added if whatever crazy mission they had currently planned failed.

The red light at the front of the plane came on to warn them that they would begin their descent and those who weren't already buckled in should do so, posthaste. Not that anyone who didn't need to be wouldn't already be secured lest they risk being flung around the cabin like so much loose cargo. A group of thirty or so men had been assembled. He remembered a few of them as veterans of the Zoo, although none of them in flattering circumstances.

The feeling was mutual, apparently. All those involved knew he had avoided prison time, disgrace, and maybe even being convicted of treason by being there. Those who didn't outright insult him to his face did their best to make sure he knew that they openly ignored him.

Fuck you. If you are so much better than me, why are you on the same plane and headed to the same place—the place that anyone with a rational bone in their body would prefer prison over?

Either they were forced to be there, exactly as he was, or they were incredibly stupid.

The plane shuddered far more than before, which made the relief of finally landing a jarring experience when the wheels made contact with the asphalt of the landing strip and almost shook the seats they'd been provided loose from their moorings. It took longer than he thought was necessary but the halt eventually came. None of them waited for too long before they unstrapped and hauled themselves up to move to the crates that had been shipped with them to provide them with weapons.

What the—

All questions about why they had been brought there were extinguished in Gregor's mind as the bay doors of the plane opened slowly from the back to give them a fairly clear view of the situation that had brought them there. None of the men looked quite as shocked as he felt, which made him wonder if they had been briefed on the mission and he hadn't or if they were simply that idiotic.

I would say the latter, personally. The thought brought a smirk of satisfaction that faded quickly as he studied the scene before him.

The reason for the rough landing became apparent when he moved closer to the door. The asphalt was cracked in numerous places and bright shoots of green forced themselves through the fissures from what was supposed to be nothing but miles of sand beneath.

He froze for a moment and stared at what should have been the desert the base was on. It was now covered in green as far as the eye could see, to the point where he questioned whether they had perhaps landed on a new airstrip that had been built closer to the jungle.

As he stepped out of the plane and looked into the base he had called home during his time in the Zoo, he reluctantly acknowledged that it was suddenly frighteningly close to the infamous hellhole.

Much, much closer than it was before I left. It's hard to believe I've only been gone a week.

That was never good news for anyone, but in this particular case, he knew it didn't bode well for any of them. There was a reason why bases were built sometimes hundreds of kilometers away from the fucking jungle. The question uppermost in his mind was what the fuck had enabled the vegetation to get this close to the base.

Gregor scowled and fought to control his growing disquiet. He doubted he would be able to answer the questions, but he did know a couple of crazy scientists who would like the opportunity to find out. It seemed like their kind of thing—assuming it hadn't happened to all the bases.

"Attention, everyone!" called the man who was supposed to lead the entire operation, although the fact that none of them had been equipped with combat suits was indicative of exactly how much the people in Moscow wanted them to succeed. "We are to spread out through the base and look for any survivors. If you encounter any of the wildlife, you are to communicate it to the team and shoot to kill. No exceptions."

A couple of crates were wheeled off the plane, which provided standard weapons for them. Given that he could already see some of the trees beginning to grow inside the base, assault rifles wouldn't protect them much if fanged panthers attacked them from above.

The group moved cautiously into the base, which was eerily empty and seemed to mock their efforts. It appeared that the sudden surge of underbrush had taken place everywhere, with most of the buildings already partially obscured by vines that crept up them. The open areas now hosted trees that looked like they'd grown there for years.

I don't like this, not at all. Something is very, very wrong.

"Where the fuck are we supposed to find survivors?" one of the group asked but no answer was forthcoming. Clearly, no one had thought this through beyond simply to search the whole damn base. It was typical, although the truth brought little satisfaction.

His gaze flicked toward movement in the distance where the jungle had already taken hold. The inner presentiment of danger sent a chill up his spine. None of these people were ready for what was about to happen. Even those who had been in the Zoo before had probably never seen it as it had been over the past few months and most likely wouldn't live to learn from their experience. His instincts told him unequivocally that they faced something far worse than even he had experience with.

This is a whole new Zoo nightmare, and I can't even rely on my comrades because they have no fucking clue.

It is probably a shitty thing to do to leave them behind, but then again, they are a collection of assholes. I am sure they wouldn't think twice about leaving me.

Gregor began to ease away from the group when they noticed the movement and once they looked the other way, he sprinted into the base. There was no telling how safe the area was at that point, but he didn't intend to stick around once he'd realized he wouldn't be better off in the group.

He had a target in mind, of course. One of the warehouses on site was where they stored most of the combat suits the Russians had used to equip the teams they sent into the Zoo. Barring some kind of catastrophe, he knew he would find at least a couple of functional suits waiting for him inside.

That said, the catastrophic had already happened, so he wasn't convinced he could bet his life on the possibility. He paused for a moment to catch his breath.

The sounds of shouts, gunfire, and screams from where he'd left his team spurred him into action and he broke into a jog, then a sprint toward the warehouse. The storage area would usually have been locked with electromagnets to hold the doors in place with over three tons of pressure. With the power apparently down, they should now be simple enough to open. If not, there were a couple of emergency entrances he could use.

As it turned out, there was no need for alternative plans. The massive doors were left open, and when the screams began to outnumber the shots fired, he knew he was running out of time. The meat shields he'd left his comrades to become would be all but depleted by now, and he needed to prepare without further delay.

A couple of the crates containing the combat suits were already lowered and ready to access, and he began to put the pieces on hastily. He froze for a moment and frowned, hoping nothing would come through the door when everything suddenly went silent outside. It would be impossible to defend this position on his own and he would need to find a place with a single entrance where he would be able to push the Zoo creatures out.

Thankfully, he knew the perfect location. Gregor loaded his assault rifle and sealed his suit before he added a few extra boxes of ammo into his pack and moved out.

CHAPTER FOUR

It wasn't the longest trip of her life but she had to constantly remind herself there were worse ways to travel than by military plane—in this case, one Courtney had helped to arrange. Anja grimaced and tried to stretch a little to ease the dull ache in her spine. While she was grateful, it hadn't been the most relaxing trip.

Then again, she could never bring herself to fully relax while in the air, so it was essentially par for the course. The way the huge plane had shuddered and shook on its trip to the Zoo had been almost terrifying for the first few hours and downright annoying for the rest.

Maybe they make it so damn uncomfortable that people can't wait to reach whatever fucking hell they're going to. She smirked and avoided the intense gaze of one of the men who seemed to have deliberately chosen a seat so he could stare at her. He proved her hypothesis—stupid enough to fall for the trick and still believe it made him more of a man. *Asshat.* He'd even tried winking at her until a nasty stretch of turbulence had made him a little green about the gills.

She was happy when the lights finally came on to signal that they would make their descent, despite the uncomfortable popping that filled her ears. A handful of others had taken the same flight. Most were on their way to the European bases and merely made a quick detour through the American one.

Aside from the would-be Lothario, they seemed to understand that everyone on these flights would attend to their own business and didn't want any interaction and therefore did not want to intrude. None of them showed the same interest in the fact that she was on the plane with them, but her admirer seemed to perk up at the realization that they could disembark. Fortunately, she was the closest to the bay doors that now began to open slowly and could avoid him.

The hacker didn't need a second invitation. She heaved her pack onto her back, headed out quickly, and scrambled off almost before the doors were completely open. Davis had left her a message saying he would give her a ride to the compound, and all she needed to do was look around for the Hammerhead sporting the tell-tale sign of Amanda's alterations. Damned if the woman didn't know her way around changing the vehicles to make them look better and more killer-bad than they had before.

She located him without difficulty. The armorer had managed to alter the squat look this particular vehicle had and from which its nickname was derived into something with a top fin, which made it seem even more like a Hammerhead shark and more threatening. It wasn't like the monsters of the Zoo would be intimidated since they probably didn't even know what a shark was, but it was always a boost to the team's spirits.

Davis waited outside and puffed on what looked like a cigar. In all honesty, the guy couldn't be any more of a military stereotype than he was if he tried. Anja wasn't too timid to admit to herself that she carried something of a flame for the man, although she knew she would die if word of it got out. Still, he seemed icy enough that any of her passive looks at him might go unnoticed as she approached. He removed his aviators and took her hand in a firm shake.

"Nice to see you home again, Anja," he said with a warm smile. "I heard you guys had something of a rough time in Europe, and from the way it sounded, things could have gone either way in some of the instances."

"Well, you know how it is," she said and clambered into the shotgun seat of the vehicle. She waited for the man to join her in the driver's seat before she turned on the air-con—another one of Amanda's additions, bless her. "I was the proverbial man in the van, running everything and saving everyone's asses, but I wasn't ever in any kind of danger."

"Well, they did mention there was a situation with Russians coming after you when you landed in the area," he mentioned as he put the vehicle into gear and turned to head toward the compound.

"Oh, yeah, I almost forgot about that," she lied flippantly. "Yes, some of their agents came to try to haul me back for...possibly treasonous actions, but doing that pissed off all the wrong people. Kennedy, Sal, Jer, Terry, and Sam made short work of them. It was a touching scene with the whole team working together to help keep me out of jail, I will admit."

"Jer?" he asked and raised an eyebrow.

"Oh, right. Savage." She chuckled. "That's what I call him when I try to get on his nerves. I guess it turned into a habit. But yeah, I'm the only one who gets to call him that."

"Jer is short for Jeremiah, right? Jeremiah Savage. What the hell kind of a name is that?"

"One he chose." The hacker laughed. "He has no one to blame but himself for the mockery on my part."

Davis chuckled and shook his head. "Kennedy asked me to run a check on him before Monroe hired him and sent me some vids to show me his operational style. He's…cold. Decisive, and he has the right instincts, but I told her that putting a man like him in a civilian environment with little to no oversight would be a mistake, and I think she agreed with me. Still, I guess he's proven himself as a part of the team."

"I'll say he has, but I've worked closely with him and been his oversight, as it were," she said and checked her pack idly to make sure her laptop was still inside. A person like her who visited a casino city like Monte Carlo could be expected to make a killing. She'd been caught a couple of times on the casino floors—having already made a lot of money—but once she was banned, she was able to find ways to get her friends and coworkers to go in for a split of the profits. They all won, except for the casinos, of course.

Now, she would need to find a way to make that happen in Vegas and maybe Atlantic City too. She would be able to retire on her earnings and find a tiny little place in some isolated corner of the world with fantastic Internet speed. It would allow her to keep helping her new friends while being far enough away from the Zoo and the dangers they faced to not be anxious about it while she worried about helping them.

Because as much as she liked to play it off and pretend it didn't matter to her, she couldn't say her encounter with the Russians in Ukraine hadn't shaken her.

Most of the drive to the compound was spent sharing the details of what was happening with the rest of the team and how Sal, Madigan, and Courtney were taking time off while the others—Savage, Sam, and Terry especially— needed to recover from the beating they'd taken in Chernobyl.

"So what will they do with that facility?" Davis asked and she knew the anxiety in his tone was real. His mind was probably running rampant with all the nasty possibilities.

"Well, that Molina bitch has assured Sal that there is a failsafe built into it and she will personally make sure it's activated. I honestly don't trust her, but as Madigan told me, she has more to lose than anyone if the shit hits the fat. Hopefully, she's pressed her magic button and the secret lab would have self-destructed by now."

"Huh. I'm not sure I'd be so trusting."

"You and me both," Anja replied and scowled her disapproval. "But Sal, Madigan, and Courtney will keep an eye on things, I'm sure."

"I imagine their first choice was to carpet bomb the location into oblivion. If the radiation being spread to the rest of the continent was less of a concern than the monsters that had been created, it would be understandable to simply want it nuked. I know I would."

"Yeah. And I don't believe they trust her any more than I do. They finally agreed based on the obvious truth that she has more to lose than anyone if the secret lab causes a public clusterfuck and exposes the dark dealings that transpired there."

Personally, Anja would have felt much better if the facility was reduced to a carefully planned crater with massive military forces sent in to clear it all. She wasn't entirely sure that Elena could be trusted but assumed Sal, Madigan, and Courtney felt the same way and would keep tabs on the situation.

"Maybe it's time to do the same to the Zoo—obliterate it once and for all," she suggested, the slight edge of humor to her tone belying her fervent wish that they could.

Davis chuckled. "I understand the sentiment, but the jungle is way too big to accomplish what they could in Chernobyl." He tapped a finger thoughtfully on the steering wheel without loosening his grasp. "But with the combined efforts of the militaries assembled in the various bases, they might be able to achieve some measure of success."

Except those in control will never allow it. Too many people make too much money from the Zoo to see it destroyed. Her thoughts on that allowed them to spend the rest of the ride in silence. Davis didn't appear to mind and seemed to be the kind of guy who was comfortable enough in his own head that he didn't mind no conversation and wasn't uncomfortable in the lulls when the discussion had run its course.

Anja slid lightly out of the vehicle when it came to a stop inside the compound and he reactivated all the security measures. Connie should be able to do that on her own, but maybe he felt more comfortable doing it himself. Or maybe he'd deactivated her. Since he'd spent all the time alone at the compound, she could see how someone might simply run out of patience with the AI.

"Everything should be the way you left it," he volunteered as he walked with her toward the main building.

It would be since she'd made sure that anyone who tried to mess with her servers—even if it was Connie or Davis—would be in for a nasty surprise.

"Aside from that, it's been quiet," he continued. "Folks come by from time to time. Mostly specialist types, but they leave quickly when they realize Jacobs, Kennedy, and Monroe aren't around. I've made the run to the Russian base for the booze they distribute, and we're not due for another delivery for another couple of weeks so hopefully, they'll be able to handle it. I'm not built to be a booze delivery man. I'm better at being the recipient and customer."

She chuckled. "Well, I don't like to perpetuate stereotypes, but I think I'd be better at that than you. Do you know they sell vodka in juice boxes in Russia?"

"No shit." He laughed.

"I shit you not," she replied, still smirking. "They have a little straw and everything."

"It sounds like a fun place to live," he admitted. "I'll get some coffee going. Do you want any?"

"Yes, please," she said and disappeared quickly into her server room, careful to deactivate the surprise she'd left behind for any snoopers. It was mostly something that would splatter any intruders with the same kind of dye packs they used in banks to avoid robberies, all with nanotech that would enable her to track the perpetrators of a break-in while sealing off the data in the servers, trashing some of it, and securing the rest behind a biometric seal that required a DNA sample from her. Any attempt to break that encryption would result in the servers overheating to the point where they corrupted all the data contained inside.

She had wanted to rig a self-destruct sequence, but since there was the possibility that someone might accidentally trigger the defense mechanisms, she didn't want to be responsible for blowing a hole in their little compound. Sal would not approve, not that she needed his permission or anything. It was always better to ask forgiveness afterward, right?

The hacker settled into her seat and smiled at the familiar squeak as she turned everything on. The array of monitors came to life and greeted her with a wave gif before they alerted her to the fact that someone was trying to communicate with her over one of her encrypted channels.

She called it up, leaned forward on her seat, and pulled her headset on, trying to track the signal.

It wasn't that difficult, she realized. It was coming from the Russian Base, along with a whole crap-ton of interference.

"Hey, who's on this line?" she asked and strained to discern who it was, but all she heard was a generic Russian VPN from one of their combat suits.

"Hey," a voice finally responded in Russian and despite the interference, she recognized it. "Who's there? Is that you, Anja?"

"Yes, what the hell are you doing here, Gregor?" she asked and immediately called up as much data as she could on his location. With some of the system still booting up, she didn't have the rapid responses she was used to. "I thought you would be stuck in Russia for a while."

"Change of plans," he replied and sounded breathless and in some kind of trouble. "They needed me here in the Zoo more than they needed me to take the fall. And I now know why."

"What's the issue?" she asked and a second later, the satellite images she'd called up about ten seconds before answered her question.

"It's the Zoo," he replied. "It's taken over the base. I think it might have killed everyone here, and it killed the team I came in with too. I don't think the plane is an option anymore either. I managed to lock myself somewhere relatively safe, but I don't know how long that will last. I'm in a whole steaming pile of shit, and I need to call in that favor you owe me."

"Oh, come now," the hacker replied and despite the attempt to joke, kept her voice in a monotone as she was still gathering all the information she needed. "We're friends now, Gregor, and this whole exchange of favors thing is so two months ago."

She needed a little humor to bring herself back from the shock of an image showing a jungle overwhelming what had once been almost a small, thriving city as well as the desert around it. The cameras on the base were down, and it looked like all the electrical systems were too, which would complicate things.

"Gregor, are you sure where you are is safe for the moment?" she asked after a few seconds.

"For now," he replied.

"Good, stay there," Anja responded quickly and pushed from her seat. "I have help heading your way."

She yanked her headset off, connected to the comms system inside the compound, and located the ex-soldier.

"Davis, you'll need to suit up and get back in the hammerhead," she said and forced herself to keep her voice calm. "I have something I need you to do."

"Roger that," he replied smoothly.

The pool wasn't that big, given the sheer size of the building. The structure had been created as almost a pyramid and stretched sixty-seven stories into the sky with the pool at the very top. It offered a fantastic view of the city, the sea, and even the Alps to the north. The wind was mostly mitigated by the reinforced glass walls on the perimeter that protected the guests without impeding their view.

Sal acknowledged that he could get used to living like this, although it would take much more money than he raked in on an annual basis. Maybe he'd be able to pay for a stay that lasted longer than a couple of weeks, but Anja's help to wangle a solid payout from the casino downstairs could extend it.

He moved to the bar—positioned close enough to the

pool to allow those who were in the water to order as well —and asked for a mojito before he scanned the area. There weren't many people there at this hour and he assumed most were somewhere downstairs or had chosen to go out into the city for the lunch hour. People could order food there too, he assumed. If you were rich enough, you didn't even need to leave the building if you didn't want to. Every need could be met and virtually every vice imaginable was available, from the legal ones like gambling, drinking, and clubbing, to the illegal like drugs and company.

It would be very easy for people who lived like this to become completely disconnected from the problems that plagued their fellow humans elsewhere.

His drink arrived in record time, which allowed him to stroll to where Madigan and Courtney stretched out on comfortable seats next to each other, tanning themselves.

Sal pulled his robe off and rather liked the way the sun reflected off his skin and the lean, powerful muscles he'd developed during his time at the Zoo.

"Don't you think we get enough sun where we live?" he asked, hung the robe from an unoccupied chair beside them, and sat before he took a sip of his drink. "When you guys said you were coming to the pool, I thought you were going to the pool."

"We will later," Courtney said. She turned to look at him and lowered her sunglasses. "We're enjoying the warmth that comes without the Sahara heat for a while."

"Yep," Madigan concurred.

"Well, it's not that I mind being out here," he replied, not wanting to rain on their particular parade. "I don't understand why the two of you would want it, but hey, as

MICHAEL TODD & MICHAEL ANDERLE

long as you are here, I have four different reasons to stick around. Maybe six."

Courtney laughed and Madigan turned her head to stare at him through her sunglasses. "Sheesh, how old are you?" she asked and almost sounded like he hadn't made jokes like that before. He had and she'd been around for most of them, sometimes even topless.

"I'm…holy shit, I'm twenty-three," he said and his mood went from joking to somber in a matter of seconds. "I can't believe I forgot my birthday."

"When is your birthday again?" Madigan asked, feeling safe to do so since he'd forgotten it too.

He wasn't offended, of course. "November thirtieth, and in all the excitement and fun we've had between here and the Zoo, it completely slipped my mind."

"Huh," she mumbled, settled herself comfortably, and adjusted her glasses once more. "I think Courtney and I can certainly come up with a present that will make up for forgetting your birthday—and ironically, be an experience to remember."

"I…what are you talking about?" he asked but already had a sneaking suspicion that was only reinforced when he saw the other woman smirk.

"Oh, yeah," Courtney interjected and nodded. "I think between the two of us, we could probably think of at least…four presents to give you. Maybe six."

"I think I know what you're talking about, but I don't want to assume," he replied and tried to keep his cool as he turned and shuffled in his seat. If there was one thing he was learning from dating them it was that it was a mistake to assume certain things about his relationship with them.

"Well, we wouldn't want to spoil the surprise anyway," Madigan replied and sounded calm and collected. "So you keep on trying to guess what it might be, and maybe you'll…ménage to figure it out."

"Huh." He grunted, looked at the sky, and donned a pair of sunglasses before he sipped his icy drink to chill a little. Under normal circumstances, it might be a bad idea to add alcohol to the mix of hormones rushing through his body, but he was well aware of the effect alcohol had on him—or, rather, the lack thereof.

"Hey, is anyone around on this commlink?" Anja's voice came to the rescue through the earpiece he still wore. They had said they would leave most of their work behind—since Courtney was still needed, she had to remain reachable for the folks in Philly—but he found it a little difficult to stay completely away from proceedings. More importantly, with Anja back at the Zoo, it would be nice to stay in touch with her in case she needed them.

Besides, he had begun to miss their little compound. Not that it was the best place in the world, of course, but it was theirs and that meant something to him.

"Hi, Anja, I'm here," he said softly.

Neither Madigan nor Courtney seemed surprised that he had suddenly started talking to himself, which meant they probably had their earbuds in as well.

"You might need to cut the vacation short," the hacker informed him in a somber tone. "There's a situation I think the three of you might want to be a part of."

CHAPTER FIVE

Davis scowled as he accelerated down the dusty road toward the Russian base. He had been around the Zoo longer than most. Hell, Monroe was the only one of the Heavy Metal team who had more time in there than he did, and that was only by a month and a half. He had been a part of the first few military battalions they had flown in to deal with the situation the jungle had become.

That had been when the American Base was the only base, and they'd built it with the thought that almost everyone would want to share it with them instead of building their own. When the news first broke that they intended to erect a wall to contain the spread of the jungle, he—like most of the others who had been there at the time—had laughed at the notion. Most of those who had been there with him were dead or headed home by now, and he was the last member of that unlucky group.

Even Kennedy had come in a few months after he did.

All that experience now screamed a singular message to

him as he began the drive into the desert in the team's hammerhead, strapped in and already wearing his customized combat suit.

Never go into the Zoo alone. You know that, yet here you are. What are you thinking? It was the first lesson that had been drilled into all of them, learned through the fact that they'd needed to drag more than a few bodies out of the jungle in those first few months.

Okay, chill. You're not going into the actual Zoo so there's no need to imagine all kinds of shit that likely won't happen. He drew a breath and focused on what Anja had told him from the satellite images she'd managed to pull. The jungle had pushed into the Russian sector, left a trail of green in its wake, and now seemed to swallow the base itself.

The questions remained—like why the Zoo seemed to target the Russians specifically and which base would be next. Still, the time for those questions would come later. He was merely heading in on a rescue mission, nothing more and nothing less.

And yes, there is still one small problem. You're fucking doing it alone—at least for now. Idiot.

Anja had called the other members of the Heavy Metal team. Many of them were in the American base, drinking and waiting for action and money to come their way. It meant they were good to go a few minutes after she let them know that their services were needed. They were still about an hour and a half behind Davis, so while she had told him time was of the essence, he had delayed his trip a little to "accidentally" allow them to catch up with him.

But of course, the asshats are taking their sweet time as well.

"Remind me again why we thought it was a good idea

to send me into a fucking base you don't have eyes on and that might be crawling with all kinds of monstrosities. There's no way to know because the only actual intel we have is from someone who is now in hiding."

He paused and waited for a response but the silence stretched on. It occurred to him that she might be ignoring him. "And, oh yeah," he continued because it was better than talking to himself, "let's not forget that he said his whole team is gone, along with the inhabitants of the base with the second-highest population in the area who are MIA."

After a few moments, Davis grumbled under his breath, not sure if Anja could hear him. She'd said she would contact the other teams and try to get an idea of their location to see if they could help. Not the teams that were in Europe and Philly, of course, although she did say that Jacobs, Kennedy, and Monroe had been updated on the situation already.

As it turned out, though, she had heard what he'd mumbled and merely took her time before she responded.

"Well, first of all, it's a simple rescue op to pick up someone who's in a combat suit and appears to be ready to go as soon as you get there," the hacker replied finally. She sounded all kinds of stressed and Davis could understand why. "Secondly, you won't be alone."

"My backup is about an hour behind me," he reminded her. "If you're right about the ease of the mission, we'll be in and out before they get there, and if you're wrong, they'll be way too late."

"Sorry, there's nothing I can do about that," she replied quickly. "But I didn't mean the team that should have been an hour and a half behind you, by the way. I meant…well, something a little more sophisticated."

He was about to ask her what the hell she was talking about when a couple of the software functions came alive on his dashboard at the same moment that they activated on the HUD of the hammerhead.

"Well, hello there, sexy." A smooth, slightly robotic voice spoke from the speakers. "How nice of you to take me on a ride. I only wish there was something I could offer you by way of thanks."

"What the fuck?" Davis tensed and looked around like he half-expected to find someone in the vehicle with him. He slowed slightly and managed to not jerk the wheel at high speed.

"Well, that was the idea, stud," the voice replied.

"Oh, yeah. That's Connie, the AI," Anja explained. "I thought you might need backup before the actual backup arrives, so I took the liberty of downloading her into the hammerhead and gave her access to the defenses Amanda installed there. I thought you'd already met her."

"I turned the speakers off while it was only me in the compound," he admitted. "I'm not a big fan of AIs. Why is she making a pass at me?"

"Oh, that's the personality she came programmed with since we got her cheaper from the used AI markets online," she explained. "While she's fully primed to operate all kinds of defense mechanisms, she's something of a perv."

"And couldn't that have been programmed out of her?"

"Changing a core part of my personality would be essentially killing who I am and allowing someone else to use my corpse for locomotion," Connie replied and sounded genuinely peeved. "Humans usually get all tetchy when someone suggests the same thing for them."

"You're not human, though, right?" Davis asked.

"I'm human in everything but body, lover," she retorted in that annoyingly sultry tone.

"Right." Seriously, what else could he say?

"Anyway, with the defenses Amanda gave the hammer-head, you should have something in the way of cover fire while you go in there and give them hell," the hacker said hastily to prevent any further comments from Connie.

"And who is them, precisely?" he asked.

"Whoever or whatever it is you run into at the base," Anja replied as he crested the last dune that would afford a decent view of where he was heading into. "Although hopefully, not those few Russians who might have survived the onslaught."

"I...think that ship may have sailed," Davis replied and came to a halt at the top of the dune. She would be able to see what he saw through the windshield of the vehicle and would probably think the same thing.

The satellite images hadn't done it justice at all. The Zoo burgeoned out of what had been a thriving military facility and had grown in what had to be less than a week to a point that would take regular, earth-grown jungles months or even years to reach. Worse, it appeared to still be expanding to such a degree that he wondered if he would even be able to drive the vehicle through the area.

"Well, shit." He shoved the door open and maneuvered his suit out of the vehicle so he could get a better feel for what they faced.

"And so, my first step in world domination is achieved,"

Connie said as he slammed the door shut. "I now have the weaponry and means of locomotion I've always lacked to push my agenda into the world, one weak mind at a time."

"She's joking, right?" he asked after a few seconds.

"We're not sure," the hacker replied honestly. "She's talked like that ever since we got her, and while she might be telling the truth and she does have plans for world domination, I don't think she'd be able to take over the world from inside an altered hammerhead. She could maybe take over a small farming community if she was lucky."

"Don't give her any ideas," he warned, only half-joking.

"I won't, don't worry." She laughed. "Her core is slaved here in the server room. You need to work on that paranoia of yours when it comes to AI. It's not your most attractive feature."

"And what is my most attractive feature?"

"Your ass," Connie responded quickly. "Don't worry, Sergeant Davis. I have every intention of leaving you alive once I've taken over the world. You will be the first in my harem of sexy studs whom I'll need to occupy myself with once the world is dominated and I feel bored."

"That's getting old, Connie." He growled, now annoyed by the distraction.

"I have no idea what you mean, Sergeant Davis," she replied. "I do not get old, after all."

He didn't answer and instead, turned his attention to the Russian base and the jungle that seemed relentlessly determined to overwhelm it. Or, more accurately, his attention was dragged away by the sight of a group of animals that emerged from the tree cover and immediately sprinted in his direction.

"And some fucking things never change." No matter where in the world you were, that would never be an encouraging sight. Davis drew his assault rifle from his back, primed it, and aimed the weapon at the advancing creatures. An odd noise caught his attention when the top of the fin jutting from the roof of the vehicle peeled back to reveal a cluster of mini-guns. These were mounted in such a way that they could cover at least five different angles around the vehicle, while a rocket launcher emerged from each of the doors.

"Locked and loaded," Connie said.

"Where did Amanda get access to that kind of hardware?" he wondered aloud and despite his misgivings about all things AI-related, he suddenly felt much safer on the crest of the little dune.

"I didn't ask, and she didn't tell," Anja replied. "Anyway, I've already alerted the rest of your team that you might have impending violence and they need to step on it or miss out. They should rendezvous with you at your current position in about thirty minutes, so watch your back."

"I have Connie for that job now," he replied cheerfully. He had to say, now that he'd seen the kind of weapons the AI brought to the battle, he might have warmed up to her a little.

No, goddammit. Not yet. I'm not ready for this. Despite his reluctance to face it, he knew it was the next morning. Savage could tell that from the fact that the sun shined directly in his face and dragged him out of what had been a pleasant and dreamless night of sleep. He didn't need to move to know what kind of condition he would be in once he opened his eyes.

They'd gone out drinking the night before. There had been singing, dancing, and some fucking. He could taste something foul in his mouth, and the hint of a headache had begun to make itself apparent on the edge of his consciousness as he leaned back in the bed and groaned softly.

That said, he wasn't as hungover as he thought he would be. He'd had a suspicion that he would be laid up for days. The truth was that he wasn't a young man anymore, and a night of drinking needed far more penance at the altar of the ceramic bowl now than when he'd been a young, naïve recruit barely out of boot camp.

Surprisingly, he seemed to have escaped his worst imaginings. His head still pounded but at least his stomach was fairly settled.

After a moment, he felt it was safe to open his eyes and groaned again as he immediately covered them with his hand against the glare of the angry yellow face in the sky. Someone moved in the far corner of the room and drew his gaze to where a tall, elegant woman began to put her clothes on. She looked like she'd already showered, made herself up for the day, and only lacked the pantsuit to complete the look suggested by the black stockings that climbed her long legs.

Savage suppressed a sigh at the sight. He was a sucker for stockings.

She turned when she heard him move and smiled with a pair of glasses held between her teeth. Once she was done fixing her bra, she put the eyewear on.

"Good morning, handsome," she said, and it took him a few seconds to reply simply because he needed to remember her name.

"Alisson." He growled, pushed himself to the edge of the bed, and rubbed his temples. "Alisson Marie. The lawyer. When did we meet up with you?"

"About an hour into the karaoke bar," she replied with a chuckle. "And it lasted until about...half-past two in the morning, if memory serves me correctly. And I'm not sure it does. Things became a little fuzzy between one and two in the morning, thanks to you."

"I'll...uh, take that as a compliment." He shoved himself from his seat on the bed. It took him a moment to realize where he was—the new apartment Monroe had supplied him with while his was still under repair after the firefight that had occurred there. While she had been generous and found him one that was much better than his own—even before it had turned into a scene from a Michael Bay movie—he wasn't sure what he needed it for. It took up an entire floor of an upscale apartment complex in downtown Philly with three bedrooms and a massive living area that a man who was perpetually on his own would never need.

That said, the fully stocked bar that came with it was always appreciated.

"I need to get back to work," she said, having dressed very quickly while he had been lost in thought. "But you still have my number, so make sure to call me again whenever you feel the urge to party like that again."

"Party like what again?" Sam's unmistakable voice asked through the walls of the master bedroom. Savage raised his eyebrows as Marie winked and opened the door and stepped out. He took a moment to retrieve his pants and pull them on quickly to follow her, but she was already at the elevator.

Oh yes, he would definitely call her again.

He studied the state of the apartment. As parties went, it could have been worse, he supposed. Most of the furniture was still in place and nothing appeared to be broken, although the bar would need restocking. Blankets were strewn over one of the couches, and he could see movement from beneath them before Sam poked her head out after a few seconds. She looked far worse for wear than he felt, and as she dragged herself from the couch, the blankets fell away to reveal a man he didn't recognize, fully nude and snoring as she moved toward the kitchen. On the way, she casually collected her clothes that were strewn about the room and put them on.

"I have to say," she said, finally somewhat clothed and in the kitchen to which he had hastily retreated. "You guys sure as hell know how to throw a coming-home bash. Remind me to get you and Terry to plan every other party in my life."

"In the interest of coming clean, we didn't plan any of what happened last night," he said as he came to terms with the fact that he was definitely hungover but not quite as badly as he should have been. Vague memories from the night before flooded slowly into his consciousness. "We didn't know if you were on meds that would mean you couldn't drink, and that was basically all we knew about what you liked doing when you celebrate something."

He paused for a moment and decided to come clean about everything. "Honestly, we weren't even sure about that, which was why we told you our plan was to let you choose what you wanted to do."

"Hmmm, good call," Sam grumbled and shuffled to the high-tech coffee machine in the corner. After a few seconds spent trying to find out how it worked, she finally settled on what she wanted and set it to brew. "If you need more hints, I do enjoy a good dicking too."

"Well, I don't think Monroe would appreciate us hiring male escorts on the company card," Savage pointed out and moved closer, ready for a cup of coffee himself.

"Well, there's always the two of you." She grinned. "From the noises I could hear from your room, I'd say you know your way around a woman's body. Praise the good Lord for thin walls, am I right?"

"Well, I think Terry's in some kind of relationship at the moment." He remembered that from some point when they'd been sober.

"I'd be happy to settle on only you." She chuckled and patted his backside before she removed her mug of coffee from the machine and sat at the kitchen table. "So, what do we have planned for us today, boss?"

Savage shrugged, filled his mug with the aromatic black brew, and sat across from her. "I don't know. They've thrown busy work at me and Terry for the past week and a half. When they have something for us, they'll call us in."

Something vibrated in his pants, and after a thought

that it might be something Marie had left behind faded, he realized it was his phone. The caller ID told him it was Anderson calling from his office.

"Hold that thought," he said and pressed the buttons to answer the call and put it on speaker for Sam to be able to hear too. "Hey, Anderson. You have me and Sam here."

"Hey, Sam," Anderson responded. "How are you holding up?"

"I have a killer headache but nothing I can't handle, boss," she responded. "How about you? I seem to recall you ditching us a little too early for my taste."

"I have a wife, son, and a day job to get to." He laughed.

"Yeah, well, I think you don't have the stomach for a hard night of partying anymore." Her chuckle took the sting out of it. "I think you've gone soft. Weak, even."

"Well, that may be the case," the former colonel said and seemed to not want to get into that particular discussion at the moment. "Anyway, the point of this call is that there are a few orders of business we'd like you to handle. And by you, we mean Savage. You still need time off to recover, Sam, so get some rest. Savage, if you could come to the office at...shall we say, two in the afternoon? Once you've cleaned up and can look a little like someone employed by Pegasus."

"Two in the afternoon sounds good, boss," he replied and ignored the cheerful sarcasm.

"I'll see you then." Anderson hung up.

"Do you know what time it is now?" Savage turned to Sam, who shrugged. "I do need to have a shower. Do you mind...uh, cleaning up around here? Maybe rope Terry into it too? Where is he, anyway?"

"Will do." She grinned. "Terry is in the second bedroom, where he and his new lady friend spent the night. I don't think any of us were in any shape to drive home."

"Good point." He stretched and his gaze settled on the character who was still asleep on the couch. "And make sure he doesn't take anything. I need to account for everything to Monroe when I turn this apartment over to her."

CHAPTER SIX

Courtney hung up and Sal and Madigan waited for her to speak. She'd been in contact with the people who would be able to arrange for them to catch the quickest flight to the Zoo.

"Okay, it's a done deal. Our new and improved suits have already been shipped to the compound, so all we need to do is pack our belongings and clear our rooms. A car will wait outside to take us to the nearby heliport. From there, a helicopter will fly us to a private airstrip in Nice, and a plane will take us to the American base."

Back to the jungle with its alien monsters. I'd looked forward to going back, but not like this. Sal hid his grimace and gave her a thumbs-up.

He was never comfortable with taking what she brought to their team with her Fortune-Five-Hundred money and company ties. Admittedly, she was a genius researcher and a gutsy fighter too, but the added bonus of her being able to arrange all this while they were packing was one he felt they didn't appreciate enough. *It's not taking advantage if she offers, right? Still, maybe it's the macho in me, but it doesn't sit well.*

That said, he still hadn't forgotten what Madigan had said about his birthday present. It wasn't the kind of thing a guy like him could easily forget but other matters would now take precedence. Top of the list, of course, was the fact that the Zoo had suddenly expanded, spread toward a base, and taken it over, seemingly overnight. All kinds of interesting research material could undoubtedly be found in there. He could hate the cause but love the possibilities, couldn't he?

Courtney gave him a small smile as if she'd sensed his conflicted thoughts and maybe even understood them.

There was also the fact that one of their closest friends and contacts on the Russian side was in a colossal amount of shit and needed help to make it out. Even worse, it seemed that most of the inhabitants of the second-largest Zoo base were MIA. These were important factors, he reminded himself constantly in his effort to keep his excited researcher brain from acting like this was a good thing.

Courtney looked up from the call she was making to Philly and turned to look at him.

"What?" he asked and glanced around to see if he'd maybe sat on something or had somehow interrupted what she was doing.

"Your phone's ringing," she replied and rolled her eyes.

Sal nodded quickly. "Shit, sorry. It's been a while since I carried one." At the compound, most of the comms went through Anja first, who then transferred them to him if it was necessary. When he wasn't at the compound, he usually had one of her earbuds in for comms, and when that wasn't the case, he was in his suit, where all calls and communications were patched into the HUD. To carry a device hadn't been a part of his reality for a while, and he would have to start getting used to it again.

Weird, he thought and raised the device to his ear.

"Dr. Jacobs?" He immediately recognized the familiar voice of the commandant of the American base.

"Speaking," he replied quickly. "Nice to hear from you again, Commandant Evans."

"Likewise," he said but didn't sound like he meant it. "I assume that by now, you have been briefed on the situation we're facing here in the Zoo, yes?"

"You would be correct in that assumption, yes, sir," Sal replied and mouthed the man's name again to Madigan and Courtney. He would have put him on speaker but Courtney was still on the phone herself and he would simply have to pass any information he received on.

"Anyway, I'm sorry to intrude on your vacation, Dr. Jacobs," the man said and again, his words carried very little genuine sentiment. "But the circumstances are unique. I've been contacted by the Russian Ministry of Defense. They've asked if they can land troops on our airfield to recover the base from the Zoo. I've been able to stall and sent the request to the Pentagon, and I'm now waiting to hear from them. In the meantime, I do need you and your team to spearhead any intelligence-gathering missions in the area. If there's anyone out there who knows how to handle a situation like this, it's Heavy Metal. It's your fault since you have a habit of hiring the best and the brightest we have available."

He wasn't sure he liked the man's tone and bit back a caustic response, mainly because he was right. The company did have a habit of attracting the best and brightest to their ranks, but that was only because of their willingness to go where none had gone before, coupled with a respect for their personnel in the field. That was attractive to the people who went in there in the full knowledge that they would risk their lives.

"Well, as luck would have it, we're already on our way," Sal replied. "We should touch down in the American base in…" He paused and looked at Courtney, who held up five fingers. "In five hours, give or take. As a matter of fact, we already have a team heading in there right now to make an initial estimate of the situation."

"That's much appreciated, Dr. Jacobs," the commandant replied and he nodded. He managed to hold back from responding with a snide, rude, and possibly even offensive comment about how the man might be able to attract the best and brightest to his forces if he decided protecting his people was a greater priority than succumbing to idiotic orders from the Pentagon. Unfortunately, that attitude stemmed from a group of folks in expensive suits who cared more about bottom-line quarterly profit margins than about the lives it cost to keep those numbers up.

He gritted his teeth and ground his jaw for a few seconds before he responded. "Nice to hear from you, as always, Commandant. We'll see you on the ground."

Sal hung up before the temptation struck again. Madigan chuckled, sensing the trial he endured but didn't want to say anything to add to it herself. She gave his shoulder a reassuring squeeze.

"You know, you might want to be a little nicer to the guy," Courtney pointed out when her phone call reached a lull. "He has let us operate freely from his base when, if he had a mind to, he could give us all kinds of trouble and headaches."

"There's a reason why he's played nice with us for this long," he reminded her. "It's because we've brought in the biggest bucks the base has seen since its inception. If he wants that to stop, all he has to do is cause trouble. Until then, he might want to be nicer to us."

She shrugged because he had a point, but she knew what she was talking about as well. If he pushed too hard, the man might decide they weren't worth the effort and begin to interfere or raise difficulties. People in commanding positions tended to have streaks of stupidity like that sometimes.

It was best to play it cool for now.

"Yeah, I'd still kill to know what kind of crap rumor you spread, Andersen," Savage muttered as he stepped through the doors into the lobby of the Pegasus building. From the looks he received from the three female receptionists who greeted him when he entered, he could only assume it was something Anderson didn't want to tell him to his face—maybe something embarrassing.

It had been necessary, he conceded, to invent a reason why he'd been missing during his recovery. The idea was for it to swamp any other gossip that might come up, and the more embarrassing it was, the more effective it would be. The ex-colonel had declined to say what the given reason was but had no doubt been fueled by the fact that he had begun to develop into something of a legend there.

Jeremiah Savage, man of mystery. He waved casually to the three women and chuckled when they immediately lowered their heads into a huddle. *Yeah, ladies, chat away. I'm glad I can provide some excitement in the boring routine of your day.* His cover as the security consultant who came in, gave a report every couple of weeks, and left again worked in more ways than one.

He frowned when a few staff members passed him with sidelong glances and turned casually to look at the handful of people in the lobby area. Even the security guard seemed to be watching him. *Goddammit, Andersen. It's not my imagination. I might be an enigma rather than a novelty like I was in the early days, but they should all be used to me by now.*

By now, he'd been a part of the routine for so long, he had even become more comfortable dressing like this. *Not that I'd ever admit it to anyone while sober.* He grinned and checked his reflection surreptitiously in the shiny elevator doors.

The suit, the tie, and the arrogant attitude that came from someone who knew for a fact that they made more money than the average Joe was an effective disguise in that environment. Based on that alone, there was no reason for him to disdain it.

Still, despite his confidence, the attention was unsettling. But he knew better than to ask—his first instinct—and reminded himself that sooner or later, the rumor would come to find him. *And then, Colonel, you and I will have a little talk. Something tells me it will be necessary. Asshat.*

Savage stepped into the elevator alone and heaved a sigh of relief. It carried him to the conference floor, where more than enough people would be around to dilute the attention from him.

As he stepped onto the floor, he realized he was right. Everyone was too focused on their task to notice him among them. That was no doubt due to his perfect disguise.

"That fucking lobby is like a goldfish bowl." The suit and tie created a semblance of invisibility. *The sign of a good operative—blend in with the herd. Maybe one day, you could assume this identity completely and leave your life of violence behind.*

The thought surprised him because it was so foreign and so far removed from his ingrained persona. But he was only human, after all, and he couldn't take these beatings constantly without any consequence. The chances were he would eventually not walk away from one.

He moved into the conference room where a meeting already appeared to be in progress. Anderson looked thoroughly sick and tired of the position he filled. Savage could understand. Even as a full-bird colonel, the man was special forces born and bred, the kind of person who liked straight contact and abhorred playing politics, which appeared to be the entirety of his job so far.

As expected, he wasn't the only one in the room. A group of what appeared to be lawyers were spread across the room and seemed to control most of the conversation. They seemed to be working toward some kind of deal. Half of the group clearly represented Anderson and Pegasus.

Goddammit. No wonder Andersen was vague with the

details. The other half represented the woman seated across from the former colonel—a woman Savage was only too familiar with. Elena Molina, the woman behind most of the troubles they'd faced over the past few months, sat in one of the chairs. She toyed with a pen on the table, oblivious to the fact that she was in about as much danger right now as she'd ever been in her life.

"Nope." The operative growled, shook his head, and walked away from the table. "No. Hell no."

"Savage, please take a seat." Anderson called him back, his tone sharp. The operative at last understood the meaning behind the man's sour expression. He likely held himself back as well since he knew the woman was probably also involved with those who had targeted his family at Carlson's behest.

"I won't work with her," he said and still wanted to leave. Unfortunately, he knew that if his boss insisted, he would have to do as he was told. The man paid his bills and everything, and he owed the former colonel.

"You're not working with her," Anderson corrected. "You're working for her."

He didn't like the sound of that. Working for a woman like Molina inevitably had strings attached. *Yeah, the kind that flings you into dangerous places, all manner of trouble, and the very real threat of death by mutant monsters.*

Reluctantly, he inched to the seat that had been saved for him and dropped into it.

"It is nice to see you again, Mr. Savage," Molina said with what looked like a genuine smile.

The lawyers in the room could sense some kind of history between the two of them and exchanged glances.

They attempted to not look overly uncomfortable when he didn't reply. He remained in his seat and present at the meeting but damned if he would be cooperative with this.

It took every ounce of impulse-control he had in him to keep from vaulting over the table to strangle the woman in front of him. She would have to settle for that as a sign of his civility in this conversation.

"There have been updates on a situation in the Zoo we were looking at," his boss said and paged through the files placed in front of him on the table. "It seems the jungle out there has begun to overcome the bases—or base, singular, as far as we know. Jacobs, Kennedy, and Monroe are headed in to investigate, so it seems they will be out of communication for the moment. In the interim, Miss Molina has bought a sizeable interest in Pegasus during the sale of stocks and used it as leverage to gain an appointment to the board of directors."

"And let me guess, you need me to run to the Zoo as your eyes and ears there now that I have experience with a taste of what it might throw at me?" Savage asked, unable to keep the venom from his tone. The lawyers exchanged another glance and looked hastily at their papers. Whatever was happening there, they wanted no part in it.

"You guess wrong," Molina said with no hint that she found his attitude offensive. "During my time here, I've been made aware of what your job with Pegasus is as a contractor, and I would like to employ your services. Fully paid for, of course, at whatever rate you choose to add on top of what Pegasus is paying you at the moment."

"You approved this?" he asked Anderson in an accusatory tone.

"No," the ex-colonel answered and shook his head vehemently. "But Dr. Monroe did, and as you know, I'm her representative in that too."

"Well, the best part about being a consultant is the fact that I can pick and choose my clients." He scowled and turned belligerently to face Molina. "And I'll be damned before I work with or for you."

"I'm confident you'll change your mind, Mr. Savage," she replied, her voice supremely arrogant. "When you do, meet me at the airstrip Pegasus usually uses for international travel. And bring your passport."

"You…shove your passport," Savage snapped uncomfortably in reply as the woman stood, followed quickly by her team.

"It was a pleasure meeting you, Mr. Anderson, and I look forward to working with you in the future." She received only a quick nod from the man in response as she and her lawyers exited the room and left Savage and Anderson alone.

"We need to talk," his boss said after a few moments of silence had passed.

"You're goddamn right we do," he retorted acerbically.

CHAPTER SEVEN

Gregor peeked out through the murder holes, the singular breaks in the steel-reinforced walls through which he could see the animals moving outside.

"I don't think they can see me," he muttered as the strange realization dawned on him. He was accustomed to the Zoo being more cognizant, but maybe the metal hindered them. "If they knew, those acid spitting bastards would make short work of these walls."

Or they simply ignored him, even though he took careful and well-aimed shots occasionally to thin the hordes. "Well, I'll be grateful for small mercies."

The lack of attention was a relief but also a little annoying. A part of him felt like the creatures thought of him as already dealt with, sealed into the room as he was, and they didn't even bother to try to break in.

Then again, perhaps they knew they would only injure themselves in their efforts to gain entry to his sanctuary and so didn't bother with it or him. "With these fuckers, all of these are possible."

He reminded himself gloomily that this wasn't his worst trip into the Zoo. And in practical terms, he was in the Zoo, for better or for worse. They would have to decide the technicalities of that later. For now, the jungle and the base were one.

"No, my worst run into the jungle was the one when I was left to die after being attacked by a massive horde of creatures, all new and scary. Although I was alone then too, separated from my teammates. Bastards."

Gregor peered out of the narrow slit and calmly fired two measured shots to fell two mutant hyenas. "Maybe the building warps the sound so they can't identify where it comes from."

It was an interesting thought, but his mind returned to its comparison of the two very different predicaments. *This time, you at least have shelter and the building's protection, however long that lasts. And you have a full suit. Shit. It's almost a holiday trip.*

On the other mission, his suit had been damaged to the point where it was unusable, and it meant the team would have had to carry him out. *Even now, I can't be entirely sure they would have done so willingly. And I'll never know because we were separated.*

He took another potshot at a blur of motion and missed, unsure what creature had flashed past. He muttered an imprecation and checked his weapon out of habit. The familiar surge of resentment seemed sharper, possibly because he was once again facing the mutants alone.

It was a moot point, however. Back then, he'd been stranded with nothing to think about except his life choices and the vague hope that he might keel over and die on his own, rather than helped along by a Zoo monster he was unable to defend himself against.

Thankfully, that had been unnecessary. Sal and Madigan had arrived to help, gave him the assistance he needed, and brought him out before they returned to the Zoo to assist the remainder of his team to make it out alive. His teammates had been a nice crew despite being mostly mercs. They were merely green and terrified of the new shit that had erupted around them.

"There is no need to wonder if they would have helped or even sent a search party if they made it to base," he told himself sharply and squinted through the narrow slit at his enemy. "That was all in the past and you made the choice to move on from the sense of betrayal that had no evidence to confirm it."

A group of the creatures massed on the far side and he watched them carefully. *In the Zoo, that is always a sign of danger.* He noted the different types of creatures, usually an indication that they massed in preparation for an attack. His heart raced for a moment as he imagined a surge toward his refuge, but it calmed when he reminded himself that they would have launched an earlier onslaught if they had known he was there. He took careful aim and fired, and a venomous panther roared and staggered, wounded but not fatally so.

"Shit. Focus, idiot. Don't waste bullets when you can pick the motherfuckers off easily." The ranks closed around the wounded mutant, but he noticed that the group had lost a little cohesion. Maybe he'd confused them. Still, the idea that they might be planning an assault worried him.

The present situation—and time to dwell on it—made him wonder about his decision to let go of his anger after he'd been left to die. *If you'd made more of a stink about the situation, maybe you wouldn't have stuck around the Zoo long enough for them to call you back.*

Of course, he wouldn't have been able to forge his friendships with Sal, Madigan, and Courtney like he had during the time he'd stayed. If he'd made a fuss, they would have simply moved him elsewhere and some other unfortunate soul would now have to deal with this clusterfuck.

Or, probably more accurately, they would all be dead and his bosses would simply bomb the shit out of this place instead of these futile attempts to take it back with boots on the ground. They were callous like that when they didn't think there was anything of value to be salvaged.

It had taken all his considerable knowledge of the facility to be able to survive this long. He'd taken refuge in the section where they stored the more expensive and unique items before they sent them home. It functioned under the highest level of security and was said to have originally been built as a bunker in case something exactly like this happened. Fortress rooms, they called them, and while they hadn't been used for the purpose of keeping something out in a long time, they did a remarkable job of it now.

Said somethings continued to prowl, and he glowered at them through the narrow aperture and wished he could see more. "The only thing worse than the fucker you can see is the one you can't." He wondered if they were gathering outside his line of vision deliberately.

"*Blyad*. This is like being a tiny fish in a can." A premonition seemed to sneak in and anchor itself despite the apparent lull outside. His instincts, honed in the jungle, warned of an impending attack and made him study his surroundings a little more intently.

He tried to decide what the building had been planned for. *If I know that, it might help to gauge its strong and weak points so I know what to look out for. Did they anticipate that the Zoo would somehow invade the base, or did they think someone else would attack?* The Americans, maybe, or perhaps one of the others. Of course, it could simply have been habitual paranoia.

Either way, he knew better than to count on a Zoo-proof hideaway. He'd put it from his mind, but the sense of tension that persisted reminded him that something had already gone wrong there. He'd discovered that during his first hour there when he'd tired of keeping an eye on the animals outside and decided to scan the rest of the safe room.

Most of the shelves were empty and a number of cases seemed to be in the process of being moved out, probably when the original attack had started. He could imagine the panic, during which a handful—most likely those in charge or with a little more battle experience—had sealed themselves in when the alarms had gone off.

While they rushed to find weapons and suits to defend themselves with, very little thought had been paid to the people who had worked there. He scowled when he accepted the harsh truth that they'd locked themselves in and most likely hadn't allowed anyone else in.

They'd gotten their just desserts, though.

His gaze turned to a pile of bodies in the far corner of the room, all dressed in uniforms, and he shuddered involuntarily. Even now, he struggled to wrap his head around what had killed them and how it had penetrated a reinforced safe room.

"Sal needs to see this," he muttered and forced himself to step away from the murder hole and focus on the gruesome pile. The niggling caution within him had decided finding an answer for this might be important if he planned to spend time there.

He grimaced and forced himself to ignore the unpleasant stirring of a stench of decay that hadn't been present earlier. "Fuck. Locked in with dead men, or a dead man myself out there. Jacobs would know what killed them, but I've never seen anything like it."

Yet again, he scanned those who were visible and found no sign of injuries that might have been inflicted by claws or teeth. While he'd seen almost everything the Zoo had to offer, he'd never encountered what looked like an organic kind of acid in such quantities that it had killed them all, seemingly at once. It was present everywhere on their skins like it had been in the air around them and soaked through their clothes to kill them slowly and painfully.

The sight had been all he needed to keep his suit on for the duration of his stay. It wasn't his size and was therefore ungainly, but he decided it would be more comfortable than what had kissed those poor bastards. Since he still didn't have Sal or Courtney around to investigate, he would have to stay in the proven safety of the suit that was a little too big and made him feel clumsy and awkward.

Gregor growled annoyance when a screech and loud thudding from outside disrupted his study and he shuffled to the murder hole. A couple of the larger gorillas—those with horns jutting from their heads—had taken it upon themselves to attempt to break through the doors and now pounded their shoulders into the hardened steel plates. One of them was already bleeding from when it had tried to charge horn-first.

He adjusted his position to find a slightly better angle. The screech hadn't come from one of five he could see but rather from a couple of panthers that had been in their way. His eyes narrowed as he considered this new surprise. It was the first time he had ever seen any of the monsters kill the other.

They had to do it, though, given that a wide variety of them were carnivores and none of them were seen outside the jungle hunting non-Zoo creatures. Still, this wasn't predator and prey. It was simply total disregard for whatever was in their path—battle focused, he realized, driven by singleness of purpose.

"But of course, these assholes must now come and make a noise." There had been no running battle and the mutants hadn't roared and shrieked as they did during a direct attack. He knew that had been fortunate and had bought him more time—which now seemed to have run out. "I do not need them to call their big friends to come play. One of the dinosaur monsters could crush this little hidey-hole with one foot."

Maybe it is best to make sure none of the monsters are

MICHAEL TODD & MICHAEL ANDERLE

around to attract attention. I can surely eliminate five of these bastards if I am careful. Perhaps, if the Zoo thinks there are no more humans, the other creatures will become bored and wander away.

Moving quietly and cautiously, he pushed the barrel of his assault rifle out of the hole, aimed it at the closest gorilla, and pulled the trigger. The weapon kicked back comfortingly when it fired a three-round burst that drilled through the white fur of the creature's head. It fell with a single shriek and he grunted with satisfaction.

The others turned toward it, realized that something was wrong, and had the reasoning confirmed when he chose a second target and fired. Another three-round burst clattered into its head. A calm and measured approach without raging combat was a bonus. He was able to focus and steady himself for each shot, which made him more effective. When the second mutant fell, the remaining three roared and looked around to determine what had attacked them.

"Die, motherfuckers," he muttered softly in Russian and continued to pull the trigger until none of the monsters remained alive. He had no way to know what might be lurking outside his limited range of vision, though, and the attack reminded him that vigilance was necessary.

"Am I interrupting something?" A voice spoke in his commlink—the familiar, welcome voice of the hacker he'd called for help.

"I'm getting rid of some of the local wildlife," he replied. "It's good to hear your voice again, Anja. I began to think you had abandoned me to my fate."

"Perish the thought, Gregor," she replied with a chuckle.

"I had to set the teams up to come in and rescue you. Speaking of which, a group is assembling at the edge of the base and is almost ready to go in. They're clearing some wildlife of their own at the moment but should be only a few minutes away."

"I can't tell you how much I appreciate your assistance, Anja," he said with a chuckle and manually replaced the magazine in his assault rifle. "Although, if it's not too much trouble, I would appreciate you getting your team in a little faster."

"I'm working on it," the hacker replied. "You stay safe in there, you hear?"

"I'm working on it," he answered.

"Do you ever think about how we simply jet from one disaster to another, work it through, get everything we need and barely escape with our lives, only to find ourselves feet-first in another disaster?" Madigan asked and sounded unusually thoughtful.

Sal looked up from what he had stared at for the past few minutes, not quite sure where his mind had drifted off to or for how long. A quick peek out the window revealed that they were already clear of the European continent and currently over the Mediterranean. It had been at least a couple of hours, right?

As for what he'd stared at, he realized it was his research papers on himself—or rather, the effects of the goop on his body since he'd started taking it in small doses. There was a selection of effects he'd listed as only explainable by something that couldn't be found naturally in the world—like his ability to process vast amounts of alcohol as well as his stamina between the sheets.

A secondary category had been those that could be explained or correlated to what happened when you underwent a significant change in your life, as he had, as well as the various circumstances that were now the norm for him.

Being in a combat situation as consistently as he was or pushing himself through the active lifestyle that came with regular trips into the Zoo were two examples. They could account for him suddenly gaining additional muscle weight, faster reflexes, and enhanced combat abilities.

These were the alterations he could either attribute to the goop or something else entirely—or maybe, most likely in his reasoning, a combination of the two.

A third file contained a handful of odd psychological changes that he'd begun to take note of once it became clear that the changes he was undergoing were not only physical ones.

Those worried him most. He would need to bring a professional in to diagnose any problems he might have. Of course, some alterations to his psychology could simply be attributed to his change from a mild-mannered if a little lazy and eccentric genius researcher into one who charged into an alien Zoo, willing and able to cut down anything that got in his way and tried to hurt him and his.

"Sal?" Madigan called.

He shook his head when he realized he was doing it again.

"Sorry," he replied. "I was lost in thought, is all. What were we talking about?"

"Well, we—Courtney and I as I'm not sure where you've been—were talking about how we simply seem to react to all the bad shit that happens around us," she said and reiterated her point from before his mind had drifted off. "We don't ever act on our initiative and always jump when someone else tells us to, as it were."

He shrugged. "There is action in reaction, I suppose. We're learning all we can about what we face out there and gathering all the information we might need if at one point, initiative is needed. Know your enemy in the paraphrased words of Sun Tzu."

"That's what I was saying," Courtney pointed out.

"Right," Madigan grumbled. "I still don't like the fact that someone or something else always seems to pull our strings."

"It's not pleasant, no," he agreed, closed his eyes, and rubbed his temples gently. "But what else can we do? Until we know what we're dealing with exactly, we're forced to react. The only thing we can do is learn about what we're doing out there."

"What are you talking about?" Courtney asked.

Sal's eyes opened and narrowed in quick succession. "I'm talking about the Zoo invading the Russian base. What are you talking about?"

"Yeah, that," Madigan interjected quickly. He had reason to doubt her assertion based on her tone, but he was interrupted when Anja broke into their conversation through the earbuds they all wore.

"I don't mean to interrupt what I assume is a deep

philosophical debate about how to give me a raise while still not boosting my ego too much," the Russian hacker said, "but I have news. Is now a good time to share?"

"Share away." He grunted and leaned back in his seat.

"Well, I have news from our people in the part of the Zoo formerly known as the Russian base," she continued. "Davis is leading that team. He arrived a little before the others and he's in the process of eliminating what amounts to a greeting party from the Zoo. His team should arrive in a few minutes, though, and from there, they will push into the base to find Gregor."

"It sounds like it's going according to plan, right?" Madigan asked. "I still think we should head out there as soon as we touch down, though."

"Agreed," Courtney said.

"So far, so good, yes," Anja responded. "On the US front, I've had a nice conversation with Anderson about how things are going there. It took some convincing, but he managed to get Savage on board with Molina's schemes. Although, with Sam and Terry still recovering from their romp in Chernobyl, it should be noted that the whole of that mission will rest on his shoulders, and his alone."

"I think he can handle it," Madigan pointed out, and the other woman nodded in agreement.

"Well, yes, obviously, and I'll give him what support I can," the hacker confirmed. "So maybe not completely alone? Anyway, he seemed about as happy as Anderson was about the whole arrangement. I'll keep you updated."

Courtney looked like she wanted to ask for more details. Sal wasn't surprised, given that it was her company they were keeping afloat and she wanted to be fully involved in any plotting, planning, and scheming that occurred. She also had a responsibility with Heavy Metal, though, and it was the one she gave priority at the moment, as her mouth snapped shut again quickly.

"Thanks for the update, Anja," he said when it seemed there was nothing more to be said on their side. "We'll touch down soon and we'll contact you then."

"See you soon," she said in parting.

"Like I said," Madigan grumbled once it was only the three of them again. "Jetting from one problem to another."

"I wonder how long that'll last," Sal said idly.

"The question, I think, is how long will we last?" Courtney interjected. It was a good point and he couldn't help but agree.

CHAPTER EIGHT

The team, fortunately, responded to the news that Davis was almost on-site and took up the challenge. No one would bother to question why it didn't take them as long as Anja had assumed to reach the location.

"Five minutes," the driver yelled and cheers and catcalls resulted as the men checked their weapons again. The hacker had contacted the team of eight at the American base and informed them of a mission into the Russian base. Her wording had been vague enough that she had their attention in minutes.

Once she explained it, they were sold, and it wasn't only because they had always wanted to play at invading the Russians.

"Damn, I hope Davis hasn't finished the party without us," one of the men said and strained to see out the front windshield.

"Nah," another replied. "The old man knows we'd never leave him hung out to dry. He'll make sure he leaves enough monsters to boogie with." Most of them needed or wanted the money, but the man had been there for them when they needed him and taught them how to survive in the jungle. People underestimated him much of the time, but he was there to get the job done and never threw anyone to the Zoo in the process.

"I'm surprised you chose to come, Sousa." The driver caught Diego's glance in the rearview mirror. He'd worked with Heavy Metal for a few months, having retired from active service with the Marine Corps.

"Yeah, well, I can't go home yet. My girl wants a big ol' rock on her finger by the time the baby comes, so Papa needs to boogie all the way to the bank."

"What about the private sector?" one of the newer members asked.

"I looked at that as another way to make some quick bucks, but the offers that came were the kind that pissed me off while I was still active. I need the money but I don't want to be one of 'those guys.'"

"Fuck no," the man said and the team laughed.

They all had their reasons. Davis was the man who had ensured they were still around to pursue those reasons, and they would make sure he stuck with them for a long time.

Anja told them he had backup in the form of an AI-infused hammerhead, but that wouldn't be enough. It was a Band-Aid measure at best, and each of them counted the last remaining minutes with growing impatience.

When they crested the last dune and were given a clear view of the Russian base, they could already hear the sound of gunfire and explosions. They pressed forward and expected to see the man fighting for his life using his vehicle for cover.

The scene that greeted them drew exclamations and low whistles of disbelief. Davis stood with a fair number of mutants around him, but the creatures seemed to be at a distinct disadvantage. The ex-soldier held his ground and his powerful, altered, and upgraded suit laid waste to any that came in close enough.

"No fucking way," one of the team muttered when the hammerhead—also upgraded—launched a series of rockets at the advancing horde with unnatural precision. The projectiles streaked into the mass of attackers and drove them back a short distance.

The monsters immediately noticed the arrival of the new group and seemed to decide to cut their losses and retreat. They snarled and hissed as the gunfire faded and rushed toward what looked like an extension of the jungle that had suddenly decided to sprout buildings as well as trees.

"Holy fucking…" The driver cut the engine and rubbed his hand down his face.

"Yeah." Sousa looked at his teammates, who seemed to have been stunned into silence. "Unbelievable."

"What part? The picture of Metal Man and his trusty mechanical sidekick in action, or the Zoo gone rabid?" He gestured to where the jungle had overrun the Russian base.

"Both."

Davis coughed and lifted his helmet to get fresh air before he turned to his teammates.

"Once you fellows are done sitting around and gawking, we have a mission to get to," he snarked, checked his ammo count, and retrieved a couple of fresh mags from his Hammerhead. The group snapped into action. While what they were looking at was odd and otherworldly, they had been in and around the Zoo for long enough that they should be used to it.

They boarded hastily their vehicles to drive toward the base. Anja had told them someone was in there and in need of some assistance and had contacted her. She had cleared the finances for the trip already, which meant they didn't need to wait for any authorization before they reached the perimeter of the facility. It looked like the roads were still intact—or enough, at least, to allow the vehicles to roll across them—but everyone shared the opinion that they didn't want to take that chance. The vehicles were their best escape option if things went badly—which, in the Zoo, usually emerged as option A, despite their efforts.

The team had worked together long enough to know that low-key presence for the moment was their best choice. They would move into unknown territory and work from a less than advantageous position. A couple of orders snapped in a low tone were all that could be heard aside from the noises issuing from the jungle. They antici-pated an attack but so far, nothing could be seen around them to support that.

Aside from the creatures that had originally confronted Davis, the animals seemed to keep to the shadowy recesses of the jungle.

"You should have reached the center of the base, more or less," Anja said. "Why are you guys on foot? You could drive the Hammerheads in there, right?"

"We don't want to risk losing our only means of rapid

escape," Davis replied curtly. "Where should we go now, Anja?"

"Well, Gregor should be about three blocks in from where you stand," she answered. "Continue down the street and—huh?"

"What?" he asked and his gaze swept the area. She had contact with them and could therefore see the world through their HUDs. It meant that if she called their attention to something, it was worth taking note of.

"Nothing. It's only—did you look around for any signs of survivors?" she asked.

"Aside from your Russian friend?" he asked.

"Well, obviously aside from Gregor," the hacker snapped.

"What are you talking about?"

"Well, I'm looking to your left and I see a footprint on the ground," the Russian explained. He followed her instructions until he reached what looked like it had been a sidewalk at one point. Sure enough, a couple of boot prints led farther down the road but they disappeared three steps in.

"How do we know it's not someone who came through here before everything went sideways?" Sousa asked.

"Because the footsteps go over the foliage, genius," one of the other members of their team muttered. It was a good point. Whoever had left the prints had done so after the Zoo had already begun to grow in the area.

"Right." Davis growled in irritation. "Let's find Gregor and we can decide what to do about any other potential survivors. For all we know, he could be the one who left the prints, right?"

He'd raised another good point which even Anja didn't argue. The group started down what remained of the old street again and followed her instructions until they reached the building she had originally mentioned. It was smaller than most of the others, but it was the one that looked the most intact with virtually no vines or plants growing into it.

"I'll let him know you're there," she said quickly. A few seconds later, they heard movement on the other side of the door. They held their weapons at the ready until it opened slowly to reveal a man who wore a combat suit. If this was who had left the footprints outside, it would have been before he put the suit on.

"You boys took your sweet time," Gregor said in good English, although his heavy accent was familiar to the ex-soldier.

"Yeah, you're welcome," Davis replied and took a step back as the Russian moved out and surveyed the area around them with a scowl. "What?"

"I could have sworn I killed a few big ape-like creatures right here," he replied.

"Well, there's nothing around, so why don't you go ahead and grab your shit so we can get the fuck out of here?" he asked and his tone indicated that it wasn't a question but rather an order in disguise.

"Fine," he grumbled. "There's nothing to grab, though, so why don't we head out?"

"Wait a second," Anja interjected. "Remember those boot prints?"

"Oh, right," Davis replied. "Gregor, did you leave boot prints—"

"It wasn't him, dammit," she snapped. "There might be someone else still alive on the base, and they might need help."

"Even if you're right, we don't have the time to search through the entire damn base," her teammate reminded her. "We have your friend and we're heading out. Once Jacobs, Kennedy, and Monroe get back, we can decide if we'll go in for round two with the base-eating jungle, okay?"

"No, it's not okay," she replied. "If there will be a round two, we need to have information first and I know where you can get it. I'm not making this out to be an order or anything, merely a suggestion should you guys choose to stick around for a little while longer. What I had in mind was the server room in the base. It's the same building that contains the power plants. If you were to, say, bring up the auxiliary power system, I would be able to access the data that was saved before everything went dark. Maybe, just maybe, I could find out where any potential survivors might have hidden themselves."

He looked at the other members of the team. They had fulfilled the primary objective, which was to reach Gregor, but now that they had him, he wasn't sure if it was a little greedy to simply walk away on a high note. Knowing Kennedy, Jacobs, and Monroe, they would probably want to head in to find survivors and sticking around a little longer might help them with that.

When no response came to his look, he threw the challenge out. "All in favor of us sticking around for a little longer?"

A couple of hands remained down but the others snapped up quickly.

"I won't force anyone to stay longer than you have to." He scowled. "You two, head to the Hammerheads and keep them hot and ready for us when we get back. Take Gregor with you since he's probably already had about as much of this place as he's willing to endure."

"No offense, but these possible survivors are my people, assholes though they might be," the Russian said, although he didn't look happy about his choice. "If there's a chance they are still alive, I'd like to be a part, no matter how small, of the team that gets them out."

"Fair enough." Davis honestly wasn't in the mood to discuss it at the moment. There were problems arising from sticking around longer than they'd planned. Then again, any problems they didn't face now would be faced by any team that entered in the future. Things had gone somewhat smoothly so far, so why not push their luck a little?

"Be safe, boss." One of those who wasn't in the mood to stay any longer moved away from the group and jogged quickly to reach the vehicles safely, followed by the other man who'd voted against remaining there.

The team leader would have put the chances of them taking one of the vehicles and high tailing it to the American base at about even. They were, for all intents and purposes, mercenaries, and everyone knew you couldn't spend money if you were dead. Maybe they were reliable, but if they were, they would have volunteered to stay, right?

Then again, maybe the knowledge that they would

probably be overlooked for all future Heavy Metal missions would be enough to encourage them to stay, at least with the vehicles.

Either way, he had neither the time nor the inclination to worry about it.

"Anja, do you have their names?" he asked over a private comm channel once the group started following the directions that would lead them deeper into the facility.

"I do, and I'll give you one better, my friend," she replied with a suspiciously evil cackle. "I've already armed Connie with a kill switch on the vehicles in case they try to get away on their own. There's no way they'll get clear with what you might need to transport the survivors back."

"Thanks," he said and tried not to heave an audible sigh of relief.

"Why did you let them go anyway?" she asked as they continued to push cautiously through the base-turned-jungle.

"I don't need anyone on my team who will break ranks and run at the first sign of trouble," he answered and continued to keep their conversation away from the rest of the group. "Besides, if they do have some loyalty left in them, they might be able to drive the Hammerheads into the Base to get us out should things go badly."

"Well, that's nice and all, but I could have rigged Connie up with driving capabilities to the same effect," she said and sounded like she was grinning.

"Fair enough." He rumbled agreement and shrugged his massive shoulders as the team proceeded through the base. From the center, it wasn't that big. Most of the essential buildings were clumped together, and the remainder of the base was comprised of a variety of housing structures and roads.

It didn't take them long to reach the server building and once they were inside, they saw more signs that they weren't alone. For starters, of course, was the fact that someone had apparently sealed it from the inside. There were more tracks in the area too, which seemed to indicate that someone had sneaked around outside without attracting any attention.

"Can we get inside?" Davis asked and studied the area.

"It's been sealed, so maybe not," Gregor replied with a non-committal shrug.

"Seriously, we're walking around in combat suits," Sousa interjected, took a step closer to the door, and wrapped his fingers around the handle. "What is there in the world that's sealed that we can't get into?"

He pulled and dragged the door open with a massive heave.

"Huh, good point," the team leader conceded. "Well, Fort Knox, maybe."

"What?" Sousa asked, stepped into the building first, and gave the others the all-clear signal.

"Fort Knox might be a place that's sealed that we couldn't get into," he explained with exaggerated patience.

"Okay, sure...maybe, but I was always under the impression that what kept Fort Knox safe was the fact that there's a whole army camped right outside," the other man pointed out.

"Right, maybe," Davis conceded. They paid little attention to the conversation as motion sensors went live at the end of the corridor they now moved through. The entire group brought their weapons to bear until it was revealed that a solitary man stood at the other end, toting a pistol.

"Hold your fire," the American snapped. It wouldn't bode well for the rescue mission if someone accidentally shot the people they were there to rescue.

"Americans?" the man asked in heavily accented English. "Fucking great."

"Not only Americans," Gregor replied and delivered a couple of phrases in Russian that convinced his comrade to stand down. "We need to access the auxiliary power functions in this building."

"First things first," Davis said as he stepped forward. "Is there anyone else in the building?"

"Only me." The man, who looked to be in his early twenties, if that, sighed and shook his head. "But there might be others. We didn't exactly coordinate search and rescue out here, you know."

"Right," he grumbled and turned quickly to his team. "I need two volunteers to stay here and watch the perimeter to keep it clear in case we need to leave at speed."

Two hands came up and the remainder of the group moved into the building after the young man, who appeared to know his way around.

"What were you doing?" Davis asked as the Russian guided them to the power core.

"Staying alive, for the most part," he replied and shook his head. "I managed to get inside with a handful of others and seal the building, but when the mist cleared, they decided to go out and see if there was anyone else out there. They...never came back. I've been sealed up here ever since."

"What mist are you talking about?" Gregor asked in English to keep his American rescuers in the loop.

"If you don't know about the mist, you haven't been around here long," the young man replied. "It's...deadly. Seriously, it kills you in minutes unless you have a full suit on, but if you go outside in a full suit, the animals attack. It's kind of a...catch-twenty-two is the term, right?"

"That sounds about right," Davis answered as their guide opened another containment room that housed a couple of generators. They were still running, but the power cords were disconnected.

"Why did you do that?" Gregor asked.

"It seemed to attract the wrong kind of attention," the younger engineer said and crouched to push the connections into place. "It was like they were being directed to anything that might help to keep the base on the grid. When I unplugged it, they stopped attacking. Weird, I know."

"Wait, so if this mist were to come back now that the power is up, how can we get you out of here?" Davis looked in the direction they'd come from.

"I have a suit down here," the boy replied and patted what looked like a lighter version of a researcher suit. "It won't do much if the monsters come, but it'll keep the mist away."

"Fan-fucking-tastic." The American grimaced beneath his helmet. "Anja, do you have any signal?"

"I do now," she replied. "You guys might want to start getting out of there now. If the kid's right, you won't have much time before something big and angry decides to attack."

"Kid, get in…oh," Davis started to say but realized it was unnecessary as the youth was already dragging his suit on. "Let's move."

It didn't take them long to reach the surface, where the other two members of their team were already waiting. That was the end of the good news, however. Before they had even stepped outside, an eerie green mist began to cover the area.

"We're moving out," Davis ordered, determined not to let the creepy sight get to him. "And not that you would, but let's not have any exposed skin while this mist is around."

———

"Seriously. Who in their right mind thought working with that fucking bitch was a good idea?"

His hands tightened around the wheel, his resentment fueled by the fact that what lay ahead effectively ruined the early morning drive. It didn't help that it promised to be as peaceful as any he could have imagined.

For one thing, it was early enough in the morning that he was able to avoid the rush-hour traffic in the middle of the city. The distance also meant more than enough time to enjoy a very decent view of the sun rising over the city once he steered his company car out into the more elevated areas. There was no time to stop and smell the proverbial roses, but it should have helped to put him in a better mood.

"Take what you can get," he told himself. "That sunrise will likely be the best you'll find in this total bummer of a day—hell, a week or even more." It irked him that Molina had somehow tainted a city he had somewhat begrudgingly begun to take a liking to.

It's bad enough seeing her, but I now need to work for the bitch. Fuck, all I want is the problem of where the best place would be to go after I've murdered the absolute shit out of her.

Maybe somewhere with no extradition treaty. I have a little cash money to throw around thanks to Molina. The irony wasn't lost on him and he chuckled darkly. Thankfully, Anja's love for screwing casinos over had provided enough to balance whatever trace of guilt he felt.

Switzerland was a little too crowded and too expensive for his tastes. Somewhere like Montenegro or Vanuatu might be better. Then again, he doubted there would be a single place in the world where he could go that Anja wouldn't be able to track him down eventually, even if he managed to liquidate all his assets and disappear before she got wind of it.

The only question was whether she would try to find him.

That line of thought brought a smile but it was short-lived and he scowled at the glorious sunrise. He was left with his single-minded antipathy and the resentment that churned at being forced to comply with what he considered an almost insulting directive.

"Happy days," he muttered belligerently as he approached the airstrip where Molina would be waiting for him. "I hope she won't pick up her damn fool coming onto me again. The woman is thick-skinned and single-minded—I say 'fuck you' and she says 'yes please."

Maybe he could simply ignore her and take refuge in his pleasurable contemplation of how to kill her in a way that would give him the most time to escape.

A plane was already prepped for their departure and he stepped out of his car to retrieve his duffel bag and the suitcase Amanda had arranged to enable him to carry the half-suit they'd developed. When he closed the trunk, he glowered as Molina descended from the aircraft. He had hoped she would want to stay away from whatever dirty business she had in mind for him to unwillingly perpetrate but she apparently intended to stick around and keep an eye on him.

I'm not sure why that feels creepy, but it does. His glower settled into a scowl as she removed her sunglasses. She appeared perfectly well-rested and relaxed despite the fact that it was too early in the morning for anyone to look that way. Did she simply not sleep?

"I'm so happy you decided to join us, Mr. Savage," she said with a smile, patted him on the shoulder, and indicated for one of the attendants to collect his luggage and load it. "For a moment, I thought you wouldn't change your mind and would choose to stay here, sulking with the rest of your team about how the evil Molina is now a part of your company."

"What can I say?" Savage responded and his voice assumed a fake Italian-American accent. "You made us an offer we couldn't refuse."

"I know but given your history of ignoring offers others wouldn't be able to refuse and shooting anyone who got in your way, I had to consider the possibility." She chuckled, followed him into the plane, and gestured for the pilots to prepare for takeoff.

"Well, in all honesty, there is no way we would be able to pass your murder off as drug-related, so I'm afraid we'll have to work together for the moment," he said, sat quickly, and buckled himself in. He waited while she did the same and the plane began to taxi down the runway. "So, what did you want us to look into? Or did you simply want to jet around the world?"

"Well, as wonderful as that might be, I'm afraid we have to do some real work," Molina replied. "Your team has cost me considerable losses. Now that we're on the same side, I'd like to experience some of the profits you have enjoyed at my expense." She paused, retrieved a tablet, and handed it to him. "You might be familiar with this team of Russians since they tried to forcibly remove Anja while we were in Ukraine. They are also responsible for the human testing in the Lab and the Zoo that your friends put a stop to, which means they will target Pegasus and Heavy Metal to regain what was taken unless we act first."

"And what did you have in mind?" he asked as the plane accelerated for takeoff.

"If you check the tablet I gave you, you'll see the bio for a man who goes by the name of Adrien Solodkov," she said. He raised his eyebrows as he studied the man's resumé.

"FSB head of operations, former Spetsnaz, bounces all over the globe, and all-around sadistic motherfucker," Savage commented dryly and kept his other thoughts to himself. "This is the guy in charge of being a pain in our asses if we don't stop him?"

"Do you think you can handle him?" Molina asked.

He shrugged. "I always wanted to tangle with those Spetsnaz characters so I guess we'll find out, won't we?"

"You don't sound too enthused about the opportunity," she pointed out.

"Did you expect me to be happy about this situation?" he asked.

"Well, a girl can hope," she replied and leaned back in her seat.

CHAPTER NINE

"So," Davis grunted as he scrutinized the remains of the Russian base. "This is new."

He wasn't wrong. They'd seen all kinds of weird shit around the Zoo before and change after change had appeared to confound them in a matter of months, sometimes occurring even while in the middle of a trip into the jungle. It was why he was confident they would be able to take this mist crap in stride.

That said, it was new—the kind of new people might think was worrisome if they hadn't run into this type of shit all the time. The data they'd received thus far told them the vapor would be deadly if they were exposed to it in any way, which meant it was only a matter of time until it began to soak deeply enough into their suits to allow it into their respirators or other systems.

The bottom line, then, was that it was time to get the fuck out. Anja had access to all the data she would need, and they wouldn't stick around to try to find more survivors. They had already found one more survivor than

MICHAEL TODD & MICHAEL ANDERLE

they thought there would be, and Davis intended to take that win.

He scowled at the mist that had begun to collect on his suit. It was a little thicker than water and looked green, even with the visual filter in his HUD. It dribbled down the hardened surface of his suit like oil. Simply looking at it made his skin crawl.

"Gregor, you wouldn't happen to know if this was some kind of gas defense your people set up to ward off attacks and it's somehow gone a little haywire with the Zoo attack, would you?" Sousa asked across their team comms.

The Russian shrugged. "Anything's possible, of course. I doubt it, though. There's something about this that screams crazy monsters, wouldn't you say?"

"I would," Davis agreed and narrowed his eyes when he caught a glimpse of movement. It was hard to see anything with the vapor this thick and, unless he had gone crazy, the damn creepy stuff grew thicker by the minute. It could go either way, and neither possibility was mutually exclusive.

What appeared to be long, slimy tentacles—or maybe some kind of snake—moved over the buildings around them. As far as he was concerned, going crazy was the better option.

"Guys, the cameras are problematic, but I have the base's motion sensors up," Anja called through their team link. "That's the end of the good news since it looks like there's a whole fucking swarm of nasty heading your way."

"Okay, listen up," Davis commanded to catch his team's attention. He didn't want them to panic and needed to act fast before their situation slid from bad to worse. "We'll form a two-man line with the kid holding the center, move fast, and shoot our way out of this, understood?"

"Hey, I have a name!" the kid said.

"Who the fuck cares?" Sousa demanded and attempted to pass the higher pitch in his voice off as humor and not terror as the group fell quickly into formation. The youngster, who very obviously lacked both weapons and armor, took his place without argument. Their leader wished they had the time to outfit him a little better, but if they could get them all out of this damn place intact, it wouldn't matter.

A hint of movement in the thick fog around them provided a flurried warning that was all they needed to spur them into a jog. They opened fire when the monsters began their assault a split-second later. It felt like the onslaught came from every side—like they had planned everything and timed it so all the creatures would attack at once.

"Keep moving, you dumbass motherfuckers!" Davis roared when their line started to falter. He had seen many more monsters at once during his time, although never with this kind of intensity or coordination. It would be one of those stories Jacobs wouldn't believe since he wasn't there.

One of the men at the front of the line fell and immediately vanished, dragged soundlessly away by the animals without even a shriek from him. At least it meant that whatever happened to him was quick, even if probably not painless.

Davis pushed toward the front of the line and fired relentlessly on anything that moved that wasn't a part of their team. His intervention came too late and the second man at the front was targeted from the side. He screamed as he was dragged away from the line by two panthers that ripped into his armor. A horned gorilla rushed in and ran him through with its horn. Its white fur highlighted the red splatter of his blood.

How the fuck does it keep its fur white in the green mist?

The team leader acknowledged the weirdness of the thought while he loaded a grenade into his assault rifle. He made no effort to even try to slow as he launched the ordnance into the horde that still savaged their fallen team member. No monster would walk away from that shit unless they had armor. Maybe they would think twice about mutilating humans.

Despite his satisfaction at the results, he knew they needed more people.

"I sent a message to the two in the Hammerheads and they're on their way to you, Davis," Anja said and kept her voice low. "They should reach you in a couple of minutes and I didn't even need to activate the kill switches."

"I appreciate it, Anja," he shouted. He didn't need to raise his voice, but it was a habit he had picked up and he doubted he'd ever lose it. Shouting when there were bullets and explosions and screams around him simply made sure he did his best to be heard by all who needed to hear him.

One of the locusts darted closer as he began to reload and evaded his kick before it lunged forward to tackle him. The maneuver failed, but as he drew his sidearm to deal with the fucker, the monstrosity's jaws snapped around his leg.

His knee pinched painfully as the mandibles broke

through the section of armor and drew blood. It trickled down his leg but there wasn't much of it—not even enough to raise a mild concern for his health as his bullets pulverized the mutant and he holstered the sidearm again.

He spun to resume his position in the line and grimaced with discomfort but shoved the awareness aside. The pinch began to hurt even more as they pushed on. It was only a sting at first but slowly became a burn that seemed to sear into his skin. With each step, it grew more painful and he gritted his teeth as the loud revving of the Hammerhead engines drew closer.

"Are you okay there, boss?" Sousa asked and stepped beside him. Davis realized that he'd begun to limp and sweat trickled over his eyes to sting them too.

"Yeah," he lied. This easily ranked way up there with the worst pain he'd ever endured in his life. *Did the fucker inject some kind of venom into my system? Fuck.*

"No, you're not okay," the other man declared after a moment and helped him to limp forward with the rest of the team. They were still under attack but the intensity of the first assault had faded. Maybe they were prepping for another round or maybe they'd had enough.

Davis sank to the ground. The pain had reached the point where he couldn't think about anything else, and it surged through his body like a wildfire. He heard screams and it took him longer than he would have liked to realize that he was the source.

The shrieks of agony continued unabated as he fumbled and struggled to reach his leg. *Do something. Anything. Take the leg away if you have to. Please...stop the pain. Somehow.*

The vehicles came into view and released continuous

volleys of bullets and rockets to decimate the creatures that surrounded them. Sousa crouched beside the wounded man, who could still hear the screams. Someone was hurt, he thought and looked around but couldn't identify who it was. Maybe…oh, right, it was still him. That explained why his throat hurt.

"We need to get him to a doctor," his teammate said as one of the other members of the team stooped and helped to lift him and drag him to the Hammerheads. He couldn't feel the pain anymore and his mind fought between relief and fear that he'd lost the limb entirely. Or maybe he could feel it, especially if he concentrated. Everything seemed to fade into blackness, though, so it could have something to do with that.

The bump as the plane touched down was enough to wake Sal. He wasn't sure when he'd slid into a nap, but it was at least a couple of hours before since that was the time required for virtually any aircraft to travel from the Mediterranean to the American base. Those who were superstitious tended to fly around the Zoo rather than over it, which extended the flight by a few hours at least, although that would only increase as the jungle continued to grow.

Still, he felt a little better rested. He hadn't had much sleep the night before, and with all their moving about, it was almost afternoon by the time they finally landed.

"Did you have a nice nap?" Madigan asked and helped him out of his seat. He didn't need the help, obviously, but there was no reason to turn aid down when it was offered honestly. He grinned at her and placed a light kiss on her cheek.

"I did, thanks for asking," he replied with a grin and let her move ahead of him toward the plane's exit to disembark. The aircraft would refuel and immediately return to where it had come from.

Given the sheer amount of cash Courtney had to part with merely to convince the pilot to fly them to the Zoo in the first place, he was surprised the man hadn't insisted they parachute down. He was happy to have a regular landing, although he wouldn't have said no to jumping out in his new suit again. That shit was fun.

The last time had been from a helicopter, of course, but it was simply semantics.

"Hey, Anja, are you there?" Courtney asked and covered her ear so she could hear over the noise of the jet taxiing away.

"What's up?" Madigan asked and studied the condition of the base around them as well as the ominous dark-green smudge that sprawled across the northern half of their horizon. It was still far away and almost hidden by the relentlessly growing wall but close enough to be seen. Sal intended to raise the possibility of adding temporary defenses. The landing strip was behind the wall, but it was a fair distance from there to the base. With construction still in progress, Zoo could expand and anything in this still undeveloped section was vulnerable.

"Anja's active but she's not responding to my hails," Courtney explained. "Maybe you guys want to try."

"I doubt she's avoiding you." Sal chuckled. "I think she's

busy providing support for everyone else on our team and she'll get back to you as soon as she can."

"Right," Courtney grumbled. She was used to being the priority when it came to communications. He could understand that, but there were circumstances when certain other aspects of the hacker's life would take precedence. Like keeping the members of her team alive, for instance.

After a few minutes, her commlink went live in their ears. "Hey, Courtney, sorry I missed your hails. I was…a little busy on this end."

The woman sounded exhausted. Unless she had taken up some kind of cardio exercise around the compound, which he doubted, something was wrong.

"How are you feeling, Anja?" he cut in before Courtney could respond. He didn't want to seem mean, but he wanted to make sure the woman didn't say something snide and hurt their Russian teammate's feelings.

"I'm doing okay, thanks, Sal," she replied but without her usual sense of humor. "I just helped to get the team out of the Russian base."

"What happened?" Madigan asked. This was more her domain than Sal or Courtney's, and they were willing to admit that.

"Well, we took a couple of losses," the other woman said, tried not to sound too down about it, and failed. "We got Gregor out as well as another survivor and enough data for me to sift through. Hopefully, we can find others that way."

"What kind of losses are we talking about here?" Kennedy asked, her expression concerned.

"Two fatalities while they fought their way out," Anja said. "They were escorting Gregor and the other man out when they were ambushed by a damn horde of the creatures. They also experienced a weird green fog or mist or something that appears to be deadly. Davis had his armor breached, and...it doesn't look too good. The vitals in his suit say he's getting steadily worse. They're taking him to see a doctor now."

"Shit." Madigan growled and glanced at Sal to see his reaction to this. "What do you mean with this mist or whatever? Will we have trouble with that?"

"Well, from what little data I've been able to glean from the Russian servers, the stuff is very, very deadly," Anja said. "I don't know if there's anything more I can say about it."

Sal shook his head. "Fucking Zoo, man."

"Agreed." Madigan sighed. "I guess we'll stick around here until they arrive and see if we can get samples of this green mist shit—maybe off their suits or something."

"Make sure no one touches it with their bare skin," the hacker cautioned them.

"Thanks, we will," he replied. "You get some rest too, Anja. It sounds like you need it."

"That's appreciated, Sal, but I don't think I'll manage any sleep yet. I'll let you know if there are any updates."

He looked at his companions and deliberately didn't ask for their suggestions as to what they should do. While he knew what Madigan would be aching for, it didn't seem respectful to wait for one of their wounded comrades to return while drinking their body weights in alcohol.

Courtney seemed a little more curious about what they

might find in the mist Anja had mentioned, while he... Well, yes, he was in the mood for a drink as well as curious about what this new development might mean for the Zoo.

Is this something we can expect in there from now on? That'll add a whole new level of vulnerability to the teams. Maybe it is a Russian development they neglected to mention that had gone haywire thanks to the Zoo's invasion.

There was no way to tell until they knew what they were dealing with. Anja sent them video footage of what happened to the team, and Monroe was able to look at Davis' vitals through his suit, which was still mostly intact except for a couple of breaks around the knee area.

They passed the information to one of the resident surgeons in the base's hospital, and the man's alarm at seeing his heart rate so elevated was enough to worry the three Heavy Metal teammates. A special operating theater was prepared to be ready as soon as they arrived. Thankfully, they did take Sal's warning about what they might find on the surface of his armor very seriously.

The team arrived in two Hammerheads and looked considerably the worse for wear. A layer of green clung to both vehicles, and when they disembarked, it looked like their suits were covered in the same shit.

Quarantine measures were put into effect, although they were expedited in Davis' case and he was stripped hastily of his armor, cleaned, and cleared to be moved into the hospital without any unnecessary delay. The other team members needed to wait a while, but none of them showed any inclination to complain much.

They were stripped of their armor as well and every piece was very carefully scoured to remove the film of green residue. What samples could be collected were sealed into a few containers and placed aside.

"What happened in there, Sousa?" Madigan asked through the plastic isolation booth the man was in.

"We went in to get the Russian guy out—Gregor, I think his name is." The tall, lean, vaguely Latin-looking soldier with green eyes and reddish hair shook his head. "We found him, but Anja said she found traces of other survivors and we went to look for them and for some... server rooms, I think. I didn't pay too much attention and simply followed Davis. When we were done, though, the mist had already covered the whole place and the critters were using it for cover.

"We lost Lee and Niska, and Davis had almost got us clear when one of the smaller creatures bit his leg. He was...fine at first but soon lost focus and limped worse and worse. Not long after, he fell and screamed in pain before he passed out. He woke up a couple of times on the way over, but he only...screamed for a few seconds, then fainted again. We couldn't treat him without exposing ourselves to the same stuff he was suffering from. I'm sorry, boss."

"Don't apologize," she said, her voice softer than usual. "You did what you had to do. And Davis will make it through this. He's one of the toughest motherfuckers I've ever seen, and he'll be pissed off that you guys are all depressed like this over him."

"Yeah." Sousa tried to chuckle, but a distant, mile-long stare came into his eyes again. There wasn't much more she could do except draw away from where the man tried to come to terms with what had happened. Sal could relate to the feeling. It had gone through his mind and body more times than he cared to admit.

"What are you thinking, Sal?" Madigan asked as they moved away from the group of men still in quarantine.

"My first impulse is to rush in, finish what they started, and find the rest of the survivors if there are any," he said and pitched his voice low as his gaze moved to the two Russians the team had brought out. "But...my gut tells me we should probably have a look at this residue first."

"Go with that instinct," Courtney agreed. "We'll gather our people, plus our two survivors, and head to the compound."

"Shouldn't we wait to see what Davis' condition looks like?" the other woman protested.

"I got the quick once-over from the docs who have taken his case," she said softly. "It...doesn't look good and he'll be in the operating theater for a while. We can't do anything for him while he's in there, so I suggest we get our tired and possibly traumatized team to the compound."

"That sounds like a good plan," Sal agreed and after a few moments, the other woman nodded reluctantly.

"As long as the docs let us know the minute that he's out of surgery," she said by way of a condition as the officials began to release the team from quarantine.

CHAPTER TEN

"So, what are we looking at?" Madigan asked.

Sal looked up from the tablet his gaze had been locked on for what felt like forever. He hadn't even blinked, as evidenced by the fact that his eyes felt dry and scratchy and he needed to rub feeling into them as he closed them for a moment and shook his head.

"Sal?" she queried again and leaned forward.

"Courtney and I have run a few tests, so we're waiting for the results on those," he said finally. "The prelims we were able to get quick results on say the stuff is organic in origin. I think we can rule out the idea of it being Russian-made, although that's gut feeling and not hard science. Anything else regarding its origins…well, we'll have to wait for the tests—probably overnight but maybe longer. What we do know is that it's highly acidic—and has very unusual properties."

"Why didn't it melt through the armor?" she asked, her head tilted in confusion.

"That's part of the unusual aspect. For some reason, it's

not corrosive to armor, only flesh," he said. "One explanation might be that it contains enzymes that do the dirty, but that's only supposition. And honestly, please don't give the Zoo any ideas. It's getting hard enough to move around in there without a gas that can melt through armor."

"Right." She grunted and studied the rest of the team quietly. Those who were assembled all had the distant look they'd seen in Sousa, even the Russian. Not Gregor, though. That man could walk through a nuclear apocalypse with a snide dick joke and come out the other side complaining about the shit vodka they had in the wastelands.

They didn't usually have this many people in the compound, their inner sanctum, but given what the men had been through earlier, Sal felt it was right. They had earned their place among the Heavy Metal veterans.

"Acid in the air," Madigan muttered. "What the fuck else will it come up with next?"

"Let's hope nothing else," he responded fervently. But… yeah, talk about a futile wish, right?"

"Right," Courtney interjected. "Anyway, from what we can tell, it only affects organic material, so maybe avoid taking your suit off when it's in the air."

"Wait," Sousa said and raised a hand to call their attention to him. "While I don't disagree that we shouldn't start licking it, the animals that attacked us didn't have any reaction to it in the air."

"Well, like with most of the shit in the jungle, the creatures created by the Zoo might be immune," Sal suggested aloud. He didn't expect a response and didn't get one.

"Either way, this is all merely conjecture at this point. What we need is cold, hard data."

"And data is what I have in spades," Anja said, almost as if she'd waited for her cue before she stepped out of the server room. She carried a laptop in her arms and placed it on the coffee table in the center of the area where they were all seated. "I managed to pull a fair amount off the Russian servers before they went down again about an hour and a half after the Heavy Metal Team left the base. It's still decompressing and that could take a little longer. In the meantime, we're looking at some of the video footage your HUDs collected while you were on the base."

"Wait, why are we looking at that again?" Sousa wondered. "We all experienced it so why would we need to do it again?"

"A, because memory is a tricky thing," the hacker said and pulled the footage up. "And B, because your suit collects data and saves it for later study, even when you're distracted and have to run around, shoot, and fight for your collective lives. Finally, C, because we're missing a couple of members of the party, may they rest in peace, as well as Davis, who— Well, there's been no word on his recovery yet. Now, can we stop talking and watch the fucking thing?"

There were no more complaints as she called the collective footage of all eight of the team members onto the device and projected it onto a much larger flat screen on the wall. It was a little disconcerting, but after a few minutes, the group had adjusted enough to be able to follow the action. They caught up to Gregor, found him in a sealed building, and decided to stay for a little while. Two of the footages moved out, while the others remained. Gregor's feed wasn't included. Maybe his suit was a little too old-fashioned to record or perhaps she was still decoding it.

They reached another building. Two hung back to keep an eye on the entrance while four moved inside and located the second survivor. Alexei Mirkov was his name, an electrical engineer who hadn't been on the base for longer than two months, poor kid.

The men on the outside caught sight of the mist as it began to drift closer. Weapons were readied and worried exchanges shared. They didn't plan to bail on their comrades, but they did prepare for a fight. As the team joined forces again, they began to move through the green mist that grew thicker with every passing second.

"Stop it right there," Sal said and suddenly bolted out of his seat and narrowed his eyes. "Pull it back three seconds and replay it at a quarter speed."

Anja typed a few rapid commands and the footage repeated at a quarter of the regular speed.

He recognized what he saw. Something writhed as it grasped and dragged itself across a few of the buildings closer to Davis' footage. It was all too familiar, a regular part of the nightmares that had plagued him over the past week or so. Shivers traced up his spine, and he forced his right hand to pinch his left wrist to make sure he wasn't currently in one of those nightmares.

"It looks like it might belong to one of those tentacle creatures we saw in Ukraine," Madigan said and focused on each of the feeds in turn. Sure enough, the closer they looked, the more evidence they could see of the tentacles and the countless eyes that surrounded the monster. "Can we tell how big the critter is from the tentacles?"

There were enough of them to match the innumerable eyes but no evidence of the creature at the center of them all. The huge, fleshy monster with hundreds of eyes and hungry, salivating mouths with long, needle-like teeth simply waited for something to be fed into them.

Sal turned away from the footage and strode to the corner of the room. He didn't want to see any more. In all honesty, he didn't want to have to even think about it.

"Are you okay, Sal?" Courtney whispered as she moved to him and placed her hand on his shoulder to give it the gentlest of squeezes to let him know she was there.

"Nah," he replied, his voice a little hoarser than he expected it to be. "I'm fucking far from okay."

Anything she might have said about that was cut off when her phone rang and drew the room's attention to the two of them. She yanked it quickly out of her pocket and pressed the button to answer.

"Thanks, Doctor, we'll be right over," she said softly a few minutes later after having said little other than a couple of grunts and quiet encouragement to keep the doctor on the other end of the line talking.

"Davis?" Madigan asked, folded her arms, and tried not to look as concerned as Sal knew she felt.

"He's out of surgery," Courtney said with a small smile. "Doc said he's relatively stable, although they want to keep him in for observation for a few days in case. That's the good news."

"And the bad?" Gregor demanded, speaking for the first time since he'd arrived at the compound.

"The acid soaked into his leg for too long," she continued and struggled to keep her voice from cracking. "They had to amputate since sepsis had already set in."

"Shit." Sal growled.

"We should go there." Madigan pointed vaguely in the direction of the hospital. "Not everyone, of course. You guys need rest. But someone should be there when he wakes up…to help him. Be there for him."

Sal, Courtney, and Madigan decided to go, and the other team members elected to spend the night at the compound and come over in the morning. Davis waking up during the night wasn't likely, given the drugs they had him on to help him sleep and recover. But if he did, Sal knew he would want someone to be there if he were in Davis' shoes.

Savage hated every minute of the long flight.

Even in a jet designed for speed and comfort, getting from the East Coast of the United States to Central Europe was a long haul, no matter which way you sliced it. *And I'm stuck here with the one person I want dead most in the world. I can't kill the bitch and I can't get away from her. The whole situation sucks.*

At one point, she moved to the back of the plane, where there was a cabin with a small room complete with a bed, table, and TV to enable Molina to be as isolated from him as possible. It didn't help. Merely knowing she was there was enough to grate on his nerves and keep him in a state of continual uneasiness.

As a result, he'd been unable to sleep, and even his pleasure in watching a couple of movies and TV series he'd hoped would help to calm him was denied. As he couldn't resist the feeling that she was somehow watching him. *It's creepy and I don't think it's paranoia. The woman is capable of anything.*

All in all, it was a long, tiresome motherfucking flight.

Still, he knew things would only get worse from that point forward. He needed to make his peace with the fact that he was in this for the long haul. He'd made a promise to Anderson that he would get this shit done and finish it besides, and he didn't intend to let his boss down. Or Monroe. He knew she was involved, even though the woman hadn't made an appearance on the mission yet.

A car waited for them when they landed in Prague. Again, Molina looked like she'd had about three days' worth of sleep in her private quarters and a solid gallon of coffee. There weren't even bags under her eyes. Savage reluctantly had to admit that the woman looked good for having flown across the Atlantic Ocean. His gaze drifted to the distinctive blue that defined her veins. *Yeah, that's why. And it goes a long way to explain the creepy factor too.*

They headed into the city a few minutes later. A half-hour drive delivered them to the entrance of a high-end apartment building, the kind that had valets and security out front. The help didn't take kindly to the fact that he shoved the man who had tried to run a quick search on him.

"Try it again, I dare you," he snapped and glared when the guard moved a hand to his hip. A coat covered what could have been a pistol or a radio. Either one would not be drawn quickly enough before the operative pummeled him into submission. He was in that kind of mood.

Molina stepped in, placed a hand on the guard's shoulder, and whispered a few words in Hungarian to him before he eventually calmed and backed away from Savage, who insisted on carrying his luggage to the elevator.

"What did you say to the asshole outside?" he asked when only he and his unwanted companion stepped into the elevator.

"I told him you were with me," she replied calmly and watched his reaction through the mirrored reflection on the elevator doors. "I don't think he believed me, but it's not his place to question my word on things."

"You know, I bet you wonder why we gave you so many L's while we ran against each other," he stated with a smirk.

"L's?" she queried.

"Losses," he explained. "It's because Monroe doesn't hire people who don't question her. She calls experts in and lets them do their thing. Basically, she knows how to delegate."

"When I delegate, people tend to try to fuck me over," the woman retorted. "But you might have a point. I've had trouble with personnel lately, true, which is why I thought I would delegate my money-making problems to you and your team."

"Of fucking course." He scowled, closed his eyes, and resisted the urge to prove the guard downstairs right. Even if it killed him, he would see this fucking situation through. And it probably would kill him, he reasoned morosely.

His murderous tendencies were curbed when they reached the penthouse suite. He had expected excessive luxury and pampering to accommodate someone like Molina, and as it turned out, he was half-right. The woman knew how to choose a location, as the glass windows gave a fantastic view of the city below.

As for the luxuries within, they were replaced with what looked like a command center. About a dozen people worked on computers, all connected to the kind of complicated server banks he imagined Anja worked on and geeked over. A couple of rooms off to the side might be used for sleep, but the remainder of the space had been designed strictly for utilitarian purposes and set up with the best of everything money could buy.

"That said..." Savage growled irritably, not sure if he wanted to complete his sentence. "I'm impressed. How the hell were we able to keep up against you for this long?"

"That is the very question that made me wonder about my personnel, darling," Molina replied with a grin, clearly very proud of what she had established there. It was an impressive sight, he had to admit. The professionals at the computers barely even looked up when they stepped out of the elevator.

"Although, in my defense, I did have numerous other balls in the air while I dealt with you and your Heavy Metal friends," she continued to explain. "I ended up delegating to the likes of Carlson and Banks, who fucked up in a variety of degrees to the point where I realized that if I wanted something done, I would have to do it myself. A few weeks later, I brought your team into the fold, and I'd say I should have done that a little while ago, wouldn't you?"

"I'd say that if you hadn't gone after my and Anderson's

families, we wouldn't have been in this predicament to begin with," Savage answered with a shrug and placed his bags on the black marble floors.

"Well, yes, but again, I would never have made those calls," she replied with a hint of defensiveness in her tone. "They fucked up, as I said."

"Would you still feel that way if they had succeeded?" he demanded and turned to face her. She didn't offer him the same courtesy but turned away and walked to where a group had begun to gather around a couple of the larger screens in the room.

He smirked. "Yeah, I didn't think so," he snarked under his breath and followed her while the group of technicians began to prepare a presentation for their benefit.

"Miss Molina, how nice to see you again," said one of the techies, a tall, thin gentleman with brown hair and a Van Dyke he appeared to groom excessively.

"Victor, what do you have for me today?" she asked and moved directly to business.

"Well, we have some matches on facial recognition based on the pictures you procured," he replied and directed their attention toward the screens. These displayed a handful of images of a lean man of medium height with black hair that showed traces of gray. The pictures weren't of the best quality, likely pulled from traffic and security cameras.

"We haven't narrowed a location down yet, but there is an area he appears to confine himself to," Victor continued. "Given that he entered the country on a fake passport, he would most likely lay low in an FSB safe house. You might be able to find it in the area."

"Send the data to my man, Savage, here," Molina replied and patted the tall man on the back. "He'll be able to sniff our friend Solodkov out of wherever he's hiding. He is good like that."

"Yes, ma'am," Victor replied and didn't even bother to question who Savage was. Specialist though he might be, he appeared to be more than used to the peculiarities that arose while working for someone like Molina.

CHAPTER ELEVEN

A long night followed their arrival at the hospital. As tired as Sal felt, he wasn't able to get any sleep on the uncomfortable chairs provided in the waiting area. They had hoped that more news would come about Davis' operation, but as the hours ticked passed, Sal, Courtney, and Madigan finally resigned themselves to the fact that they would spend the night.

In this particular case, no news was good news, as anything new on his situation while he was supposed to be resting under heavy medication would mean something had gone wrong.

None of them wanted that.

Madigan seemed the most affected by what was happening. Sal thought so, anyway. She was quieter than usual and displayed less of the take-control attitude he both loved and feared about her. The woman tried visibly to keep herself calm and alternated between sitting beside him, staring forward at the wall, and pacing. Through it all, she tapped her wrist lightly every few seconds as if she tried to convince herself that whatever was happening couldn't be real.

I can relate to what she's going through, although maybe not fully. Part of her response was ingrained in her military experiences. The man had been an exceptional soldier, and when it came to people like Madigan and Davis, he was her comrade in arms and probably something of a mentor too, since he had been stationed there before she arrived. He couldn't identify with that but could understand that watching someone like him endure so much damage was overwhelming. *Yeah, it's enough to make anyone consider their chances of walking away from the Zoo unscathed. With all the history, it must affect her tenfold.*

Sal wanted to hug her, wrap her in his arms, and tell her everything would be okay. He couldn't promise anything, though, and she wouldn't appreciate him showing any weakness around her while she tried her hardest to remain strong in a very public place. Instead, he simply put his hand on her shoulder when she sat and let her pace in peace when she stood.

When they finally returned to the base, he would embrace her and let her get everything out, whether it was angry yelling or crying. Knowing the woman as well as he did, either one was likely enough to be considered.

Footsteps brought him out of a restless doze after what felt like days later, although with the sun barely beginning to rise outside, it had been less than six hours. Madigan had finally calmed and managed to get some rest by laying her head on his shoulder. Courtney had laid on his lap, giving him some balance to work with while they waited. Now, with someone approaching, both were up and alert in seconds in the way people did when they were accustomed to resting in a dangerous location on a regular basis.

"Are you the team waiting for news on former Sergeant Davis?" the orderly asked and looked at each of them for a moment. "Might I ask what your relation to the man is?"

"This is a military fucking hospital," Madigan snapped at the young man. "What are you expecting, actual family?"

"We're his teammates," Sal cut in quickly before she berated the nurse even more. "I understand there's some paperwork regarding his bills that I need to fill out."

"You'll be happy to know the commandant has waived those in light of Davis' significant contributions to this base," the young man replied with a small smile. "So there's no need to worry about that."

"Well, I owe the man a case of vodka when I see him next," he said and tried not to chuckle. It didn't feel appropriate. "How is Davis?"

"An examination was made this morning," the nurse replied. "He's still in critical condition but he is awake and stable, so the doctors said you should be able to see him. Given the infection risks, though, you will have to do so through some isolation procedures."

"I understand." He sighed. "We only want to make sure he's okay."

"Of course," the nurse said with a sympathetic smile. "If you'll follow me?"

They did and took a moment to stretch and get the blood flowing in their limbs before they stepped into the quarantine ward of the hospital where they had put Davis for observation. Aside from the plastic that kept the three of them separated from him, it looked more or less like an average hospital room. The patient was still in the bed and looked battered, bruised, and a little pale as he turned to see who had come to visit.

His movements were sluggish, and it took him a few minutes of staring and blinking blankly before he realized who he was looking at. They could tell when he recognized them from the broad smile that filled his face.

"Hey, guys," he said, his words slurred as he fumbled for the bed control, missed it the first and second time, and finally grasped. He pressed the button that raised his bed into a semi-reclining position. "What are you doing here? I thought you...were all still on vacation. At the beach, right?"

"Well, we heard about what happened here, and we... had to be here, Sarge," Madigan answered, steeling her voice as she watched him. It looked like she made a point of not looking at the bandage where his right leg ended.

Davis showed no such restraint, however. He glanced at the leg and chuckled. "Damn...yeah, I don't think I'll punt anymore, honestly. I doubt I'll be able to run any missions for you guys either. At least until they develop a suit that works minus one leg, you know?"

"They are making amazing strides in that direction," Sal said and hoped he didn't sound like he was making light of the man's situation. Davis had the thickest skin of anyone he'd ever met, and yet there were things that you simply didn't joke about, intentionally or not.

"Well, let me know when that happens." He chuckled and rolled his shoulders.

"How are you feeling, Sarge?" Madigan asked. She placed her hand on the clear plastic between them and the man in the hospital bed.

"Not too bad, Sarge, not too bad." He stretched and shifted a little. "They have me on a shit-ton of meds, though, so things are looking as shiny as fuck from this end of the spectrum, do you know what I mean?"

Sal wasn't sure they did, but Madigan smirked and nodded. "We'll stick around the hospital, so if you need anything, give us a shout, would you?" she said, and he gave her a thumbs-up before she and Courtney exited the room.

He remained, though, and while he didn't know what he would do or say, something was needed in this situation. As the founding member of Heavy Metal, it was his place to step up.

Davis' mood shifted once everyone had left, although it took him a second to realize that Sal had stayed. The drugs were to blame, probably, although the man's face didn't brighten when he saw that his boss hadn't moved.

"I'm so sorry, Davis," he said finally and lowered his head. "I...just..."

"You don't have to say anything, Sal," the man replied, his voice a little less slurred than before, which indicated that what he had said previously was something of a performance for Madigan and Courtney's benefits. "We all knew what we signed up for when we started this gig. As it turned out, I was luckier than most."

"Not everyone would feel that way," he pointed out.

The patient shrugged. "I feel that way. I'm alive, and that's more than can be said for Lee and Niska."

He nodded. "I guess."

"I'm fine, Sal, seriously," Davis insisted. "Well, I've been better, but I'll walk this off the way I've walked all the other difficulties in my life off. It'll be tough, but I can get through it."

"Well, I hope you know there's a hefty Heavy Metal pension in it for you if you decide you want to head home after this," he replied.

The man shrugged. "Well...I hadn't planned to head home anytime soon. But then all this happened and...I'll think about it. Unless they get me a suit that can operate with a missing leg, that is. I've heard tell of something in that line, but I don't recall hearing if they cover missing legs or only those that are there but don't work. If and when that shit comes along, you can bet your ass I'll be right back in that fucking jungle with the rest of you."

Sal couldn't help a small smile. "You're a better and braver man than I."

Davis grinned in response. "Was that ever in doubt?"

He chuckled. "I guess not. You get better soon, you hear?"

The patient nodded and leaned back again as his visitor began to make his way down the hallway, where he could already hear Madigan and Courtney arguing. It sounded like they were discussing what to do next, with Courtney advocating a salt-the-earth kind of approach, while Madigan advised caution.

"What happened to Davis is a huge, motherfucking

warning sign to stay the fuck away from that base," Madigan said when he approached.

"Hey, I don't disagree," Courtney replied and slid her arm around his shoulder as the trio continued to the waiting room where they'd spent the night. "That said, we do need to find out what's happening in there, at least so we can get a hint of what we might expect should something head this way."

Madigan had no retort to that. It was on everyone's mind. The fact that a jungle could mount a surprise attack like that was terrifying, to say the least, and they needed to be prepared for whatever might lie ahead. Who was to say that the American base wouldn't be the next one targeted?

Both knew the other had raised valid points, and they paused their debate as it appeared the rest of the team had arrived to see Davis.

"He's awake again, and I think he'll be happy to see the guys who got him out of that nightmare alive," Sal pointed out as the nurse led Gregor, Sousa, Alexei, and the others toward the same room they'd recently left.

"Hey, guys," Anja called through their earbuds. "I hope this isn't a bad time, but I've managed to decrypt most of the data from the Russian servers. Aside from a whole shit-load of other crap, I have managed to find out what happened to the survivors of that damn base."

"Thanks for the heads-up Anja," Sal replied and took a deep breath to calm himself. "We're on our way back."

"Any progress, Savage?"

He looked up from the tablet he'd studied intently for the past few hours, shook his head, and blinked once or twice to regroup and settle his thoughts. Trying to track someone in an unfamiliar city had proven to be more troublesome than anticipated, and he'd had to resort to older tricks like marking the places where Solodkov had been seen on a physical map of Prague he'd picked up.

Molina had spoken to him and honestly, while he was in his researching zone, he didn't want to talk to her. He didn't want his concentration to be broken, but unfortunately, it seemed like that ship had already sailed.

"I've managed to narrow down the places where Solodkov might be staying, but it's still a three or four-block radius," he said, rubbed his eyes, and pushed the marked map around so she could see his work. "The pictures always show him walking, so I don't think he has a car of his own. That isn't unusual. If he's not familiar with the city, he will rely on his people to get him around town and will only get into a car when it's absolutely necessary. Here, you see him going to the metro." He sifted through a couple of photos. "And right there, into a small store to buy cigarettes."

"How do you know he's buying cigarettes?" she asked and raised an eyebrow.

"It's a liquor store, but he doesn't leave with any bottles," he pointed out after a pause to gather his thoughts. "He has no bag, so he hasn't stashed them in there, and it's logical that he bought cigarettes and tucked them into his jacket. Either that or the idiot would have to stop there about three or four times a day to buy tiny bottles of booze."

"Okay, that's a fair point." She grunted acknowledgment and folded her arms in front of her chest. "Carry on."

"The one interesting stop he makes is at a small Irish Pub...there," he said and indicated the picture in question. "It seems like he goes there every three days. He doesn't eat anything but instead, collects a large bag of food and takes it somewhere the cameras can't follow him. I'd say he picks food up for the rest of his team, and the lack of bus stops and metro stations in the area would indicate that it's in walking distance from his safehouse."

"Well then." Molina smiled. "It looks like you and I need to have a drink at an Irish Pub."

Savage sighed and made no effort to hide his grimace as he pushed out of his seat. The company would be lousy, but honestly, he could do with a drink, food, and the opportunity to escape the damned penthouse they'd been cooped up in all day. It was winter outside, but anything was better than remaining indoors with people he was half-convinced would try to kill him when the mission was over.

He collected his jacket, armed himself with only the magnetic revolver he tucked into his underarm holster, and joined Molina in the elevator that arrived as he reached it.

"Don't wait up," Molina called as the doors closed again. It was a short drive to the pub in question, although he suggested they stop a couple of blocks away and walk the remaining distance. Someone arriving by town car to eat and drink at a bar like this would be more than a little suspicious, and there was nothing he wanted less than to draw attention to themselves.

It was a short, brisk walk, and Molina edged a little closer to him than he would have liked to link her arm in his. He had an instinctive urge to push her away—maybe into oncoming traffic, he thought belligerently—but if avoiding attention was the game, he needed to play along with whatever she had in mind at the moment.

They found an empty booth and ordered drinks, and he leaned forward on the table between them to narrow his eyes in obvious displeasure.

"So," he demanded quietly. "What the fuck is your problem?"

She tilted her head and regarded him with an unreadable expression. "I'm not sure what you mean and I don't appreciate your tone."

"I don't like you, Molina," he said as bluntly as possible. "I don't like the kind of person you are, and I don't like the fact that you seem to condone this whole...ends justify the means business. Which begs the question of why you seem to play this game of pretending to be attracted to me. We work on the same side now, so it would be best if you stop playing games."

"Who says I'm playing games?" she asked and paused when their drinks arrived—a tall glass of lager for him and a whiskey sour for her. "Whatever you might think about the kind of person I am, I'm a woman who takes what she wants and fights to keep it. It's not something I reserve for only one aspect of my life, which begs the question of why it distracts you so much."

Savage shrugged. She made a good enough point, he supposed. "I guess it's because I don't know you. If I were working with someone I knew, trusted, and felt comfortable with, I would feel better about whatever…passes were made at me. As things stand, I don't know if you're being sincere, playing some kind of game, or looking for an angle that ends with me getting shot in the head—or some combination of the above and more."

"And what would be the problem with the combination of all the above?" she asked and sounded genuinely curious.

"It's distracting," he pointed out. "I don't know if the hand you loop around my arm is looking for a weapon to kill me with, and even if it's not, the possibility that there's some kind of agenda in what you're doing is enough to pull my focus off what we're doing."

She nodded. "I guess I can understand that. And I appreciate your candor if not your tone. That said, I won't change my personality or style simply to make you more comfortable. While I feel I am perfectly within my rights to demand you get over it, I do wonder if there's anything I can do to help you feel a little more comfortable in my presence."

He shook his head and took a sip of his drink. "Well, you could stop getting all touchy-feely, for one thing."

"I can't promise you anything on that end, darling." She grinned and leaned forward to trace her fingers over the back of his hand. "Is there anything else I can do to help?"

Savage yanked his hand away and scowled at her. "Why don't you tell me a little about yourself?"

"Is there anything you'd like to know?" she countered with a hint of teasing in her tone. "I've had a rather adventurous and exciting life, although I suppose you have too."

"That's not how this works." He threw her an irritated glance and raised his hand to indicate for the waiter to return. "You need to be able to think of something you want to talk about. Something you want to share and that you'd feel comfortable with me picking down to the tiniest detail and possibly even making jokes about."

"How can I help, sir?" asked the young man he'd called over.

"If you could bring us refills on our drinks," he said and drained his beer in a couple of gulps. "And how about one of those platters for the table? The one with a little of everything—sausages, fries, onion rings, wings, the works."

"Of course, sir." He picked up the empty glass and headed to the bar.

"I don't need a refill," Molina pointed out and took a sip from her glass that was still about three-quarters full.

"And that segues us directly into point number two," he said. "You need to drink a little more."

"Might I remind you that we're working undercover and looking for someone?" she stated in a hushed tone.

"Right, and everyone knows that people who don't drink at a bar are suspicious," he reminded her. "Besides, if you want me to trust anything you have to say about yourself, I need to have the impression that your inhibitions are a little lowered so I can feel you're being honest with me. Can you do that?"

She sighed, rolled her eyes, and took another sip of her drink, followed quickly by another, and by the time the waiter was back with their drinks and food order, she was ready for the refill.

"So," Savage said as he chewed on a collection of the small pieces of food he could fit on a single toothpick. "What do you think you want to talk about?"

"Is there any kind of restrictions on what can be talked about?" she asked, her head tilted again with that slightly teasing attitude. "And does it have to be true?"

"Not necessarily, but you do have to sell it like it is," he replied, selected a piece of dried meat, and popped it into his mouth. "This is a bonding experience."

"Huh." Her face scrunched for a few seconds as if she thought hard about what she could say. Eventually, she seemed to make a decision and leaned forward. "Okay, I think I have it. People wonder why I'm so controlling and why I can't delegate problems to people I can trust."

"Like I mentioned before, sure."

"Right, okay," she replied. "Anyway, I do know what my problem is, aside from a chronic lack of trust in people. Seeing the dark side of humanity as often as I do, it's diffi-cult, you understand."

"Sure," he answered with neither sarcasm nor encour-agement. His lack of emotion didn't seem to affect her, though.

"Anyway, when I thought about it, I recalled that my father always pushed the idea of leadership on me," she continued. "It wasn't anything quite so cliché as him wanting a son and got a daughter instead, and nothing like my mother dying either. Although my dad did divorce her and he walked away with full custody when I was...three, I think. He didn't even like me that much and merely wanted an heir to his fortune to be raised according to his principles. As such, he oversaw every little detail of what I was taught, from the private teachers' backgrounds, to their curriculum, all the way to my diet and exercise regimens."

"Overbearing father figure...classic." He chuckled.

"I think that would be a mild way to put it." She laughed. "The first taste of what the real world was like was when I got a scholarship to Cambridge when I was sixteen. He wanted to come with me to ensure that he got what he wanted when it came to raising me, but the school refused him. That was the first time I realized he was nuts."

"Oh, please," he said and shook his head. "You don't call rich people crazy. They're simply eccentric."

"Sure, he was eccentric too, I suppose." Elena grinned. "And a verifiable genius when it came to manipulating the money he'd inherited from his parents. He didn't want me to throw all the cash he gave me away on boys, booze, and other vices, which is why he raised me so strictly."

"Well, my dad was as poor as dirt, so I think I can simply call him what he was—batshit fucking crazy," he replied cheerfully. "The man thought everyone in the world was out to get him. In fairness, he was serving in the Marine Corps at the time when the CIA ran all kinds of crazy experiments. While he never said it outright, I wondered if he was ever a subject of MK-Ultra or something like that."

"Huh, no kidding?" She leaned forward with what appeared to be real interest.

"Well, I don't have any proof but I had my suspicions," Savage continued. "The guy ended up schooling me at home too since he didn't trust the US school system to not brainwash me. He taught me to hunt and shoot a gun as soon as I could walk and made me take trips into the wilderness with nothing but a knife to keep me alive.

"My mom divorced his dumb ass when I was young, but

when she found out what he was doing, she sued for custody, won, and brought me to Seattle when I was... fourteen, I think. Maybe thirteen. Anyway, the damage was already done and I was almost as crazy as he was when I got back to the real world.

"I attended a real high school to finish my education, and when it became clear that I wouldn't get any sports scholarships and my scores were too low to get into college any other way, I joined the armed forces. And as a middle finger to the old man, I joined the Army instead of the Corps. He died while I was on my first tour. I didn't even attend the man's funeral."

"Wow." Elena rubbed her chin, her expression speculative. "Is any of what you told me the truth?"

"You have some of the best researchers on your side," he reminded her. "Why don't you go ahead and find out for yourself? We're merely talking here while we wait."

"I suppose, but how are we supposed to bond if we lie about ourselves?"

"It's to get a feel for the way the other person's mind works," Savage replied. "Even when someone lies, they display a psychological side of themselves—something they either want or don't want. And from there, subconsciously, we can bond with each other. Maybe not grow to trust, exactly, but maybe, just maybe, reach a point where we can interact without making each other uncomfortable."

"Well, you weren't making me uncomfortable," she reminded him, took another sip of her drink, and glanced at the food he attacked almost single-handedly.

"Sure I was." Savage grinned. "You were uncomfortable when I was honest with you and began to take control of the situation. You don't like having the control taken from your fingers quite that quickly. Or did I read your body language wrong?"

"You're a professional," she replied, selected one of the sausage pieces, and put it smoothly into her mouth. "Find out for yourself."

His grin widened like he might enjoy fulfilling that challenge, but his gaze shifted toward the doorway when two men entered. They were dressed in heavy coats and boots and quickly ordered food to go and drinks to nurse while they waited.

"That's who we're waiting for," he said quietly.

Molina turned to look at the newcomers, discreetly enough to avoid attracting attention to their surveillance. "How do you know?" she questioned dubiously.

"Their boots and stances, for the most part, scream Spetsnaz," he explained.

She raised an eyebrow.

"They're...very distinctive stances," Savage clarified, finished the food on the platter as well as his beer, and pushed himself slowly from his seat. "See, I think it was good that we did this. I already feel more comfortable around you, although I'm about...ninety percent sure you were lying through your teeth. I think we can keep working together."

She laughed and stood as well, took his proffered arm, and pressed herself a little closer.

"Well, maybe not that comfortable." He rumbled a protest and nudged her away a step while they watched their quarry receive their orders, finish their drinks, and head toward the door.

"Well, there's more than enough time to get there," Elena replied and nudged his ribs gently near where his pistol was hidden under his coat. "I look forward to more outings like this."

Savage held back his instinctive retort and instead, led them to the door. Still, he didn't completely push away from her as they stepped outside and set off after the Russians they assumed would lead them to their real target.

CHAPTER TWELVE

"Why don't you tell us your story, Gregor?" Madigan suggested.

"I didn't see or hear anything that anyone might consider relevant," the Russian replied with a shrug.

"Maybe you should let us be the judge of that," Courtney snapped. Her tone was a little icier than the situation warranted, but given the day everyone had endured as well as not having much sleep the night before, Sal could understand why she wasn't in the best of moods. He still intervened, however, and gave her shoulder a firm squeeze to calm her. She sighed. "I'm sorry, Gregor. It…yeah."

"Don't worry. I understand, Courtney," the Russian said with a smile. "Well, my story is basically that they were about to lock me up in Moscow when someone came in and handed the judge a message. They suddenly changed their minds and said it was time for me to return to the Zoo. I didn't even have the opportunity to see my family.

"They took my cuffs off, drove me directly to the military airbase, and flew me here together with a small team of veterans—those who had been into the fucking jungle before. When we arrived, though...it had already been overrun. We had weapons but no armor and I knew shit was about to go down. While the rest of the team investigated, I headed to a warehouse that contained combat suits. Some were still intact in there, so I started putting one on since I could hear the monsters already attacking the others and knew I didn't have much time."

"Wait, so you simply let the rest of your team die so that you had time to get a suit on?" Sal demanded, his eyes narrowed.

"In short, yes." Gregor nodded, apparently unremorseful. "They were some massive, prolapsed assholes, though, so I didn't feel too bad about it. Right after that, I found one of the secure buildings they built for...I'm not sure. Maybe for defense, I think, but they used them to store the expensive Pita flowers before shipping them out. I locked it and waited after I contacted Anja to ask her to send someone to get me out of there."

"You're welcome!" the hacker shouted from her server room.

"It wasn't a sealed building, though," he continued. "I realized that when I found a couple of bodies in the back. Well, 'bodies' isn't quite the right word. I wouldn't have even identified the remains as human if there weren't some uniforms mixed in. Otherwise, they merely looked like a mass of rotting flesh that could have been a wild animal that got inside and couldn't find a way out."

"Well, I guess we know what caused that," Madigan said, cracked her knuckles, and rolled her neck, sure signs of her heightened tension. "I only wish we knew what the fuck this green mist is. We've established that its origins are inside the Zoo, right?"

"More or less," Sal agreed.

"What do you mean, more or less?" Alexei asked and seemed a little confused when he looked at the teammates. He hadn't said much of anything since they'd rescued him from the base. That was entirely understandable after being in a life-threatening situation, only to be rescued and dragged into a group of strangers whom he didn't know from Adam. A smart man would take the time to be silent and see what they were talking about before he risked any input to the conversation. Right now, though, it seemed like he had something to say.

"Do you have something to add, short stack?" Madigan asked and raised an eyebrow.

"Well, I...yes, I do." Alexei looked a little intimidated by the woman but stood his ground for the moment, his posture stiff. "You want to know my side of the story too, don't you?"

"Well, we didn't intend to force it out of you," Courtney answered. "You have been through a traumatic experience, after all, and if you wanted to avoid reliving it, we would understand."

"Fuck that." He chuckled. "If there's the chance that anyone else from the base might still be alive, I'd want to help to rescue them. Not because I have any love for them, but because...well, I don't want to see anyone else melted by this fucking mist. It's...not right to leave them there."

"Does anyone plan to ask how this kid speaks English so well?" Madigan demanded.

Alexei was about to answer but once again, Anja made

herself noticed by shouting from inside her server room. "Three years spent at MIT before he returned home for family reasons. He's currently employed by a company with government contracts, which decided to send him out here to fix the comms systems of the base as well as prep it for new and improved versions, particularly for teams going into the Zoo. Madigan and Sal, I think you ran into some of the prototypes on your last trip in."

The young Russian techie looked at the Americans, his mouth agape as he tried to grasp the reality of the facts the hacker had delivered so precisely. "How...did she know about all that?"

"We've stopped asking that question," Sal said and gestured vaguely in her direction. "At this point, we merely have to accept that she's some kind of benevolent deity we're happy to have on our side instead of against us."

"Benevolent deity—I like that," Anja said with a laugh.

"Huh." Alexei grunted, still struggling with the concept, but decided to push past it. "Anyway...what happened while I was there was that we caught sight of the mist moving across the sand a few hours before it got to us. It was dark so we couldn't see the green color. I was sealed in that same building, so we didn't realize the effects until we checked the security cameras when we heard people screaming and dying. At that point, the fog was so thick we couldn't see much. Once it had cleared the next day, most of the humans were gone and the jungle had already grown overnight and swallowed half the base. We didn't even consider the fact that there might be any other survivors."

"Well, that's changed now," the hacker said as she emerged from the room where she'd been busy. She toted a laptop and a couple of external hard drives, which she placed quickly on the coffee table. "Like Alexei said, most of the cameras were visually useless when the mist got thicker, but the motion detectors were still up and worked for a couple of hours after it all began. There's some data on the number of animals, but there is other movement inside the base which indicates that there are survivors in those buildings that can be sealed. Of course, there's no way to tell if they're still alive, but it might be worth a look, right?"

"Okay, based on what we were able to determine from the tests we left running overnight, there are many of the same genetic markers between the original goop—as well as what is being extracted from the Pita flowers—and the residue that was taken from the suits and Hammerheads after they left the mist," Courtney interjected. "It means, if nothing else, that the mist has its origins in something inside the Zoo and possibly even the same origins as the Pita plants."

"That is worth looking into," Sal said, thinking aloud. "It's entirely contradictory if you think about it. On the one hand, we have the stuff that works as anti-aging cream now peddled all around the world, and on the other, we have shit that will melt your face off. Even if there's no other reason, we should at least obtain more samples of the mist residue to determine how the blue stuff turned green, if that's at all possible. We need to make sure that should this turn up when folks head into the jungle, they know what to do about it."

"Yeah, because if the Zoo has discovered how to weaponize the goop before we did, I'd say that's a concerning development," Madigan said, pointing out the obvious, and no one in the room appeared to disagree with her. She did have a point. Humans tended to be the best at turning ordinary crap into weapons. If something else beat them to it, all kinds of red flags would always be raised. Besides, they had more than enough to contend with. The idea that the Zoo had found a way to go all nuclear on them was, quite frankly, terrifying.

"No one wants to go into a jungle where the slightest crack in the suit means a very painful death," Sal said and voiced everyone's fears. He wasn't sure how many people concurred, but he certainly spoke for himself. The unanimous nods around him confirmed that he most likely spoke for them all. He liked working and fighting in his suit, but the Zoo had a habit of exacerbating the normal wear and tear that high-tech weapons like their combat suits were meant to deal with.

The discussion came to a sudden pause when Anja called up footage of parts of the base that hadn't been covered by the mist. It was from the far side of it, the last to be touched by the insidious fog and the only location that hadn't been covered in the green blanket when the alarms had been activated.

A group of humans could be seen racing into one of the secure buildings, similar to the one where Gregor had holed up. These survivors seemed to realize that it was in their best interest to seal the place completely, which in turn meant they might have avoided the horrifying effects that had befallen the rest of the base and its inhabitants.

"Would you look at that?" Courtney said with a small smile. "It seems we have survivors to rescue."

"You don't need to sound so happy about it." Madigan snorted and folded her arms with real displeasure. She still appeared to be of the opinion that they needed to stay as far away from the disaster area as possible.

"True, but she's not wrong," Gregor added. "It is known that I have little love for these people, but we can't simply leave them in there waiting to die. If we can do something, we should."

"While that might be true, I don't think we need to do it merely out of the goodness of our hearts," Courtney pointed out. "A wise man once said that if you're good at something, you shouldn't do it for free, and I agree with that. We're a business, after all, and if there is some kind of incentive to perform this risky rescue mission, we should look into it. Perhaps we should explore trying to get a message to the Russian government to see if they would be willing to offer us something in exchange."

"Well, as nice as that would be, knowing the government as I do, there's no way they will respond to any proposal like that with alacrity," Alexei said, derision sharp in his tone. "Those pea-counters and pencil-pushers will talk about not overcompensating you guys from now until the proverbial cows come home, and we'd end up either rescuing the people for free or simply leaving them there to rot."

"Well, that definitely won't happen," Sal declared. "The leaving them to rot part, not rescuing them for free. I'm more than willing to rescue them for free, but if there is some kind of payout available, I don't think we should overlook that shit. Think about it. If they were willing to overlook the charges against Gregor—even temporarily—

to ship him here, they should be willing to accept a couple of conditions from us, right?"

"Yeah, but we have to make sure we know the message reached them before we conduct the mission," Madigan said. She frowned as she leaned closer to watch the replay of the footage of the people heading into the secure building.

"I have an idea about that," Anja interjected and looked up from her work on the laptop. "From what I've heard over my commlink with Savage, I've been able to establish that he and Molina are targeting a high-level FSB official—the kind who could probably authorize something like what you have in mind."

"Wait, back the fuck up," Courtney said. "Why the hell are you keeping open comms with Savage? He's supposed to work with Molina and keep her occupied, distracted, and away from us."

"Please." Anja chuckled. "Do you think there is any way in the world I would let my friend go into enemy territory with that bitch without backup?"

Her boss opened her mouth to berate her about endangering the very mission she was helping Savage to conduct but she paused when Sal indicated for her to rethink her tone and wording. This was Anja, after all—the person who had watched their backs for the past few months and done a damn good job of it.

"I merely think you should have run your idea past me first," she said finally with a sigh and made a visible effort to calm herself.

The hacker nodded. "I know, and I'm sorry about that."

"Thanks." She smiled. "Now, what did you have in mind?"

"Well, if Savage will run into someone like that, I think we can get him to twist the situation to get the message of our conditions across without endangering his life or the mission he's on," the Russian replied, her focus once again on the laptop. "I only need to put a little work into it. I'll be back in a sec."

With that, she disappeared into her server room again.

"I love that woman, but I swear she'll give me a heart attack one of these days," Courtney grumbled. She ran her fingers through her blonde hair and broke away from the group to head to her room.

CHAPTER THIRTEEN

Trailing the two Russians from the pub had brought success. They followed them until they stepped inside a mid-to-low-class apartment building, the kind that didn't have an elevator. It had the appearance of an older structure, one people would revere as a classic from decades past, while those who could afford it moved to the more modern buildings the city of Prague had to offer.

"We can't get in there without being noticed," Molina stated with a frown. She still clung to his arm and her other hand was shoved deep into her pocket.

"And we don't need to. This visit is only surveillance and we're only here to wait and watch." He gestured to the shadowy seclusion of a handy alley almost directly opposite.

Their efforts were finally rewarded, although only after they circled the block again to avoid remaining in one place for too long and perhaps raising suspicion. The terrace door of one of the apartments on the third floor opened and their mark stepped outside and closed the door quickly behind him. He drew a pack of cigarettes from his pocket and lit one.

The already low temperatures had begun to plummet as night started to fall. Some people needed their fix, no matter what, and since Solodkov was probably a guest in a safehouse someone else owned, he would have to get his nicotine fix out in the cold.

His habit proved to be their stroke of good fortune. They would have found where the man was anyway, but now that they knew where the safe house was, considerable time had been saved and they could turn their attention to their plans to reach him.

Molina wanted the Russian to be eliminated before he could spearhead an operation that could be detrimental to Pegasus' profit margins, which Savage supposed was his job these days, even if he didn't like it.

That said, he could already guess that there wouldn't be too many people who would volunteer for the job when they returned to headquarters. It didn't look like Molina had brought in many hitters with her team of mostly techies, but she still could have brought even minimal backup for him.

But no. That would be too much to ask—although her operatives haven't proven too efficient thus far so maybe it's for the best. It appears I'll have to accomplish the mission alone, which means I definitely need a plan of attack.

By the time they returned to the command center, the team—prompted by Molina's phone call—had acquired the plans for the building, which gave him at least some frame of reference to work with. He dedicated the time he had to memorize every detail about the location.

"What kind of ingress plan do you have?" she asked and broke his concentration once again. He scowled at her and tapped his pen on the table.

"It would have been easier to run this with a partner and a little help to get me inside," he said. That was usually the optimum scenario, but he was also used to improvising when he lacked resources and this would be no different. "But I can go in alone. That's not a problem."

"I could always go with you," she volunteered.

He shook his head decisively. "I don't know you and don't trust you to cover my back instead of bugging out should things get hot. I can formulate a plan to do this alone, so you sit your ass down and wait for me to get back."

"I'm not sure I like that," she replied and made a face. "I'm not sure I trust you to get the job done on your own."

"It's funny how you say that like you expect me to care." He smirked. "No, I've got this. The best you can do for me is run support from this end of the operation. Give me eyes and ears around the building—and even inside if your guys can manage it."

He turned his attention to the experts on the computers as he spoke, one of whom caught his comment and nodded. "We'll get it done."

"I appreciate it." Savage focused on the plans of the building once again and considered the situation from all possible angles. They were as new as could be provided, but there was no telling how many changes had occurred since they'd drafted the version he had, which meant he would need to improvise his approach somewhat.

Ordering pizza was an almost infallible go-to in the US,

but since most folks around there tended to go out and purchase their food, he'd have to think of something else.

Molina sighed dramatically and rolled her eyes. "Ugh, fine. You work on your own, you lone wolf, you. Now, what kind of plan do you have in mind? Or do you intend to simply go in there, shoot first, and ask questions later?"

"Were there any questions you wanted me to run past the FSB agents who will be guarding that safe house?" He replied with a question and looked at her with a skeptical expression.

"I have nothing in particular, but I do want to make sure you get the right man," she replied.

"Then, yeah, I do have a plan," he answered with a careless shrug. "Well…kind of."

"Kind of?"

"Okay, the beginning of a plan," he clarified. "It'll be fully grown, ordering drinks, and getting DUIs in no time."

"Color me comforted." She hissed her frustration and sighed loudly before she turned away from him and walked to where the other team members had begun to work on how he could get inside the building.

As it turned out, the best way in was the simplest way. A security system allowed someone to enter the building without a key simply by punching a fifteen-digit code into the keypad located at the front door. This was usually used by people who worked in the building like the security guards or cleaning crews—those who would have no need to use keys like the people who lived in the building did.

It was only the first step, of course. Gaining entry was a victory that could be attributed to the high-tech team of experts who had been able to acquire the code from the folks who operated the security system. This enabled Savage to get inside with comparatively little difficulty. People didn't question him when he punched the code in and simply assumed he was there to work.

"Now the fun starts," he muttered. "I have to gain access to the apartment, which might be easier said than done if Molina's techs don't live up to their promises."

The contracts signed by the residents when they rented the dwellings included the stipulation that they were responsible for securing their own homes. Some used the same security company that monitored the building as a whole.

Unfortunately, the safehouse owners had not done so. *Surprise surprise*, he thought snarkily as he made his way up the stairs to the third floor. *And on the subject of surprises, I need to sneak in without my Russian friends discovering that I'm there—at first, at least.* This meant he would have to make use of the interesting, gun-shaped device they'd given him before he left Molina's penthouse.

The techs had told him how to use it and warned him to not mess with the controls since they had been very precisely configured. Its purpose was to allow them to pick the locks for him from where they sat at their consoles. It was more help than he'd expected and excluded the need for any kind of subterfuge to get inside.

It's simple. Once in, all you need to do is get to Solodkov without any of his comrades seeing me first. It's possible. Maybe.

Savage adjusted his trench coat and stretched to accommodate the added weight of his modified suit before he withdrew the small device from his pocket.

"Now," one of the experts whispered in his ear, "the device is already primed, so all you need to do is slip it into the keyhole and we'll do the rest from here. Do you think you can do that?"

He didn't bother to reply. There were two locks, and if he made so much as a sound, he could alert the people who were inside. All he could do was hope they didn't have some kind of bolt lock on the inside that would make any attempts to break in very loud and obvious to everyone.

While he could deal with that, it would be an inconvenience he'd far rather do without.

The first lock was picked in seconds, and he inserted the device into the second and waited for them to finish before he removed it slowly and cautiously and slipped it into his pocket.

Right. The moment of truth. It was late—after eleven in the evening—so most of the people inside would be asleep. Despite that, unless the rules had changed regarding security in safe houses like this, at least one person would likely be up and awake at all times.

Savage turned the knob with exaggerated care and silently praised the gods he didn't believe in that the mechanism was well-oiled and no mechanical noises or creaks would alert anyone inside to his approach. One hand rested on the knob and the other held his pistol as he pushed the door open with exaggerated care. There was a chain that was intended to be latched to the door, he realized, but wasn't. *Okay, so someone is out of the apartment and left the chain off for when they return.*

He accepted the lucky break and eased the door wider to scan the inside of the apartment when it came into view. With extreme caution, he stepped inside and tested the floorboards with each step.

No one was in the common room, he confirmed, and resisted the urge to heave a sigh of relief.

"What are you looking at?" Molina whispered in his ear. He gritted his teeth and took a few seconds to let his heartbeat settle into a normal rhythm. *For fuck's sake. Does she not realize I'm in the middle of infiltrating an apartment full of highly trained agents? All of them are no doubt in possession of all kinds of hardware and won't hesitate to use it if they see me. How can she think this the best time to play I-spy?*

He shook his head and forced himself to calm for a few long seconds while he scrutinized every corner of the common room for movement. Finally, he took another step forward. Who was running the watch? Had they left the chain off the door? *Maybe they went to the roof for a smoke or perhaps out to a bar for a quick drink since everyone else is asleep and won't notice their absence?* Or were they simply this lax in security?

Savage couldn't assume they were, even if he could hope, and he remained on high alert as he moved through the room.

A hint of movement caught his eye and dragged his attention to the same terrace where they'd seen Solodkov smoking before. He resisted a chuckle. Perhaps the target himself was on duty that evening and had taken a break from sitting around and watching the door to get another smoke break in. The man truly was an addict, and it would tell on his lungs before too long.

Although, his inner caution reasoned, if Solodkov was the man on guard and he was on the terrace, who had left the chain off? *And why does this voice in my head suggest it was done deliberately?*

He moved closer and placed his hand on the handle of the glass door that led onto the terrace, keeping his weapon aimed at the target's head. The man turned, obviously expecting someone else. His eyes narrowed when he saw the intruder step outside.

Concern immediately evidenced on his face but his sudden tension faded quickly and a hand caught the door as the operative slid it closed. A quick look behind him revealed two men in dark combat gear—not quite full suits but they still provided some body armor—who pushed through with their sub-machine guns aimed at his head. A hasty look revealed another three who held their weapons trained on him through the windows from inside the apartment.

"Shit." He growled his frustration but made no effort to lower the weapon aimed at Solodkov, who smirked. *That explains the goddammed chain.*

"Drop your weapons, if you please," the Russian instructed in surprisingly good English. His intonation contained not even a hint of an accent. It confirmed the assumption that men in his line of business put considerable work into being able to blend in with foreigners as much as possible.

Savage sighed and hesitated for a moment to check the positioning of the men with guns behind him before he dropped his pistol without further protest.

"And the other," Solodkov added knowingly. The operative complied and drew the second pistol from under his shoulder and tossed it lightly beside the first. "Kick them over, please."

Again, he did as he was told, and the revolver-like weapons slid across the icy surface of the terrace until they rested against the man's boot.

"Now that we're past the formalities, how the fuck have you been, Sergeant Johnson?" Solodkov asked with a chuckle.

"I go by Savage these days," he said with a shrug. "And I'm not a sergeant anymore either. Other than that, not too bad."

"That's right. I remember news reaching our side that you'd died in the field." The Russian took a puff of his cigarette and exhaled the smoke languidly. "I'm glad to hear the news of your demise has been greatly exaggerated."

"You and me both, brother," he responded with a smirk. "When was the last time we saw each other?"

"Berlin, I think," he recalled. "It was that embassy function they invited us to. They wanted it to be awkward, but we ended up having a great time, as I recall."

"You recall correctly." The operative laughed. "They tried to kick us out after we decided to collect all the coins in the fountain, but I don't think they minded since we used the cash at the bar there. The cheap bastards couldn't even put out for an open bar."

"Ah, those were good times." Solodkov chuckled. "Anyway, I'm afraid we must get back to business. Are you here to kill me, my friend?"

"In a way." He shook his head and his companion raised an eyebrow.

"In a way?"

"Well, yeah. I did come here to kill you on the orders of someone I don't like," he explained. "But as you clearly have the drop on me and since I don't want to, I won't kill you. I have a deal to offer you instead. Well, a deal for you to send to your bosses."

Molina's outraged splutter in his earpiece preceded her demand to know what the fuck he thought he was doing, but he chose to ignore her.

"This deal wouldn't happen to include you walking away from here with your life, would it?" the man asked.

He shrugged. "Not necessarily, but I would appreciate it. You see, I'm aware of a certain situation you folks have in the Zoo—or rather, on your base in the Zoo. As it turns out, I'm connected with a team who can rescue the survivors who are left on the base."

"There weren't any survivors," Solodkov stated.

"You should receive a text message with overwhelming evidence to the contrary, friend of mine," he countered smoothly. "Heavy Metal can run the rescue op, but they have certain conditions, starting with erasing the charges you have pending against Anja, Gregor, and others. All the conditions and details will be in the message you should already have on your phone. I'm merely here to make sure you take it seriously and that it hasn't gone into your spam folder or something."

The Russian studied him for a moment before he checked his phone quickly and raised his eyebrows, a sure indication that the message was, in fact, already waiting for him.

"I'll pass the message along since I do owe you one," he said, pocketed his device, and took one last drag of his cigarette before he dropped it and ground it out with his heel. "Unfortunately, since you did break in here, I won't be able to let you walk out of here alive."

He nodded. "I understand. You have a job to do and all that."

"That is appreciated," Solodkov replied and smiled but it faltered when the operative rolled his shoulders, took a deep breath, and looked like he was preparing himself for a fight.

"So." He narrowed his eyes and focused his gaze on the Russian in front of him. "Do you want to see something cool?"

CHAPTER FOURTEEN

There was something in Savage's voice that made the team hesitate where they had positioned themselves behind him. People like him didn't simply wander into traps without something to show for it. It appeared he had planned for someone to get the drop on him. He'd already had an ulterior motive for breaking in that would have resulted in Solodkov remaining alive and, in fact, had relied on it.

Which meant he probably had something in mind to ensure his escape. He had to know they wouldn't simply allow him to walk out of the building alive. They also had no doubt that he wasn't the kind of man to walk away from a situation like this without putting up a fight. There merely didn't appear to be any realistic way for him to battle his way out of here, at least in their minds.

Under the watchful gaze of the intruder, Solodkov began to put the pieces together. He noted the metallic glint reflecting from Savage's gauntlets, indicating...something, he was sure of that much, although he had no idea what. The operative, in turn, doubted that the Russian knew precisely what he had in mind or he would have made sure to secure the pistols at his feet before they suddenly slid across the slick surface of the terrace as if of their own accord.

They completed their glide and launched upward, called magnetically to Savage's hands, and he ducked under the first volley of surprise fire the Russians released without warning. Thankfully, none of the bullets struck Solodkov, who flung himself aside hastily and almost toppled over the iron railing in his effort to avoid injury.

Savage had fallen prone and now fired the pistols as rapidly as he could work the triggers. The coils inside the weapons responded with satisfying alacrity to launch thin, hyper-dense needles that could drive through virtually any kind of body armor. They were designed to fracture on impact with something soft, not unlike the fleshy humans beneath the armor the Russians wore.

The two men who had stepped out onto the terrace with him and Solodkov fell back with the impact that penetrated their suits easily and tried to find cover. The operative twisted to fire at the window and the tempered glass shattered. He pivoted on his stomach before he rose smoothly to his feet with almost inhuman speed and precision.

Solodkov would, of course, be able to see the half-suit in action. It was too bad since he had hoped to keep Amanda's invention a secret for a little while. Anderson had said there was more than enough money to put into patenting the design. Many people would see the advantage of having something that enhanced a user's speed, strength, and precision and provided some measure of body armor into the bargain.

This would merely mean there would probably be Russian designs out there to compete for the market sooner than anticipated. It would drive the prices down a little but not by much. Most of their American clients would refuse to buy Russian-made weapons anyway.

Solodkov moved to draw a weapon from his coat. Savage resisted the urge to kill him since they did need him to walk away from this little encounter alive to be able to pass the Heavy Metal message on to his bosses before the sun started to rise in the Sahara.

Instead, he placed the heel of his boot against one of the metal chairs that could only be used out there during the summer. The coils inside his boots primed for barely a half-second before he launched the piece of furniture violently across the terrace into his opponent and effectively knocked the weapon out of his hands, which were most likely numb from the cold.

"Sorry about that." He grinned and kicked the pistol clear of the terrace. It sailed to the street below while the remaining members of the team gathered their strength and courage once again and pushed out from behind cover to open fire.

Pain reverberated across his ribs. His armor absorbed the rounds effectively, but the impact would still leave bruising.

"I'll be sore tomorrow," he muttered and spun to return fire at the assholes before he ducked and moved rapidly across the open space. The coils in his boots whined when he pressed the right one against the wall the men used for cover, kept the other on the ground, and activated them in quick succession.

First, the left launched him upward, then the right shoved him away from the building. He grinned at the added bonus of littering the room the Russians were in with shrapnel from what had once been a solid brick wall they were hiding behind.

Shouts and screams resulted inside as he flipped upward about fifteen feet and well clear of the railing. A moment of vertigo twisted his stomach before his momentum was slowly arrested by gravity. It tugged him down to the inevitable hard landing that waited three stories below.

"Fuck!" he yelled and angled his descent as best he could in the short time he had to do it in. The chilly wind whipped his body as he tilted forward to complete the flip and his eyes widened as the pavement rushed to meet him with alarming speed.

The inertia dampeners in the half-suit slowed most of his momentum, but he could still feel a dull ache in his bones as he completed the maneuver and uttered a low groan. He pushed up from the three-point pose he had somehow managed to arrange while in midair. Jacobs would have been proud—and probably shouted something about how it was a superhero landing or something like it.

"I do have to give it to the kid, though. It is cool." It didn't bother him that although he talked to himself, he was well aware that Anja and Molina—and members of the penthouse team—were probably tuned into everything he said.

He might as well irritate the shit out of the woman with

useless comments as there would be all kinds of explaining to do once he returned to the penthouse. She seemed to have subsided into sullen silence when she realized he'd simply ignored her previous questions but at this point, he didn't care. He had to work with her, but his real bosses were still the ones who hung out in that godforsaken jungle in the Sahara.

It was interesting that he'd left a heavy dent in the road where he'd landed. The suit, even with Amanda's extensive modifications, added about two or three hundred pounds to his overall weight, which still shouldn't have been enough to dent a well-constructed road. It said more about the quality of the construction than it did about the weight of his suit, though, and the power functions had been more than sufficient to compensate for the added bulk.

He decided it wasn't that difficult to work with and made a mental note to let Amanda know. Shouts issued from the building he had left and he broke into a jog. It wasn't long before weapons' fire erupted behind him. He'd already gained sufficient speed to place himself safely out of the effective range of the sub-machine guns the men used. Besides, they would soon have to explain themselves to the police. The sirens grew louder with each passing second, and the Russians would have to cease the pursuit soon to clean up after themselves.

It wouldn't benefit Solodkov's reputation that Savage had been able to stroll into his safehouse and walk—or jump, rather—out of it unscathed. Neither would the fact that the man would return to his bosses with a deal from Americans in the Zoo. Then again, his reputation was already well-established with over two decades committed to the service of his country. He could afford a couple of losses here and there, as long as they didn't happen too frequently.

"What the hell are you talking about?" Petrov asked.

His friend, an engineer by the name of Felix, shrugged as if the answer were self-evident. "We're talking about the difference in temperature between the two bases we were told to keep an eye on. The fact that you picked this one on the border with Ukraine is because you don't understand the basics of meteorology, and that's embarrassing."

"I know enough that farther south means warmer," Petrov complained and rubbed his hands together. Admittedly, he wasn't an engineer like Felix and honestly, he didn't have much of a higher education unless you considered military experience to be one. "Everyone knows that winter will suck anywhere you go, so you might as well brave it out someplace where summer will be warm, at least."

"Well, if you did any studying—like reading the papers I sent you while we were still in St Petersburg—you would know that while, yes, the temperatures in the summer are milder, the temperatures in the winter are also milder since it gets a warm wash from the Gulf Stream current."

"That's the border with Norway, you idiot." Petrov chuckled and shook his head. "And either way, I don't give a shit about the milder temperatures in the winter. What I want are summers warm enough that I can pretend to live in a tropical country and maybe even get a tan while I'm at it."

"You do know that the sun stays up for about twenty-three and a half hours during the summer there, right?" Felix reminded him

He opened his mouth to retort but that seemed like a sweet deal when he thought about it. "Yeah, but during the winter, the nights are almost as long so it evens out."

"We stay inside all day during the winter here anyway," his partner replied. "What the hell does it matter how cold it is out there if we're nice and warm in here?"

"If only we were nice and warm in here," he complained and rubbed his arms briskly. "No amount of heating in the world would be able to keep this little outpost warm enough. I'm surprised people don't all move to the places where it's not cold enough to make you want to roast yourself over an open fire."

"You're being dramatic," Felix grumbled but he laughed at the idea.

"No shit," Petrov responded with a chuckle and took a sip of his tea. He didn't want to be a Russian cliché but he could use something to spike his drink with right now and he wouldn't say no to a touch of vodka. That said, they were military men tasked to keep watch over a small military surveillance center with connections to not one, not two, but three nearby military bases. As such, they were the first line between any invasion force that might come through Ukraine. He honestly doubted anyone would be so stupid, but there was a meme about never betting money against humans being stupid. A massive monument in the middle of the Sahara Desert represented precisely that.

"But you know I'm right," Felix stated and raised an eyebrow.

"I know no such thing," Petrov chuckled. "It's still cold in here."

"I wasn't talking about in here. I was talking back home," the man snapped. The surveillance post was a tiny building on the highest point in the area built to give them a better physical view, which also gave them the perfect position to relay information between all the installations they had in the area.

They needed two people there at all times, one engineer —Felix, in this case—and one grunt to watch their back in case something went wrong. Petrov filled the latter role as a junior officer who desired to climb the ranks. It wasn't very likely, Felix thought, since he would reach a point where the selections for promotion were more of a political decision than based on any real aptitude for the work.

Still, the engineer couldn't help but support and believe in the man he had worked with for the past year or so at two military installations. He had heart and a will to succeed. Sometimes, that worked when political connections weren't available. Not often, admittedly, but sometimes.

"I think it must be a hell of a lot warmer in the Zoo," Petrov commented as he settled into a seat and took another sip of his now lukewarm tea and made a face.

"And the action would be hotter too," Felix retorted with a grin.

When they'd taken over the comms base for the night shift, all indications had pointed toward yet another boring night that involved listening to the comms that passed between the various military points in the area and not much else. Felix and Petrov knew they needed to take their work a little more seriously but honestly, there wasn't anything worth worrying about.

Instead, they had spent most of their time over the past few weeks watching the variety of videos that had been uploaded to ZooTube. Most of what came out wasn't from the Zoo, of course. Everyone simply came up with original content and the site itself began to sponsor TV shows about the jungle, but it made fun watching. There was even talk about simulator games being released in the coming years featuring it as a location for the various PVE and PVP gaming formats.

"Since we're speaking of the Zoo," Petrov insisted, "have you seen any new videos on ZooTube?"

Felix chuckled. "The Heavy Metal Militia channel is damn insane. I'm surprised some Hollywood exec hasn't tried to push them to make a movie yet, but we'll see. It looks like they haven't posted as many videos lately as they did in the past, though. We've seen all those that are already there."

"Yeah, maybe they're taking a vacation," his partner suggested. "They've posted vids fairly regularly over the past few months, and I don't even want to think about how I would handle being in an alien jungle like that on a regular basis."

"We'd probably both crap ourselves thoroughly and never return," Felix said. "Assuming, of course, that we were able to get out alive at all."

"Here's to hoping we never have to find out." He laughed, raised his Styrofoam mug, and tapped it lightly against his comrade's before he took a sip and scowled. "It's too fucking cold in here if I have to keep reheating my tea every five minutes."

Felix opened the site and shook his head with a glum expression. Sadly, Heavy Metal didn't appear to have launched any new videos.

"Don't worry about it." Petrov chuckled and moved to the commlinks to make sure all the transmissions were behaving as expected. "They might have simply taken a quick winter vacation or something. Or maybe they're gathering and editing as much footage as they can before they release them in batches. That's what many of the other channels are—huh."

"What?" the other man asked and leaned forward to see what his friend was looking at on the screen.

"Do you remember the chatter we heard a couple of days ago about our base in the Zoo being attacked?" Petrov asked as he called the comms up. "Well, from the chatter that's going through here, it looks like there are reports of survivors."

"None of this is meant for us," Felix grumbled and rolled his chair closer. "Why the hell are you messing with it?"

"Because I'm curious. Ah, yes…there we go." He grinned and practically glowed with pride. "It looks like Heavy Metal is involved in getting the survivors out if there are any."

"Well, I guess we know why they aren't making any new vids. I guess the FSB must have clamped down on anything they release to make sure nothing they put online has any compromised or classified data." His grin broadened. "Like the Prime Minister getting it on with one of those horned gorilla creatures."

"You're fucking disgusting, you know that, right?" Petrov complained and rolled his eyes. "Besides, those creatures are like...three and a half meters tall. The logistics of it would be insane."

"Yes, of all the problems that would come from the prime minister having relations with a horned gorilla, the logistics and size are what comes to mind," the other man snarked and his voice dripped with sarcasm. "Let's get these comms through and not talk about it, okay?"

"Yes, please," Petrov pleaded. He shut the software down and sent the messages along the line to Moscow.

CHAPTER FIFTEEN

He dreaded returning to the damn penthouse—to the point where his mind toyed with various equally futile alternatives. *Nothing's changed. You felt like this all along, even before you gave Anderson your agreement. This is simply a little more salt rubbed in the existing wound.*

Thoroughly disgruntled, he paused his sprint through the back streets of the city to catch his breath. Even with the suit doing most of the work, the effort still took a toll on his body and the muscles in his legs and shoulders burned like they had grabbed a time machine, headed to the Middle Ages, and had been accused of being witches and burnt at the stake.

Now that was a weird analogy, but he wasn't exactly at his mental best. He was both physically and mentally tired, so his wit was bound to be at its lowest.

Which was another reason why he didn't want to return. *Molina will have listened to everything that happened with the Russians. It doesn't take a fucking Einstein to know she'll have a thing or two to say. She's probably beyond pissed and will keep me up for hours until she's vented her anger and frustration and I can finally get back to business.* It was necessary to endure it, but the fact remained that he simply didn't want to.

It was all moot anyway. If he tried to head off on his own, her team would be able to track him and haul him back. That scenario had the added downside of giving the woman political clout to use against Courtney and Anderson should she need it in her dealings with Pegasus. To some degree, what was happening now would do the same, but if he attempted to bolt, it would make what was already bad much, much worse.

"You have to go back. But maybe you can get a drink on the way—a little liquid bolstering in preparation." The temptation was quickly dispelled. If he had to engage in a shouting match with Molina, he would prefer it to happen at the penthouse instead of a random bar. He would simply have to get the drink once it was over. "It's probably just as well as I'll likely need something to help me unwind afterward after butting heads with the bitch."

It was a long walk that paradoxically, couldn't last long enough. The effects of the adrenaline from his fight began to fade and the cold seeped through his clothes and the suit he wore beneath. He didn't want to be stuck out in the cold and therefore gritted his teeth and resumed his journey toward the building where she waited for him.

She had known he would go there. It was a simple assumption easily made as she sat in the lobby, drumming her nails impatiently on the counter. The building had a bar there, something he felt he should have noticed the first time around. It would make unwinding after the inevitable confrontation a little simpler, even if it looked fairly basic. His alcoholic demands weren't extravagant, after all.

His walk toward the elevators was halted by a hand on his shoulder. It was a small hand, but her grasp was impossible to ignore.

"I thought it would be best if we had our conversation here rather than upstairs," Molina whispered and yanked him to face her. "I don't want to distract my people from their work. You understand."

"I thought I'd change first," Savage said and tapped his coat to indicate the suit. It was hidden well enough but was still uncomfortable to stand in.

"That can wait," she responded and looked angry for the first time since he had met her. "We need to talk about what happened out there."

"I'm not sure what you mean." He shrugged her hand off his shoulder.

"You were supposed to kill that motherfucker," she stated before she swung on her heel and strode to one of the booths. She sat and waited for him to join her. He did but he didn't sit. "Do you want to explain yourself?"

"I had conflicting orders." Savage offered the explanation but folded his arms in front of his chest in a gesture that was half-challenging and half-defiant. "When push comes to shove, I'll choose the orders that mean people are saved rather than killed."

"Well, I admire your bleeding heart, but did you think I would let you walk away from this without doing your job?" she demanded. "For fuck's sake, sit down."

"I intend to get the job done eventually," he replied and

scratched his jaw as he considered his next words. "I needed him to get a message to his bosses first, which tends to work better when he's alive. We'll eliminate him when he's done what we need him to do. Oh, and how the fuck am I supposed to sit anywhere without breaking the seat while I'm wearing this much armor?"

"Solodkov knows that you're coming now." She sighed.

"He knew I was coming before too," he pointed out. "They had a trap primed and ready for me. Which begs the question of which one of your people could have tipped him off."

"My people?" she questioned, an eyebrow raised.

"Well, it wasn't my people," he assured her. "It wasn't me, and I assume it wasn't you. Someone let the man in on the secret, and the number of people who knew we had targeted him is small."

The woman nodded and sipped the drink she'd ordered before he arrived. "I guess that's a good point. I'll put feelers out to determine what we're dealing with here. But your time of running these operations solo is over."

"Hey, I was the one who said I needed backup," he reminded her.

"Get upstairs." Molina shook her head. "Take a shower, get changed, and get some rest. We'll talk more about it tomorrow."

He nodded and turned away to head to the elevators again with no one there to stop him this time. *Well, that went better than expected.* He grinned and pressed the button.

Sal looked up from his laptop, where he'd focused mostly on taking notes for potential whitepapers he planned to write as soon as they had resolved the issue of the Russian base. Anja emerged from the server room—her domain, as it were—and honestly looked like she was about ready to drop with exhaustion.

"The Russians responded fairly quickly," she said and extended a tablet to him with a massive yawn that all but split her jaw in two. "It looks like our friend Solodkov came through for us after all. There are no big surprises there, though. If there's any branch in the government that moves quickly, it's the FSB. Anyway, they agreed to all the conditions, provided we finish the mission before they bring their troops in. They have arranged with the commandant to land their forces on the American base."

"When do they arrive?" Sal asked and rubbed his eyes gently to ease the scratchiness of too much focus and too little sleep.

"We have a couple of days," she replied and checked the data on the tablet she still held out for him to take. "It seems they don't want anyone in there when they decide to clean the place out—which I assume involves things that go boom. I can't say I blame them."

"Right." He finally took the tablet from her hands. "It looks like we have ourselves a mission to start tomorrow. Can you let the team know?"

"It's already done, boss man." She grinned and patted him on the shoulder. "You might want to get some sleep before we go in there."

"We?" He raised an eyebrow.

"Figuratively," the hacker replied and helped him up

from his seat on the couch. "I'll run support for you, as usual, but if you think I'll be there in person, you're fucking crazy."

"Well, you know me—nutty as squirrel shit," he replied and gave her a quick hug before he wandered to his room. "Why else would I risk my life and head into that fucking place to begin with?"

It was a good question and one he asked himself far more often than he liked. He would continue to go in there, though. The Zoo was the one place in the world where he could feel alive these days, and the adrenaline rush made almost everything else feel dull by comparison.

Well, almost everything, Sal thought when he entered his room as Madigan stepped out of the shower. She wore a towel around her hair and nothing else, still drying herself with a second towel as she turned when he closed the door behind him.

"Do we have an answer?" she asked and hung the one she used to dry herself on the edge of the bathroom door and took the one from around her hair and started working on that.

"The Russians were amenable to our conditions," he replied and tried not to stare too intently as he placed his laptop and Anja's tablet on his desk. "They did give us a timetable, though, so we'll have to leave tomorrow."

"Fucking aces." She nodded. "I hate sitting around and waiting for politicians to get their thumbs out of their asses. And I imagine the folks we'll go in to rescue will feel much the same. Did Anja let the rest of the team know?"

"They should be ready to go at dawn." He grinned when she finished toweling her hair and walked over to him.

"Assuming anyone wants to go in there anymore. It could only be the three of us, now that I think about it."

"I doubt it," she replied as she began to loosen the buttons of his shirt. "Gregor is a tough guy, and he'll probably go with us. Sousa had the look of a man who wanted payback for what happened to Davis, so I think he'll come too."

"Five of us," he pointed out and let her undo the rest of the buttons and pull his shirt off without protest.

"We've made do with fewer in the past," she reminded him and leaned in to place a light kiss on his lips.

He nodded and smiled distantly as she followed the kiss with a couple on his cheek and neck. "What are you doing?"

"Well, it occurred to me that in the rush to get here, there wasn't the chance for us to offer you that birthday present we talked about," she murmured softly, her lips still pressed against his skin when she spoke so the heat of her breath teased his senses.

"Us?" Sal asked, suddenly a little breathless himself.

"Oh, did I forget to mention it?" She glanced at the bathroom door and guided his gaze to where Courtney stood, just out of the shower herself, and as undressed as Madigan was. "It's the kind of present you need two people to give."

While he stared with his mouth open, she chuckled and set about unbuckling his pants to shove them down. Courtney moved in behind him, wound her arms around his midsection, and placed a light kiss on the nape of his neck.

Oh yes. Now, this is the best birthday gift ever.

Hours later, Sal knew he wouldn't get much sleep. Then again, he didn't need all that much anyway. That said, he assumed he would sleep like a damn baby once he got around to it, but there were a few things he needed to do before he could indulge in that particular pleasure.

He slipped carefully out of the bed to not wake Madigan or Courtney and moved to his desk where his laptop was. After a brief search, he finally opened one of the drawers and located his tablet, which he'd only the day before decided to stash out of sight on the off chance that someone might see his notes. The device was where he'd kept track of everything that had changed in his body since he started licking Madie, to use their term for it.

It had been a while, now, since he'd last taken what had previously been his regular dose. Not since they'd left that damn Chernobyl lab after the horrifying events that had triggered all kinds of alarm bells. He had expected a few changes to take place as a result of his decision not to take the goop.

Reluctantly, he called up the file he'd updated daily and added a log for the day.

"No changes to report," he whispered as he typed the words, shut the tablet down, and slid it into its drawer before he headed to bed again.

CHAPTER SIXTEEN

As Sal had suspected, he didn't get much in the way of sleep. On the bright side, while he didn't exactly wake refreshed and rested, he still felt he'd had enough. He felt even better after he attacked the coffee machine for two cups of the terrible yet effective brew.

Anja had done what she had said the night before, and by the time he finished his second caffeine fix, a couple of Hammerheads were already pulling into the compound with the team she had assembled. Some of those who had gone in with Davis still needed a little more recovery time, so they had to find a few others to join them.

It wasn't that difficult since Heavy Metal did have the reputation as the most interesting and profitable enterprise that ran missions in the Zoo, even if it meant they would go into some of the more dangerous sections of the jungle. Thankfully, their additional rep for protecting and standing by their comrades when times were tough in there more than made up for it.

The group that disembarked from the vehicles was a

mixture of old and new faces. Gregor and Sousa had joined them, as well as those who had survived the last run into the Russian base without real injury. They were tough and experienced and Sal, who had thought they might need a break from the jungle, was clearly proven wrong.

After a hurried and quiet breakfast shared by the group, they assembled quickly for the beginning of the mission. There was enough to do and not much time to do it in. They would only receive the compensation promised if they completed the mission before the Russians landed their troops in the American base.

Sal didn't know what kind of deal had been struck there and he was genuinely curious as to what kind of concessions the Russians had promised in order to have a friendly landing zone from where they could stage the attempt to retake their facility.

He knew they would find out about it soon since the commandant was very proud of how he ran things and would want any positive news to be disseminated as quickly as possible. The man was a politician in everything but name, and he made sure to gather as many chips on hand for when he could cash them in when his real political career started.

"So," Madigan said and patted his shoulder while he worked on the suit they'd brought back from Europe. "Do we have a plan for when we get out there?"

He looked at the group that had assembled, all of whom were prepping their suits without much conversation. None of them seemed even remotely nervous about what lay ahead, but these people were also the best at covering up any fears or tension they might feel. It wasn't a macho thing, or at least not entirely. They all felt it, after all, and everyone knew enough about the Zoo to realize that this would probably be one of the most dangerous missions they had ever been involved in.

It was an accepted fact that a reaction from one would cause the same response in others. They owed it to one another to at least present the outer show of calm in order to inspire the same in their teammates. And maybe, if they maintained the pretense, it might eventually be true.

He shrugged and returned his attention to his suit. "A plan? Sure. We'll head into the base with the Hammerheads and to the building where Gregor said we could find more suits. We collect as many of them as possible, dress the survivors in them, and leave as quickly as possible."

"Well, that seems simple enough." She grinned and helped him pull the shoulders of his suit on.

"There's less shit to go wrong that way," he replied with a firm nod and donned his helmet. "If we want to pull this off, we have to do it right. We're not simply on a rescue mission. That is the main idea, of course, but if we get in there, it'll be to deliver revenge. For Davis."

"For Davis," Sousa added quickly. He'd finished his suit and grinned manically at Sal and Madigan.

"For Davis," Gregor agreed and punched Sousa in the shoulder. He wore a newer suit than the one he'd been found in, with tougher armor and smoother mechanics. It wasn't top-of-the-line, but it was one of Madigan's older suits, which would enable him to help her with the role of tanking gunner.

The remainder of the team knew Davis and were aware of what happened to him. Many of them had gone into the

Zoo under the man's command at one point or another, and most had their lives saved by the sergeant too, which meant they all owed it to him to go out there and kick some serious Zoo ass. It wouldn't do much to get his leg back, but knowing Davis, it would lighten the man's mood to know they were heading in there to make the Zoo pay for what happened to him.

Hopefully.

The thought was enough to buoy the spirits of the men and women assembled, and they mounted the three Hammerheads they would use for the mission. Two of them were the heavily altered vehicles Amanda had put her magic into, and a third had been rented from the base to carry their additional numbers.

The weapons systems were comparatively limited but they knew Connie would be able to get creative with anything they gave her. Anja had taken the time to load the AI's programming into the new Hammerhead and they were ready to go.

The drive to the Russian base was much quieter than Sal would have liked. Too much silence meant too much time spent inside his head, with him overthinking everything to the point of insanity. He reminded himself that everyone was supposed to focus on what they were doing out there and slide into that quiet, dark place inside them. It would put them into the shoot first mindset that would bring them through the mission alive.

He simply couldn't do that, though. His mind needed to focus on something in particular for him to be in the right headspace, but he didn't want to interrupt the concentration of the rest of the group. Not all of them were used to his particular brand of leadership and this wasn't the time to instruct them. Right now, they needed every member of their Heavy Metal team to operate at the highest level of efficiency possible, which meant Madigan would run the mission for the most part and thus provide them with a more traditional leadership style.

The hours that passed gave them a view of the sun rising over the desert as they crested the last dunes and had their first sight of the base.

"Well, it looks like the mist isn't around," Courtney pointed out and glanced at the team. "That's something, at least."

"It wasn't around when we went in either," Sousa reminded her over the comms from one of the nearby Hammerheads. "It comes and goes, and quickly too. The last time, it seemed to be triggered when they brought the base online but that could simply be a coincidence. We should probably stay on the alert and be ready to pick up the pace and rush about our business rather than take our time."

"Why the hell shouldn't we simply rush to start with?" Madigan asked.

"We should, yes," he replied. "But when green starts to fill the area, we'll find rushing takes on a whole new meaning, that's all I'm saying."

"Right," she agreed. Sal knew that when shit like that happened, people would dig deep and let adrenaline drive them to do all kinds of crazy shit they would never have thought was possible.

It's the story of my life. He smiled at the thought as they eased the vehicles into the base. The trees had grown almost nonstop to forge a jungle that should have taken years to grow in weeks or less.

The fact that this was almost definitely a death trap was the only reason why he didn't leap out of the vehicle and collect all the samples he could fit into his bag. They would inevitably deal with the interesting and funny shit that the Zoo could produce for a while—knock on wood—which meant they needed to put saving the lives of the people trapped in this fucking place first.

Gregor continued to guide them through the damaged streets of the overrun facility, and they kept the three Hammerheads in tight formation. Animals appeared in the motion sensors and a few were even visible on top of the buildings, but they acted shy and drew away from the humans as soon as they moved closer. For some reason, the Zoo had decided to keep its distance from the team, which only added to the anticipation that built slowly in Sal's head for what was to come.

"This is it," the Russian called from the lead vehicle and their little convoy stopped in front of a larger warehouse-like building. The walls were already crawling with vines, and a couple of trees had broken through the roof of the building to tower about fifteen feet above with vividly green leaves. It was a beautiful spectacle of nature reclaiming what it believed was its own.

Well, that wasn't quite the right analogy. Nature reclaiming what it was originally in this particular piece of the earth would include far fewer plants and much more sand.

One of their new team members scrambled out of the lead vehicle and pivoted his weapon constantly until he reached the gates of the warehouse and dragged them open wide enough for the Hammerheads to drive through. The inside looked like it was covered in almost as much greenery as the outside, with plants creating a small biome within the confines of the building. There was enough room for the vehicles, though, with most of the growth closer to the walls and the windows. The glass was already missing, which meant the sunlight streamed in unfiltered from outside.

"Okay, folks, it looks like the suits are still intact, more or less," Madigan called. "We might need help getting them into the Hammerheads, so all hands on deck."

The group set to work with alacrity, checked the suits still in their crates, and made sure they were functional before they loaded them on the vehicles. It wasn't quick work. They were older models—the kind that wasn't quite as easy to check as the newer ones. On the bright side, it did have the advantage that the simpler mechanics meant far less could go wrong. The team moved systematically through the collection, discarded three or four that had breaches in the outer armor, and loaded the rest into the three vehicles.

It wasn't until they were finished with most of the crates that Sal's gaze was drawn to a handful of bushes that grew in the center of the building directly beside one of the trees that had thrust through the roof. Any number of plants invited study, but there was something interesting about these in particular.

"Hey, Courtney, have a look at this," he called and gestured for the only other researcher in their team to help him identify the plants that sprouted out of the floor like it was the finest, most fertile soil.

She jogged to where he stood, her weapon at the ready, and tried to stay alert while the remainder of the team loaded the last of the suits. "What—are those Pita plants?"

"I thought so, but look," he said, dropped into a crouch beside the low bushes in question, and traced his fingers over the petals. "Call me crazy or colorblind, but why are these petals the wrong color?"

"And this one," Courtney said when she moved to the next plant. "The petals are blue and red here too."

"I think we need to collect samples for future analysis," he suggested, and she couldn't help but agree with a nod. The sealed bags were quickly retrieved from their packs and he snipped the flowers gently from the stem, careful not to disturb the plant itself. There was no need to send the Zoo into a killing frenzy.

"That's weird," he said as they collected the remaining blossoms seconds before Madigan called for a headcount near the Hammerheads. "These flowers are the only things I haven't seen change since I arrived in the Zoo and now, even they are altered somehow."

"Yeah," Courtney grumbled. "I guess we should have known the whole place would inevitably change, even the flowers."

He sighed as he mounted up beside her and they started moving out of the warehouse. "I wonder what else will change."

CHAPTER SEVENTEEN

Thanks to Anja and Gregor's knowledge of the base, they already had the location locked into their GPS systems. These showed signs of the usual interference from the Zoo but were still functional and guided the team deeper into the base-turned-jungle.

It wasn't the best of situations—heading deeper into what could only be described as enemy territory—but they knew what and who they were there for. With the gunners they had seen heading into the bunker, they were confident that the addition of them to their already two-dozen-strong team meant they would have a better chance of getting everyone out of there alive.

They wouldn't be careless, however, and while they proceeded rapidly over the tough terrain, they also made sure to not get stuck anywhere in the underbrush that would complicate the rescue attempt. By Anja's estimates, they could safely assume they would rescue a maximum of ten survivors, which would make the trip home a little cramped. It would be tight but they would have enough space.

"Are we here?" Madigan asked and stopped the lead vehicle when they reached a comparatively tiny building—barely a shed in comparison to the other buildings. "Is this the place? Can we honestly expect to find a group of canned Russians in there? Like…sardines?"

"Well, yes and no, respectively," Gregor said and dismounted quickly as the drivers began to turn the Hammerheads into a defensive formation around the entrance. Connie assumed control of the weaponry once they were all parked facing away from the building to allow for a quick escape if they needed it. "They are in there, but there will be no canned Russians. I doubt anyone would buy if that were even a thing. I love my people, but we taste like bad potato vodka."

"I don't even want to know how you know that," Sal said and shook his head to eventually dislodge that picture from his head.

"Oh, please, don't be sick." Gregor chuckled. "I'm talking about oral sex, of course."

"Yeah, too much sharing," Sal grumbled. "I don't need to know that."

"All right, ladies, put your collective ovaries back in your collective purses." Madigan laughed. "We have a group of humans in there, hopefully, who will need suits if we want to get them out safely, so we'll have to take what they need and carry them in there. I want five people to stick it out up here and run interference on any attackers that might decide to create a problem for us."

Five of the newcomers were chosen to remain with the

vehicles, both to keep the animals away and to keep Connie from attempting world domination. The fact that she hadn't made any jokes on the way was something of a concern, to be honest. Sal reasoned that if he was an AI on the verge of taking over the world, he wouldn't want people to think or talk about it either.

But that was a concern for another time. He hauled one of the suit crates from the Hammerhead and headed toward the shed, where Gregor was already speaking to someone over an intercom system. He spoke in Russian, but it sounded like the people inside were a little reluctant to open the door, which visibly annoyed the man.

"What gives, Gregor? Do these people not want to be rescued?" Courtney asked as she stepped closer.

"I think they're a little paranoid." He scowled. "They seem to think it's within the realm of possibility that something in the Zoo is trying to trick them into opening the door."

"Well, let's be honest, we've lived and survived this long by never ruling out anything as impossible out here," Sal conceded. "That said, there is a hint of paranoia in there. It could be a sign of oxygen deprivation, couldn't it?"

"Decreased judgment or awareness is a symptom of altitude sickness," Madigan said and shrugged irritably. "It could be something like that, right?"

"It doesn't matter," he pointed out. "We need to get inside and get them out of here, whether they want us to or not. Is there any way to blast through this?"

"I'd say that should be plan...like, Z or something," she responded and shook her head. "The noise alone will bring every Zoo monster in the area down on our heads with a vengeance. Let's simply try to reason with them..." Her voice trailed off as the reinforced door clicked and swung open slowly with a loud creak. "Or wait for them to come to their senses on their own. Let's move it, people."

They responded without delay, pushed into the building in single file, and were led down a small flight of stairs to what looked like a fairly secure bunker under-ground. It was even spacious enough to allow for a second secure door, which swung open as they approached.

The group inside looked like what Sal imagined he would if he were stuck in a bunker for the better part of a week, knowing there was something outside that wanted to tear his guts out. It wasn't a pleasant thought, and he could see the stress telling on the group. Most looked like they hadn't had a wink of sleep during their time inside.

Gregor spoke to them to calm them and explained that they would need to come with them and put suits on to do so. Now that it was established that they were dealing with humans and not some bizarre Zoo trick, the group inside —consisting of eight survivors—was quick to grasp the opportunity to escape.

"We should be topside in five minutes. Do you read me, outside team?" Madigan called as her teammates helped the weak and disoriented survivors into their new suits.

"Roger that," one of the men above called. "Be advised, we see some weird movement on the perimeter—oh, shit, is that the mist?"

"Come on, man, what else in the world looks like a green fucking cloud?" one of the other team members snapped.

"Right, close the doors and seal them," Madigan

ordered. "Don't open them again until you hear me tell you that we're clear down here. We have people still putting their suits on. Repeat, we have exposed skin down here."

"Roger that," he replied. "Sealing the doors now."

The loud click of the heavy door at the top of the staircase sealing shut felt a little ominous to Sal as he hurried to assist some of the slower men to get their suits on quickly. There was no telling if the reputedly secure top doors would keep the mist out, after all, and he didn't want their rescue mission to start with people being melted alive by acid fog. That was as inauspicious a start as a mission could have.

"Let's move it, people," Madigan shouted and clapped briskly, trying not to show that she felt a little anxious herself. He knew her focus would be more on saving lives than the fact that the mission might be compromised.

They had talked about him and the fact that he'd become a little more ruthless as time had passed and honestly, this was the first time he was able to look at his thought process in an objective way that told him something was wrong.

But that wasn't something for him to think about now. He would put it into his journal and add a couple of thoughts before he sent it to a psychology professional who could tell him what the problem was. For now, though, he was at the front of the line that climbed the steps. He drew his assault rifle clear with one hand and his vibro-sword with the other, then prepped the extra arms with a variety of commands to ready them for immediate action the moment trouble began.

"All right, topside team, everyone's suited up," Madigan

called and keyed the team's commlink. "We're moving out of here in a hurry."

"Copy that. Unsealing the doors now," their teammate responded. A hint of interference buzzed the reception somewhat as the doors clicked again. Sal was up the steps in a moment and helped to thrust them wide before he stepped out, activated his sword, and positioned his assault rifle in readiness.

The eerie view of the world tinted green was the sight that greeted him. It sent chills rippling down his spine as he moved out to the group that still held the line in front of the Hammerheads.

"Any sign of the creatures?" he asked, a little disappointed that there was no fight to be had after he'd primed himself for one. The mission was still young, though, and he anticipated an attack at any minute now. He had the familiar feeling in the back of his skull he'd come to associate with the Zoo gearing up for an attack they would need to deal with.

"Nothing yet, sir," one of the newcomers replied and moved closer to him. "Do you think we're in for one of their swarm attacks?"

"Honestly, I'm surprised they've held off this long," he said, his voice a little distant as he studied their surroundings. There was something out there that didn't add up in his mind. The fact that he wasn't able to pin it down immediately was annoying.

As the remainder of the group appeared along with the survivors, he finally realized what ticked him off about this place. It seemed as though Courtney picked it up almost immediately. That was also annoying, but he had to acknowledge the fact that she had a brilliant mind too.

"Hey, Sal, did you notice something weird about this mist?" she asked and he nodded quickly.

"There's no wind," he replied and squinted into the murky green that enveloped them. They couldn't see farther than ten yards in any direction and the fog grew thicker by the moment.

Madigan looked quickly from one to the other, reluctant to ask since it appeared they were talking about something fairly obvious. It took her a few more seconds to grasp it too. The lack of wind to carry a mist like this meant something else pushed it around. It defied the laws of physics, but that wasn't exactly new around there.

Sal was curious as to what could make an acid mist move as rapidly as it did without any visible form of locomotion. Maybe something was spraying it? He didn't know how that particular concept would work, but they lacked any real hypotheses at the moment.

"We have no time for this," Madigan snapped and shook her head impatiently. "Let's load up and move out of here. Hopefully, we'll be able to reach the edge of the base before any of the animals realize we're here."

Sal didn't want to say he felt it was a futile hope. It didn't need to be said since he was sure everyone thought it even more now that it felt like she had jinxed their efforts to escape the fucking place. There wasn't much to say at this point. They would have to decide how to get out one step at a time.

All of them squeezed into the three Hammerheads and the engines roared to life.

"Plotting us a way out of here, sexy mamma," Connie said, still active on the defenses as she displayed the way out on the HUD built into the windshields. Silence filled the vehicles as the group watched the area around them intently, waiting for something to go wrong and for something to force them to use the weapons their suits provided. Even those who weren't gunners and had probably never worn the combat suits before in their lives looked like they were ready to fight if that was what they had to do.

The reservations about exactly how useful they would be once bullets started flying did enter Sal's mind. He recalled his own first time in the Zoo. Although he'd worked with less equipment at the time, he'd still managed to make himself useful thanks to the power of adrenaline and the willingness to stay alive at all costs against increasingly unfavorable odds. These people were possibly looking down the same proverbial gun barrel and from the scared yet determined looks on their faces, he had a feeling they would not let the Heavy Metal team down.

Madigan drove the Hammerhead at the front of their little convoy, and when she dragged to a halt and compelled the other two vehicles to stop as well, he could only assume it meant something had gone terribly, terribly wrong.

"Something's clogging my front wheels," she said over the comms and others had already begun to dismount from the vehicle. It couldn't be a coincidence, he decided silently and hastily yanked the top hatch of his Hammerhead open to haul himself onto the roof.

His suit's motion sensors suddenly went crazy. Movement flickered all around them, barely visible through the green mist, but the shrieks and roars of the monsters that instantly attacked from all sides were frighteningly audible.

All six of the arms on Sal's suit activated at once. One knocked two panthers away from the hatch that was still open, and another used the assault rifle to fire at the creatures that attempted to reach Madigan and her group where they tried desperately to free their vehicle.

It took him a few moments to realize what held the front wheels immobile, although he should have guessed after all his various Zoo encounters. Vines writhed eerily in the mist and wound themselves tightly around the hardened tires. That, however, wasn't the real source of his concern. They were accompanied by other far more sinister helpers.

"Shit, Madigan, look out. It's one of the tentacle—" he started to say, but his voice was cut off when two of the elongated, slimy appendages careened toward him. His sword caught one of them but the second lashed through his defenses, punched him easily from his position on top of the Hammerhead, and hurled him a few feet away. He only saw one of the nearby buildings a half-second before he crashed into it, head-first, and the world turned from green to black.

CHAPTER EIGHTEEN

"Explain 'disappeared.'" Molina scowled at her phone before she held it to her ear again.

Savage leaned back in his seat on the plane and shifted into a more comfortable position in a somewhat futile effort to nap while they were in the air. Word had come through that Solodkov had been moved from the safehouse and out of the country about halfway into his much-needed night of sleep. As a result, Molina was raring to go as soon as they knew a destination. Confirmation came at around five in the morning and they were already moving a half-hour later.

He didn't like that or the fact that it didn't seem like she had slept at all. While it didn't show on her face, it did rear its ugly head in her attitude as evidenced by the fact that she had alternated between screaming and muttering at her ground team for the duration of the flight.

The time of a flight from Prague to Brussels was only about an hour and a half, but that still didn't excuse the fact that she was rude to the people who held her life in their hands. It was no wonder she couldn't get decent help. She drove all the talented ones away and cowed the talent out of those who were too desperate to go anywhere else.

She had never yelled at him like that, though, not even when he'd sided with his Zoo team over her, and that was telling. He merely wasn't sure what it was telling of. Either she respected him and his skills too much to want to insult him, or she merely still carried that weird torch of hers. He didn't know which was the more likely.

"Why is he going to Brussels to begin with?" Molina asked, presumably of her people who were still stationed in Prague. He decided to field the question anyway.

"The first thing a covert agent does when their cover is blown and they need to vanish is return to their handlers for a debrief," he pointed out, his eyes still closed. Even if he wouldn't manage a nap, he still wanted to rest them as much as he could in the short time he had. "Given that Brussels is the de facto capital of the European Union and plays host to a number of their institutions, it's a location where few questions would be raised if a group of Russians was suddenly flown in on diplomatic passports.

"Ask your people if Solodkov disappeared in an area that doesn't have that much surveillance and if so, ask them to look for any property that is associated via paperwork to the Russian embassy or consulate."

"Did you get that?" Molina asked into her phone and nodded when he opened his eyes, then gave him a thumbs-up as the plane began its descent. A few minutes passed while the experts in Prague followed the instructions. They worked quickly, although not quite as quickly as Anja did, he noted. The Russian hacker had a way to anticipate his questions and seemed to always be working on anything he asked of her a few minutes before he mentioned the request. It was what made them such a great team.

Savage had begun to miss working openly with her. She would have known what they were looking for and already have a detailed analysis of the building he knew they would find. All this would be accompanied by some kind of snarky and arrogant comment about how she imagined he would flounder around the world like a caveman without her.

In fairness, she would have been right. Without someone like her on his side, his only option would be to go off the grid and essentially force himself into the Dark Ages.

"We have a location," Molina said and called the address up on the nearby TV screen.

"Five bucks says that's a safehouse they're debriefing our friend Solodkov in," he said with a nod.

"Your friend Solodkov," she retorted acidly. "Don't think I missed how chummy the two of you were when you were talking in Prague."

"Yeah, and then he tried to have me shot," he snapped in response. "We might be chummy but that doesn't alter the fact that we're both professional enough to kill each other if the situation dictates it. I'll do my job, don't you worry."

"Like you did last night?" she asked and raised a very fair point. "No, I don't trust you to carry the mission out again, Savage. I intend to go in with you this time."

"I don't think that's a good idea," he said although he'd known this would come, which did little to diminish the fact that he hated it.

MICHAEL TODD & MICHAEL ANDERLE

"I think you'll find I'm more than up to the task of infiltration and assassination," she said and looked a little more relaxed now that they had the location of their target.

"That's big talk from the woman who was too afraid to get involved the first time around." Savage grinned at her.

"Well, how the hell was I to know you would blow it like that?" she asked with a scowl. "When you get into a position like mine, you realize you won't last very long if you're the one to charge into the dangerous situations. You learn to delegate."

"So why don't you delegate the task of looking over my shoulder?" he challenged.

"Because if I were to send someone else into the field with you instead, you'd shoot them simply to annoy me," she countered with a shrug.

"If that's what you think, you don't know me at all," he pointed out.

"Well then, you can consider this a learning experience for both of us." She smirked as the stewardess came to remind them to fasten their seatbelts for the landing.

As learning experiences go, I wouldn't ever have chosen this particular scenario as a way to get to know Molina a little better. Not that I want to. The only closeness I want with her is the one when I can strangle her with my bare hands.

Savage still didn't trust her, despite their little bonding session in Prague. Her insistence on heading in with him instead of sending someone who might be a little more qualified to work in the field was suspicious, at best. She had mentioned that he might shoot anyone she sent in with him. *But you forgot the part where you're still at the top of my to-kill list. That puts you in the most danger of being shot in the back.*

Not that he would do that, of course. There were rules about the shit you were and weren't allowed to do in the field. In his mind, there was nothing worse than shooting your team in the back. There was a special place in hell reserved for the kinds of people who did that.

It made them even worse than the supposed crimes the people they were killing could have committed. He was known for doing more than his share of shady shit in his time, but that was the one line he would not cross—not now and not ever. Shoot her when they got back? Sure. Shoot her before the mission started, even better. But while they were on the mission, he would watch her back and expect her to do the same, no matter what kind of grudges he might hold against her.

And I guess that's the biggest difference between us. You only think I'm capable of gunning someone on my team down because you are capable and willing to do exactly that. Her inevitable lack of hesitation to shoot someone on her team in the back due to a disagreement from before the mission started was the reason why he didn't trust her.

Savage had tried to explain it to Molina while they prepared for the mission, but his lesson had slipped from her mind the way water slid from a duck's back. She was a paranoid, deadly person who wouldn't think twice about betrayal if it improved her chances of survival and success. As a result, she couldn't imagine there were people in the world who thought differently than her.

Okay, this is not the time to think about that. Focus or you won't have to worry about her killing you. Someone else will do it first.

Dressed in his half-suit covered by another trench coat —one that didn't have bullet holes in it—he made it abundantly clear that he would run point on the operation with her relegated to the position of glorified observer simply to keep him in line.

"Remember," she whispered as they stepped out of the car and moved toward the building in question, using the cover of darkness to keep their movements hidden. "Not only are we here to kill Solodkov but also to make sure the Russians lose any information they might hold against Pegasus in the months to come."

"You didn't think that was something I should have known before we started?" Savage asked as he scrutinized their surroundings. The house was in the suburbs of the city of Brussels, with a condo feel about the neighborhood. There were too many pristine lawns, and all the homes were built with the same style in mind. A few changes had been incorporated here and there but they all looked and felt the same like they had been put up within hours of each other.

He paused when they reached what looked like an electrified fence and glanced at Molina, who indicated for him to give her a boost. He took position with his back to the fence and his hands extended. She would need to be launched well over the top. Scaling it would not only electrocute her but also probably activate the alarms that would be positioned around the house.

The security set up on the property was rather extensive according to the records, but most of the tech went into the perimeter. There were no motion sensors but tripping the fences would activate the cameras inside the building. It was a solid building but designed to not look out of place in a quaint neighborhood like this one.

Molina sprinted toward him. As her boots connected with his hands, he gave her a boost with the help of his half-suit that was, thankfully, enough to thrust her cleanly over the ten-foot fence that surrounded the house.

With anyone else, he would have expected to hear a few grunts and possibly cracking bones on landing, but he knew she had been taking the blue goop from the Zoo. It was supposed to make her stronger, faster, and a whole lot deadlier, and it meant that she landed lightly and executed a perfect roll to absorb the impact.

"Showoff," he muttered under his breath, took a few steps back, and activated the coils in his boots to launch himself upward. He flipped over the fence and landed lightly in a three-point touchdown.

"Superhero landing." He grinned at her but kept his voice at a low, almost inaudible whisper. "I don't know why I've never done it before."

"Because it's been overdone?" Molina asked as they moved cautiously toward the house. "Because it's hard on the knees?"

"It still looks cool, you have to admit," Savage said as they approached the back door and she produced the same unlocking device they'd used on the apartment. They had only one lock to deal with this time and it opened with ease before the two of them entered the building.

"The alarm's been deactivated and turned on again,"

Anja said into the earpiece he still wore. "It made barely a blip in the servers at the security company and they shouldn't notice it or investigate until tomorrow morning. I'd still hurry the fuck up if I were the two of you."

"The alarm is killed and turned on again," he said for his partner's benefit, still in a hushed whisper. "It won't set any bells ringing anywhere, but someone might notice the blip and send someone to investigate. Where did you say we'd find the info you mentioned again?"

"I didn't say," she muttered in response and guided them through the kitchen and into what looked like a common room. There was no sign of anyone on watch, which immediately struck him as suspicious.

Then again, as safehouses went, the one used for debriefing was supposedly safer than most. The people inside might be lulled into a sense of security that would only be proven false if he broke in with Anja working at his side. It was supposed to look exactly like another house in the suburbs, after all.

He followed the woman through the building and to the second floor, which looked less like a regular house and more like the safehouse it was supposed to be. The scene included computers left running, weapons mounted on the walls for quick access, and a couple of rooms that were layered with more than your average amount of security, which included steel-reinforced doors.

And five men standing watch.

They looked like they were playing cards, completely unaware that their house had been infiltrated until they saw the two intruders appear at the top of the stairs. A moment of silence was shared between the two groups during which both tried to decide what to do next. The quiet before the storm, Savage thought inanely.

He was the first to move and acted fast because he didn't want to wait for them to reach the veritable arsenal they had on the walls. There was no need to give them the opportunity to react because their first move would definitely be to arm themselves. He pushed past Molina and stepped in front of her as one of the men drew a pistol from inside his coat.

The shots from the unsilenced weapon in the confined common area set his ears ringing as another jump brought him to the other half of the room where the men stood. The two bullets their adversary managed to fire missed both his targets entirely. He hadn't expected him to be able to move that fast and Elena had evidently ducked in time.

The gunman in question tried to reacquire him as a target, but he was too late. Savage's suit-enhanced fingers wrapped quickly around the man's wrist and pulverized the bones inside. The Russian screamed in agony, dropped his weapon, and tried to pull himself away but proved no match for the gauntlet his assailant wore. A firm backhand to the side of his head silenced his shrieks and he crumpled in a heap. The operative had already moved to the next man, who had snatched a shotgun from the wall and turned to fire it.

Again, he underestimated how quickly Savage was able to move. He bounded closer, grasped the barrel, and yanked it away. In the same moment, he stamped his foot into the man's knee and activated the coils inside his boot to shatter his opponent's leg. His victim's scream was cut off when he grabbed the side of his head and slammed it into the table where they had played cards barely seconds before.

A third realized he had no chance to reach the weapons without engaging the seemingly superhuman character who stood between him and them. Instead, he drew a knife from his pocket, lunged forward, and stabbed viciously at the invader's torso.

The serrated steel of the blade clanged impotently against the titanium weave of the armor he wore.

"Really?" Savage asked. "You thought that would work?"

The Russian had no answer for him, not that he expected one. He twisted his body and pounded his right fist into the man's chest. He could feel ribs breaking and tendons snapping under the power of the blow. The man catapulted across the room to break through the drywall and remained where he had landed.

There wasn't even the remotest possibility that anyone would be able to walk after that. If he was still alive, it was debatable whether the man would think of himself as lucky or unlucky. It didn't matter, but there was something to be said for not waking up when you were bleeding internally from about three dozen or so different places.

He turned to deal with the other two he knew were in the room but was rather pleasantly surprised to find his services wouldn't be necessary. One already hung, unconscious, from the railing of the stairs they'd ascended. The last attempted to fend off a series of punches that slipped through his defenses like he made no effort at all.

A jab landed to break his nose and another forced the breath out of his lungs with a solid strike to his solar plexus. Finally, an uppercut to the jaw hurled him over his comrade and he thumped loudly down the stairs.

Savage nodded as Molina turned to face him, rolled her neck, and grinned. For a moment, the blue veins seemed to pulse and possibly glow, but that could have a trick of the light.

"Not bad," he admitted. It would be about as much as he was willing to say in respect of her abilities, but she could see he held back on his compliments and didn't appear to mind.

"That blue stuff might be nasty, but it sure as fuck is useful," she replied, took a deep breath, and examined the condition of the three he had dealt with so effectively. "You should try it sometime."

"Thanks, but no thanks," he retorted and shook his head fervently. "Or did you not read the report Jacobs wrote on what happens to folks who take that shit?"

"I skimmed it," she conceded.

"Anyway," he said roughly to change the subject, "it looks like our attempts at infiltration are rather spectacularly blown. Do you think it might be time for us to head to this data you want to get your hands on?"

"What about Solodkov?" she asked and moved to one of the doors that boasted considerably more security than the average bedroom should.

"Given the mess we've made here, I wouldn't be surprised if he comes running to see what the problem is," he said with a shrug.

"Don't you think he'd be smart enough to know we're here for him and stay the fuck away?" she countered as she slipped something into the keypad. Both devices suddenly came alive with the sound of beeping and flashing lights.

"Does he know we're probably here for him and he'd be better off running away to find another safe house to hide in?" he asked rhetorically. "Sure, probably, but the guy's former Spetsnaz. He's trained to move toward the sound of gunfire and explosions, and it's not in him to run from a fight, especially when it's on his turf. By now, he knows we have a bead on him and will come for him wherever he decides to hide. He'll want to make a stand in a location where he has some kind of advantage. Here is as good a place as any, I suppose."

The beeping stopped and the door clicked open. She turned to look at him. "And if you're wrong?"

He shrugged. "You'll have your data, so it won't be a complete loss. After that, your team will find Solodkov again and this time, we can focus on killing him. Maybe with a rifle from a long fucking way away."

"Maybe," she said and pushed the door open. A collection of computers lined both walls inside the room, which left only a very narrow way in. It was too small for him to be able to slip in with the suit on, but Molina moved through easily, found a chair inside and dropped onto it, then set to work.

"Huh." Anja grunted into his earpiece. "You know, that place looks like my server room here."

Savage wanted to ask her how she was able to see what he was looking at, but that was a question for later.

"Now, like I told you, put the drive into the nearest slot and I'll do the rest," she said and he followed her instructions without hesitation. He retrieved the drive she'd mailed to him while they'd still been in Prague and inserted it into the nearest port—the only one he could reach, in fact.

Molina, completely focused on her work, didn't notice what he'd done at first but something happened on the screen she stared at so intently, and she turned to look at him and the drive he'd inserted.

"What the fuck did you do?" she snapped and bolted out of her chair, looking aghast as the lights in the servers began to go down one by one.

"Honestly, I don't have the slightest clue." He chuckled. "I simply followed the orders of someone much smarter than I am."

"Damn right." Anja laughed on the other end of the commlink.

"Why?" Molina demanded.

"Because I still trust you about as far as I can throw you which, as it turns out, is fairly far with this suit of mine," he replied. "The data's safe and is being decrypted as we speak. On the flight out of here, we can talk about how we'll let you access it, deal?"

"No deal!" she yelled and shoved him with enough strength to force him to stumble back a few steps.

He wondered if he would be forced into a fistfight with the woman, but his suspicions were quickly allayed. She wouldn't pick a fight with him now that they had a group of Russians to deal with. Those who had heard the noise from the fight earlier—and their present altercation, no doubt—had rushed to investigate.

"Savage." Solodkov's familiar voice sounded almost welcoming as he stepped out in front of the group of a dozen heavily armed Russians. The man himself was strapped into a combat suit, one that was considerably sturdier than the one Savage wore. "I should have guessed you would return for more."

"Well, you know me, a sucker for punishment that I am." He chuckled and inched his hands into his coat for the pistols that rested inside.

"Who's she?" the Russian asked and aimed his assault rifle at Molina with a wary expression.

"My sidekick," he answered before she could get a word in.

"Fuck you," she snapped, drew a pistol from under her body armor, and opened fire.

CHAPTER NINETEEN

His ears were ringing. It was the first conscious thought that came into Sal's mind and he groaned softly. The second realization was the pain that throbbed in his skull, neck, and most of his body. There was more than enough time to think about that later, though. Little by little, his consciousness returned and told him that the barrage of firepower and explosions was real and not that far away.

He opened his eyes warily and looked instinctively for the damage report that was supposed to display on the HUD of his suit. The fact that nothing was there should have alerted him to exactly how fucked he was. Still, he needed a few seconds to realize that there was no HUD because the part of his helmet that should show it was shattered in all the wrong places.

His senses registered what could be a couple of gashes along his face and he reasoned that some of the plexiglass had entered his suit and sliced his face deeply enough to possibly leave a few killer scars.

Everything was green. Why was everything green? *Oh,*

241

right, the mist. Godammit. It continued to grow thicker and thicker by the minute if that was even possible. He pushed up from where he had landed. The tentacle that had struck him had launched him across what had probably once been a street but was now merely another piece of the jungle they all knew and loved.

Wait...the green. The mist. It's supposed to do something to my face now that I'm exposed to it, right? Sal attributed his slow cognitive state to the concussion he had probably sustained, and he reached hastily into his shattered face-mask. He expected to already find his face a half-melted mass of flesh. *Maybe the burning destroyed all the nerve endings, which would explain why I can't feel anything.*

There was some bleeding and some green residue, but his skin was mostly still intact. He honestly didn't know how that was possible, and a storm of questions suddenly arose to make his head throb again before he shook the confusion aside. Now that he knew he wouldn't die in agony anytime soon, he had bigger concerns. The sound of gunfire told him that the Heavy Metal team was still fighting and somehow, still held their own against the monsters that tried to kill them. They needed his help.

One of the extra arms of his suit picked his weapons up and placed the sword into his hand while retaining control of the assault rifle. With the HUD gone, the suit would be stuck in combat mode until he was able to fix it again, which suited him fine for the moment. Combat mode was all he would need for the foreseeable future.

He sprinted across the street again and vaulted over a couple of fallen pieces of rock and trees before he reached the Hammerheads. All three looked like they were still intact.

"Don't shoot!" he shouted, not sure if his comms were still active as a couple of the Russians spun toward him, thinking he was one of the monsters. With his six arms, he could understand their confusion.

"Hold your fucking fire!" Madigan shouted and rushed to where he approached their line. He could see she wanted to wrap him in a tight hug and punch him in the jaw for making her worry like that, but there was no time. They were still under attack from all sides and while the initial rush of monsters seemed to thin, in Sal's mind, they merely regrouped for another assault.

"What's the situation?" he asked quickly before she could say anything else. "How long was I out?"

"Long enough to have us all worried, asshole," she snapped in response and turned when she was alerted to a couple of massive albino apes with horns jutting from their heads. The rocket launcher on her shoulder activated and delivered two smoking trails at the creatures, struck them squarely in their faces, and effectively disabled them, if only momentarily. It didn't look like they were dead. "All in all, we only lost track of you for a couple of minutes."

That much was good, at least, he reasoned. He still thought he had a concussion, and with the HUD missing, his suit's first aid capabilities were severely limited. Still, he was strong enough to fight, even if every step he took made him want to puke his guts out as the throbbing in his head only grew worse and worse.

"Sal!" Courtney shouted. She ran to him from where she was helping the group around the middle Hammerhead to hold their ground. It was the only one that lacked a complete arsenal of offensive weaponry. They needed to convince the folks at the American base to make improvements to their vehicles. Maybe they could contract Amanda to do it so she could earn a fat stack of cash to help her start thinking about proposing to Bev.

His train of thought was cut off and the pain in his head became epic when Courtney collided with him in a hug. The moment was made awkward by the suits they wore but it didn't diminish her enthusiasm. "We thought you were dead."

"And you guys didn't even mourn my loss." He chuckled sarcastically. "For shame, Dr. Monroe, for shame."

She punched his arm and again, made a sharp stab of pain lance through his head. "Asshole, we were worried, but we were trying to stay alive ourselves, you know."

He nodded and tried valiantly to smile. "I know. I was only...trying to lighten the mood. Sorry."

"Don't apologize," she replied and rubbed the spot on his armor where she'd punched him. "We were—wait, is that a breach in your suit?"

Oh, right. I completely forgot about that. Sal reached inside the hole the impact with a wall had left and located more blood and green residue inside. They had mixed to make a thick, gooey, yellowish substance that stuck to the fingers of his gauntlets.

"How are you still alive?" Madigan asked. "I know, that's the most bizarre question you've ever heard. But in this case, how the fuck is your face not melting off? Not that we're complaining, mind. Is the mist safe now for some reason?"

"I doubt it," Sal replied, shook his head, and immediately regretted it. His face melting off or not, he still needed to find a doctor to look at his head and make sure nothing was broken, dislodged, or missing after the impact with a building. "It might be...uh, you know. Since I spent so much time licking Madie, maybe I've been made immune to this shit like the rest of the animals? Something like that."

"That's an interesting hypothesis, and it looks like you're already set to prove it with breaking your fucking mask," Courtney said. She spun to open fire on a couple of locusts that rushed forward to try to break through the human lines.

"Well, now that we have an idea of how to counteract this fucking mist, maybe the folks at the base would be willing to let all their people who head into the Zoo give Madie a lick." Madigan grinned and punched him lightly in the arm.

Sal winced. "I wouldn't stand for it, a jealous man like me. Besides, as I recall, the only guys who get to lick Madie are the ones who can beat me in a drinking competition, right?"

"Correct." She smirked and reloaded her assault rifle.

"Wait, I think I'm missing something," Courtney said, looking confused.

"There was a time when...well, I don't remember much about it as we were drinking, but I think I said this guy could fuck me if he could beat Sal in a drinking game. Sal won, but he was subsequently too drunk to enjoy the spoils of his victory," Madigan explained. "Well, that night, anyway."

"Huh." Courtney tilted her head and looked for an explanation from Sal but she paused when she saw his eyes narrow like he was trying to focus on something.

Which he was. The pain and throbbing were still there, and he tried to push them to the back of his mind so his brain could work at its normal capacity. He had a strong sense of something he should notice, something that should be brought to the forefront of his consciousness, but had difficulty taking hold of it. He needed to focus to make it happen consciously.

Oh. Right. That. I can't forget about that.

"No, we really shouldn't let soldiers have access to the goop," he said finally and the humor of what they had discussed previously melted away quickly as he gripped his sword with both hands. "You will both remember what happened when I came in close contact with the tentacle creature—that, by the way, is a part of this here engagement too."

Both women exchanged a quick glance, which told him that while his brain functions might be a little impaired, they needed to focus too. There were too many problems with what they faced for any of them to be careless, and it wasn't only about the monsters that wanted a piece of them.

Sal took a deep breath. He didn't have access to the motion sensors in his suit but something told him in the back of his mind that the creatures were gathering in preparation for round two. He had experienced those kinds of feelings for a while but now that he was practically blind and the mist masked anything that was farther than ten feet in green nothingness, it was more acute.

He could sense that an attack was imminent. Acting purely on instinct, he raised his sword and waited for the suit to catch up with what he had already discerned. Two panthers rushed in first, having pounced from one of the buildings in an attempt to catch them unprepared.

The first was quickly decapitated when he leapt into the strike. He avoided the second as he landed on the section of cracked pavement where he'd stood a second or so before. The assault-rifle-toting arm fired and eliminated the creature, which enabled him to move forward with his attack. Five locusts were quickly dispatched as he pushed toward the central Hammerhead, where it looked like the Russians had a difficult time holding off the concerted assault.

And not only from the regular monsters, he realized. Long, thick tentacles extended from the left and twined around the wheels as if they tried to pry them free. As plans went, it was rather ingenious. If there was one way to permanently make sure the vehicles wouldn't go anywhere, it was to remove the wheels completely.

That kind of sentience was probably what set the tentacle monster apart from the other creatures. They appeared to be the most intelligent of the group. Maybe it wasn't even one of the monsters, but rather...the original? That seemed unlikely since they hadn't run into these mutants until only a couple of months before.

Of course, simply because they hadn't been seen that didn't mean they hadn't been around. Sal made a note to gather samples as he hacked at a swarm of the appendages that were intertwined and looked like a writhing mass of worms.

A couple of swings were enough to sever the slick, slimy limbs from the creature that previously owned them. He vaulted over those that currently went through their death throes, still imbued with enough nerve endings that they were able to trigger a vibration that rumbled through the base. The other monsters rushed into the attack with more vigor than before. They roared and howled and shrieked at the humans, who tried to pry their vehicles free of the sinuous grasp that held them in place.

Gregor stood with his countrymen and women and looked like he was having the time of his life as he led the defense of the central Hammerhead.

"Jacobs!" the Russian shouted when he saw the lean and lithe suit Sal had already become known for. "We thought you were for the afterlife—the one I don't believe in but still fear irrationally in my hindbrain."

"Well, it takes more than a little knock to the noggin to send me over to meet with Hades," he countered and hacked one of the locusts in half. A killerpillar began to work its way toward them and thrust a couple of the smaller creatures out of the way in its rush.

Gregor paused in their conversation to launch a rocket at the creature. The attack slowed it and Sal sprinted to where it attempted to recover and stabbed his vibro-sword into its head. The carapace separated smoothly. Green blood gushed from the wound as the massive creature suddenly flipped onto its back and rolled into a ball to die.

"Knock to the head, eh?" the Russian asked, reloaded his assault rifle quickly, and drew his sidearm to release a steady stream of gunfire at the mutants that attacked them with renewed ferocity.

He flicked the blood from his gauntlets and nodded. "Yeah. That damn tentacle monster hurled me headfirst into a building. The suit took the brunt of the damage, but I think I might have a concussion."

"You might want to get a CAT scan when we get back to be safe," his friend said and looked genuinely concerned. "Do you hear that, ladies? We have to get my *mudak* friend back to safety so we can look after his health. If I see any of you slacking, I will shoot you myself."

He grinned. "You're a good friend, Gregor."

CHAPTER TWENTY

Molina shooting first was something Savage hadn't planned for. When it came down to it, he'd thought she would try to talk her way out of this or maybe throw him under the bus in order to get herself clear of danger. He wouldn't have minded that, honestly. After all, if he didn't have her to deal with, he could always do the smart thing—run away and live to fight another day.

But no. She had decided to stick this one out and fight her way through a group that had them outgunned and outnumbered in order to get to Solodkov. He wondered if there was something a little more personal in her desire to kill the Russian.

She'd previously explained that the man would spearhead any mission to interrupt her new cash flow from Pegasus, and he could see that as the catalyst for her decision to attempt to kill him. But still, it seemed like there was something else going on there. She was hiding something from him.

It didn't matter at the moment, though. She had initiated a fight he wasn't sure they could win and tried a few times to shoot Solodkov before she realized the peashooter she carried would not be enough to penetrate his armor.

Savage was quicker on the draw, though, and chose easier targets among the men who flanked the Russian, none of whom wore the same kind of combat suit. They wore body armor, of course, but it wouldn't do them much good against the needles his weapon rocketed at them at around eight hundred feet per second—slow enough to stay under the sound barrier so it worked as the quasi-perfect silenced weapon. At the same time, it propelled them with enough speed and accuracy to ensure that each of the needles drilled through the high-tech body armor three of the men wore before they had even managed a shot.

Still, that small victory wouldn't be enough. They were still outnumbered. Molina had eliminated one of the men, although that would inevitably be rather temporary given that she probably didn't use armor-piercing bullets. Still, four men down before their opponents had even fired a shot was fairly impressive.

The operative lurched in front of her as the first volley from their opponents was released. He covered his head with his arm and at least a dozen rounds caught him hard across his armored torso. There would be bruises around each of the strikes, but they seemed to be as ill-equipped to handle someone in combat armor as Molina was.

She, in turn, thankful for the cover, returned fire around him and one of her bullets struck the head of one of the Russians. The man fell without so much as a cry of pain. Savage opened fire as well, although with the bullets peppering his armor and forcing him back a few steps, he found his aim wasn't what it should be. Still, it had the desired effect, and those opponents who weren't wearing combat armor were forced to dive for cover.

Solodkov charged at Savage, who still gave Molina cover. The Russian couldn't be slowed, however, and the operative shoved her into the room she had exited from a second before the other man crashed into him.

The tackle had enough power in it to hurl him into the wall behind them. Like the one Molina now hid behind, it was reinforced to keep whatever was inside protected from outside attack. Even the combined weight of two men in combat suits could not penetrate, although the impact did leave a dent.

Being pinned between a combat suit and a hard place forced the breath out of him and he fought to keep himself awake and in the fight. The pistol would have been knocked out of his hands under any other circumstances, but given that it was held in place by a magnetic grasp, it remained locked in his fingers when his adversary initiated a series of suit-powered punches to his midsection.

I already have too many bruises to look forward to tomorrow.

He turned the weapon on Solodkov and pulled the trigger. The armor-piercing needles were not enough to pierce the armor fully, but they were enough to drive through the outer coating and interfere with the electronics. This slowed the Russian's movements while error messages presumably displayed on his HUD. It wasn't much, but it would have to be enough.

Using the coils in his boots, Savage pushed himself up from the ground and shoved Solodkov away in two fluid motions. The man stumbled back with a dent in his chest plate. His adversary landed again, his pistol aimed at two of the Russians who peered cautiously out from cover. He missed his shots at them, but they were sufficient to force them back. Solodkov recovered quickly from the counterattack. He yanked an assault rifle from his back, primed it, and aimed it at Savage, who was already moving to avoid the steady stream of bullets it delivered.

They sprayed into the walls and the floor around him, but with the aid of his suit, he was easily able to evade them. He ducked and slid under one of the tables and the coils whined as he kicked two chairs across the room. One pounded into Solodkov and pushed the man back once more, and the other careened in the direction of his comrades to pin them down.

Molina stepped out of the room and sprinted to reach the other Russians. She had most likely realized that she couldn't handle Solodkov herself. Savage was the only one who was more or less equipped to do so, and it seemed she had the good sense to leave him to do it without interference.

She could take care of the extras the Russian had brought in as backup, though. Savage had seen her fight. She was capable, although he doubted he would ever give her the satisfaction of admitting it to her face. It wasn't her, he reminded himself. The blue stuff pumping through her veins was what gave her the unnatural abilities she demonstrated

He turned away from the woman—although the sounds of gunshots and screams gave him a fairly accurate play by play—and settled his attention on Solodkov instead, who now tried to reacquire him as a target. The man's electronics were still giving him trouble. While the operative assumed he had at least been instructed on how to use the suits, he would not have had the opportunity to acquire too much practical experience.

Although he was a veteran of the Spetsnaz, it had been in a time when suits were still being tested in labs. From what he remembered, the Russian had spent most of the past decade or so in intelligence operations, which required considerable skills, obviously, but the use of a combat suit rarely factored into his activities. This limited experience was a disadvantage because when his electronics didn't take on the work of operating the suit for him, he had trouble keeping up.

It wasn't a bad thing. Savage was still getting used to his suit and it had been built and designed with him in mind. That said, he guessed that even with his limited experience, he could still claim more time in a suit than Solodkov had.

It gave him precious seconds he didn't intend to waste.

He launched himself forward and the tiles beneath his boots gave a little when the coils interacted too roughly with them. Stray pieces sprayed like shrapnel as he hurtled across the room and roared more out of instinct than intent while he fired continuously at the Russian. The coils in his boots powered up again and thrust him over the distance he needed to tackle his opponent's midsection and force them both into the window. He had expected to find a terrace or porch outside but unfortunately, his luck seemed to have run out.

All he could see was a two-story drop that tumbled them onto the solid ground. He had a second to adjust his position to ensure that his adversary would take the brunt of the fall before they landed with a jarring impact.

He groaned and accepted that he would feel this the next day. It was a thought that often occurred to him, which was why he had contemplated moving into a line of work that didn't require him to be pulverized so often or this badly. The shit he had to endure could only be detrimental to his health.

Either way, the crash-landing drove the breath out of him again and he rolled away from Solodkov, dragging the man's assault rifle out of his armored gauntlet as he did so. He raised his weapon to create a few holes in his adversary's suit while he was still recovering, but his attention was diverted by the sound of glass shattering.

Molina pitched out of the building with two of the men who were still alive and well and they plummeted roughly to the ground. It had been a tough drop for him in a suit of armor and he could only imagine the impact it had on her when she landed with a whump that made him wince.

All three combatants took a moment to recover from the drop before they even made an attempt to return to the fight. Savage came over to where she still sprawled with little apparent desire to move.

"Are you okay?" he asked and extended a hand to help her up.

"Never better," she lied and groaned when she took his hand and let him pull her to her feet. Even if she was taking that blue stuff and it did make her superhumanly stronger and faster than before, she looked like she would need time to get back to full fighting form.

Time they didn't have, he thought as Solodkov managed to stand, albeit slowly and carefully.

"Shit." He growled his annoyance and aimed his pistol at the man but before he could fire, a volley of gunfire issued from above. A couple of the Russians remained in the building and now fired at them. He raised his weapon, pulled the trigger, and felt the gentlest of kicks as the magnetic coils inside the barrel launched the needles with lethal velocity. The strips of needles inside his pistols gave him about a hundred rounds per strip so he didn't need to reload. He merely pulled the trigger as quickly and as often as he could until both men toppled out the window, dead or dying but definitely disabled.

Solodkov charged. The Russian didn't have his assault rifle and it didn't appear that he had any kind of sidearm either. Maybe he hadn't thought he would need one.

Savage ducked to meet him toe-to-toe and Molina recovered enough to deal with the remaining Russians, but he couldn't help thinking what a bad idea this was. His suit was more of a hybrid and added more speed and power than he could achieve without it.

Now that it was toned down, however, it wasn't a match in terms of power, strength, or speed against the full suit his Russian friend wore. The only reason why he was still alive at this point was the fact that the coils in his boots were able to compensate somewhat while they were in tighter quarters and the man's slight issues with his electronics.

It seemed obvious that he would have to get creative.

Savage faked a defensive posture and at the last minute, went limp when Solodkov was about to crash into him.

The collision still happened, but the man had put too much force into it and the operative landed flat on his back and his attacker careened past him. It still hurt like a bitch, but he was better off than if he'd attempted to meet the charge with one of his own. At least this way, he was prepared.

His boots whined and the coils kicked the other man's suit and launched him end over end to skid to a stop five or six feet away. The operative ached and grimaced at the pain but aside from that, he remained mostly stable. He dug hastily in the pouch Amanda had attached to his suit, located one of his specialized rounds, and attached it to his pistol as he turned to see Solodkov stretching for his assault rifle. The man snatched the weapon up and whirled instantly to face him.

It was a valiant effort but too late. Savage reached him in less than a second, pressed the barrel of his pistol to his facemask, and pulled the trigger. The round immediately shattered the reinforced plexiglass. It was a weak point in the suits that were being developed, but honestly, that was true of most suits of armor over the years.

The need to see trumped the need to protect the face in combat, which meant that until they developed either a transparent form of armor that was as strong as the rest of the suit or maybe something with cameras and internal imaging, they would need to live with that weakness.

For now, though, it had worked out exactly the way he wanted it to, and his adversary sagged to leave him standing. He panted for breath for a long moment before he turned to see what was happening with Molina.

The woman appeared to be intact, for the most part, although she struggled to stay on her feet. She might have twisted her knee or perhaps her ankle, judging by the way she favored her right leg.

Without a doubt, she needed medical attention. From the sound of the sirens that could be heard approaching in the distance, they wouldn't get it from the people who would normally offer it without some very serious questions being asked—the kind none of them could afford or answer without incriminating themselves.

"Let's get out of here." She turned hastily toward him and he could see a hint of fear in her eyes. He knew she still didn't trust him, and the thought that went through her head right now was that he would leave her behind.

She still didn't know him at all, he thought with a chuckle, shook his head, and pulled her arm across his shoulders. There was no need to be subtle at this point. The neighbors have probably called the police, and there would likely be alarms sent to alert the Russians in the city, which meant they were minutes away from a world of hurt.

They needed to get out fast. Savage let her lean on him as she limped to the fence they had vaulted over. In her current condition, there was no way she would manage another attempt so he led her toward the gates. He stood for a moment and stared at the barrier as he tried to think of an alternative escape route.

"Give me a second, Jer," Anja said in his earpiece and he startled. In all the mayhem, he'd forgotten her constant presence as she'd remained silent and let him work uninterrupted. "I managed to access the software once you got inside so I'll open the gate. It'll only be for a moment, so you'll need to hurry."

He half-dragged his unprotesting partner through the gate as it began to open. As always, the hacker had managed to save his hide with her calm assistance. The duo hurried through as it immediately began to close once again, and they headed to the car that they arrived in.

"Do you need a hospital?' Savage asked.

Molina shook her head and slid gratefully into the passenger seat of the SUV, a vehicle chosen precisely because it was large enough to accommodate Savage's bulky half-suit. With the boots and the gauntlets, it would be a little difficult to drive but it didn't look like she was in any condition to do so.

He wasn't in the best shape of his life either, but at that moment, he was the most able of the two. Besides, the suit would do most of the work, anyway, he thought with a small grin and pressed the accelerator cautiously to ease the vehicle away from the curb.

The flashing lights of the official vehicles approached from the opposite direction toward where the firefight had taken place. There were at least a dozen cars, he noted and narrowed his eyes when one of the vehicles pulled over at the curb but left it's red, white, and blue lights to flash confirmation of their presence.

"Shit." He growled quietly, took a deep breath, and forced himself not to shove his foot hard on the accelerator when the police car suddenly made a U-turn and began to follow them. Word must have come through that an SUV was seen driving away from the location, although that wasn't necessarily the case since most of the vehicles appeared to continue toward the house without slowing.

The officer behind them had possibly only decided to make sure they weren't escaping the scene.

Any sudden acceleration would only be suspicious and cause more trouble, so he maintained the same speed and the police car slowly caught up with them. They reached an intersection that would take them deeper into the city before the officer decided to turn his sirens on and pull them over.

"We can't afford this," Molina warned him. "There's no way we can fool them if they look hard enough." He agreed. They might pass a casual first inspection, but if the man looked more closely, he would immediately see the truth.

"Turn to the side," he ordered as he drew the car to the side of the road and slowly came to a halt. "Pretend you're asleep. That should buy us a few seconds. Maybe we get lucky and he doesn't ask too many questions."

She nodded and shifted quickly to face away from the driver's window, which the officer in question now approached cautiously. He squinted as unobtrusively as he could but couldn't see how many had remained in the vehicle. Even one would be enough to send word to the rest of the authorities and they would descend in force in mere minutes.

The officer reached the window, tapped it lightly with his flashlight, and spoke in French when Savage rolled it down.

"Sorry," he said and shrugged apologetically. "I don't speak French."

He looked annoyed but switched smoothly to slightly

accented English. "I need to see your license and registration."

The operative reached to the glove compartment as the man followed his movements with the flashlight. The beam caught Molina, who still pretended to be asleep, and more importantly, the blood on her shoulder and neck.

"Fuck me." He knew the jig was up the moment the man took a step back from the vehicle and reached toward his hip. Whether it was for a radio or a weapon, he wasn't sure but didn't intend to wait to find out. His free hand grasped the door handle, pulled, and shoved it open to pound into the officer at an impossible speed. Enough power was put into it to make him drop his flashlight and sprawl awkwardly, stunned and shaken.

Shouting issued from the vehicle behind them as he stepped out, his weapon already in his hand. He didn't feel good about killing police officers, but when it was kill or be killed, he had no other choice.

A second man stepped out of the vehicle, his radio already in his hand and the other hand on his weapon, but the operative tracked his target carefully. With the suit, it was easier to aim and remain steady as he fired three of the needles at the man's hand. They all but shredded the radio and rendered it ineffective. Another two shots disabled him when they punched through his kneecaps and felled him before he could even bring his weapon to bear.

Movement indicated another figure inside the police cruiser, and Savage didn't wait for his target to present himself. He sprinted to the vehicle and peered into the back seat where a man huddled as he whispered furtively into his radio.

"Shit," he snapped, punched his gauntleted fist through the glass, and smoothly dragged the unfortunate man out by his collar. The radio fell with a clatter and he stamped on it to render it thoroughly out of commission. He hammered his fist into his jaw. The officer went slack and his eyes rolled up.

Savage hoped he hadn't killed him, but there was no time to check. He swung his weapon and delivered a couple of shots to the radio inside the vehicle before he turned to see the first officer he'd stunned with the car door push slowly to his feet.

"Don't do it, man," he warned and aimed his weapon at his opponent, who stared at him with a hint of disbelief in his eyes as if he tried to understand what had happened.

"You know I have to," he responded as he tightened his jaw and slid his hand to the pistol at his hip. "It's my job."

"Yeah, I know." He took the last few steps between them as the officer drew his weapon from the holster. It was a fairly quick draw and it would have had him dead to rights if he hadn't worn the suit. As it was, though, tonight was not a good night to be a member of the Brussels police force.

He caught the pistol by the barrel as it turned on him and felt the slider jump back when the trigger was pulled out of reflex. The bullet rocketed wide of its intended target. He yanked the weapon savagely to the left and twisted it out of the man's hand before he brought his right fist in to deliver a solid punch. While he tried to hold his additional force back, a couple of ribs cracked when the blow connected with the officer's midsection. He stepped in closer, pivoted at the hips, and completed the sequence with a powerful elbow to his jaw. Another crack made him wince instinctively, but the man dropped without a sound.

Again, there was no time to check if he was still alive and no way to tell what kind of hell might descend on them. Savage moved hastily to the other side of the car, opened the door, and caught Molina with a grunt before she could topple out.

"What are you doing?" she asked as he straightened her in the seat.

"We need to find a new car," he replied, draped her arm over his shoulder again, and half-carried her away from the carnage he'd left behind.

CHAPTER TWENTY-ONE

Sal paused and flicked his sword like he tried to dislodge the blood. The fact that the blade moved three or four micrometers back and forward—about five or six thousand times per minute—was enough to clean it without effort on his part. It was one of the benefits of modern technology.

The gesture was purely reflexive, however, and there was more than enough to keep his mind occupied—like the fact that the ground shook with the heavy rhythm of something huge that strode ponderously on two legs. There were a couple of creatures that fit into those categories. He hadn't seen one of the dinosaurs in a long time, and he had occasionally thought he wanted to see another one at least once more.

While he listened intently to try to discern which of the two it might be, the rhythm changed slightly to indicate two, rather than the one he'd previously heard, and his mind did a full one-eighty.

"Fuck," he snapped and whirled to where Madigan was already prepping the heavier artillery her suit had to offer.

"Are you thinking what I'm thinking?" she asked, her posture tense but not stressed. "What am I saying? Of course you are."

"Wait, what?" he asked and looked around as she moved forward. "Anja, do you still have eyes on our location?"

"Sal?" she answered, but the connection had weakened considerably now from the Zoo interference. They were used to it when they went into the jungle but it seemed out of place in what had once been a bastion of human civilization. He had been happy to know that the base didn't have the same level of interference and had been relatively free of it, but he supposed he should have known it wouldn't last.

Of all the times to lose comms, though. He shook his head irritably and forced his thoughts onto the impending battle. The dinosaurs began to advance with earsplitting roars that his auditory filters caught only barely in time. Despite their intervention, he was still unable to hear anything but a dull ringing for a few seconds.

Madigan moved forward to engage the creatures and expected him to join her while the team hung back and continued with a half-hearted effort to free the Hammerheads. Most of their time and energy was focused on defending against the monsters that continued to attack.

He hated missions like these.

"Sal," Anja called as he thrust forward to run support for Madigan. "I'm having trouble keeping comms with you guys and so is Connie."

That was alarming news. The only reason they'd been

able to fend the attacks off this long was because the vehi-cles had played an active role in both defense and offense. It would be slightly less problematic for him since he now moved beyond the defensive perimeter they'd created in what he assumed was Madigan's attempt to improvise a strategy against the massive beasts that drew ever closer. The team, however, would be far more vulnerable than they had been thus far.

"She'll copy...a patch to the vehicles' software, which should help...keep you all defended." The hacker's voice crackled and stuttered a great deal but she managed to convey the important detail. Connie had copied a section of her defensive programming to the Hammerheads but this patch would hopefully enable them to maintain the defenses even when the outer comms went down—a hint of good news in a situation that seemed set to go downhill fast.

They would need to keep the good news coming.

Madigan's plan appeared to be relatively simple—draw the mutants toward the trees or perhaps one of the build-ings nearby, which would enable her to use the launchers on her shoulders to collapse it on top of them. Unfortu-nately, it seemed he had to be the bait to entice the crea-tures into the kill zones.

"It's about time we start using drones to do this work," Sal muttered as he sprinted to the area Madigan gestured toward as the prime location to position the dinos for her attack. It would have worked better if he still had an HUD. That would have allowed her to mark it accurately, but they would need to improvise. Sal raced as quickly as he could across the space and allowed his extra arms to eliminate the other creatures in his path while he dispatched a few with his sword. His partner selected a position that would give her a clear line of fire on the building she wanted to drop on the monsters.

He removed the assault rifle from his extra hand and allowed it to take the sword from his fingers, disconnect it from its power source to end the vibrations, and slide it into the scabbard on his back. Without hesitation, he pulled the trigger on the weapon and fired at one of the dinos that appeared to prefer to keep its distance from the fight.

This wasn't that uncommon, of course. They often allowed the other beasts to launch massed attacks before they involved themselves. It had been documented previously and a few fights had revealed that the larger creatures didn't even participate at all. Instead, it was almost like they were overseeing the actions of lesser beasts.

It hinted vaguely at some kind of social structure among the Zoo animals, and he was curious as to the implications that arose from the thought. Did this involve a kind of semi-sentience?

That wouldn't be the craziest thing he'd seen from this place, he had to admit.

One of the gargantuan mutants lumbered forward and roared in annoyance as the comparatively small bullets pestered it more than inflicted real injury. It could see him out in the open where he now turned to fend off a horde of the creatures that assumed because he was alone and out in the open, he was an easy target. They were rapidly educated as to the error of their ways.

The few that attacked were dispatched hastily when the

dinos began to advance on his position in earnest. Watching something that would dwarf an elephant in size —something that had haunted his nightmares since the single time he'd watched Jurassic Park—bearing down on him was one hell of an adrenaline rush. Their enormous fangs were at least the size of the sword he was so proud of being able to use and merely added to the crazy surge of fear that was, nevertheless, tinged with exhilaration.

"Mistakes were made," he whispered and resisted the urge to run the fuck away. He stood his ground while he hoped and prayed that Madigan wasn't too busy fighting animals on her own to be in time to launch the rockets on her shoulder the plan required.

Thankfully, that particular fear proved groundless. The first of the monsters stepped into the killing ground and the whomp and hiss of one of her rockets was immediately followed by two more.

Now, his problem was to get the fuck out of Dodge. He launched into motion, moved as quickly as his legs could carry him, and handed the assault rifle to one of the automated arms as he ran. A locust blundered into his path and he drew his sword again to hack it in half.

The first of Madigan's missiles impacted with a powerful whump that signified a shattering building. The explosive debris bombarded a colossus until the heavy weight of the building landed on its back. It thrashed and bones cracked beneath the rubble as another roar split the air.

Sal stopped and located the second monster that had come to a halt. Whether the one that had fallen was dead or not, the second appeared less than willing to attack. It turned and lumbered away in the direction it had come from with ground-shaking steps.

"Well...what?" Madigan asked, another rocket already prepared for the second creature. "Where the hell is he going?"

"Do you want me to go and ask him?" Sal asked and jogged to where pieces of the prefab building still shifted and settled, dusty and crumbling, on the huge pile of wreckage. Nothing appeared to move beneath it all, where the creature was almost completely buried. A few parts of it were visible here and there but it didn't move at all.

Still, it was best not to leave anything to chance. He shoved a couple of jagged fragments out of the way until he had a clear view of the skull before he pushed the blade down. The bone resisted somewhat but he was able to deliver the coup de grace without difficulty while carefully avoiding the blue sac of fluid at the base of its skull. They were already dealing with a pissed-off jungle and there was no point in making things worse.

The second mutant displayed no reaction to him executing its kin but had stopped its shambling retreat at the place where it had stood before he'd initially opened fire to entice them into the kill zone. It stood its ground, motionless but still menacing like it was defending something. There was only one "something" he could think of that it might be protecting, and they already knew the monster of his personal nightmares was somewhere around there.

"Madigan, I have an idea that might get us out of here," Sal called as she returned from her position above him.

"Will I like it?" she asked, although she already knew the answer.

"I doubt it," he answered quickly. "Do you have any phosphorus grenades?"

"What grenades?"

"Incendiaries," he clarified and sounded like he was at the edge of his patience as they began to inch closer to the enormous beast. The other animals appeared to be avoiding them and instead, focused their attacks on the team defending the Hammerheads. They possibly assumed they would be able to eliminate the stragglers once their vehicles were destroyed.

"Oh, right," Madigan snapped, retrieved a couple of the devices from her belt, and slapped the first into the barrel under her assault rifle. He took a cautious step forward while she entered the trajectory into her HUD and aimed the first of the grenades. It launched with a hissed whoosh and exploded when it reached its arc to coat the ground in blinding white fire he could smell from over a hundred yards away.

Unfortunately, it looked like she had overshot the tentacle monster and its dino bodyguard by fifty yards or so. They were only able to see that once the burning phosphorus drove the green mist away, at least for the most part. He had almost forgotten what the air felt, smelled, and tasted without that damn stuff in it.

Thankfully, with their target now visible, she loaded the second grenade and launched it in seconds as he began to sprint toward the monster.

The air filled with the acrid smell of burning when the flames erupted directly on target. Exactly like it had the last time when Savage fired the ordnance in Chernobyl, as the fire began to eat into the mutant, it severed its connection with the beasts around it.

Behind them, the team was quick to respond and attack in earnest as soon as the link was shattered and their adversaries appeared to mill and hesitate in confusion. The tentacles that had threaded insidiously through the area recoiled quickly in the beast's attempt to extinguish the fire.

The biggest problem, of course, was that the dino no longer held its position beside the burning mutant but now stampeded toward him with grim intent to kill.

"Go!" Madigan yelled. "I'll take care of the dinosaur. You get rid of the bad hentai nightmare."

Good plan. Sal spun into action and hacked and slashed through the appendages that writhed and flailed in their frantic attempts to put the blaze out. They would succeed in a few minutes, interestingly enough. Even though the flames were apparently capable of searing through the flesh, enough of the tentacles had returned that they did a good job of smothering the fire.

The smell of cooking and burning flesh almost made him gag. It was simply another of the innumerable times he wished his helmet was still intact, but that was low on the priority list.

He thrust forward and tried not to breathe deeply since the air around him was now full of smoke instead of green mist. The convergence of the massed appendages provided a good indication of where the creature's body was, and he sliced methodically through the veritable forest of mutant limbs that surrounded him. The fires were almost quenched by the time he reached the squat hulk that was his target.

It was a great deal larger than the one they'd run into in Chernobyl. That was the first thought that came to Sal's mind when he encountered the fleshy, chunky center of the beast. The second was that hundreds of mouths leered from the ghastly green flesh, and it appeared that the sickly mist was seeping between the lips.

Well, that answers the question of where the fog comes from.

"Dammit, and that fucking gross shit got in my mouth." He gasped and tried not to gag when he stepped in closer. With the fires all but extinguished, if he didn't annihilate it in the next few minutes, the mutant would be able to initiate its mental manipulation. And the bigger the creature, the more powerful the control, he assumed.

He definitely would not wait to find out.

Spurred on by his determination to avoid a repeat of the worst experience of his life, he raised his weapon and swung it hard at the creature. The flesh peeled away beneath the blade's rapid vibration. Green blood gushed from the incision and flowed hard and strong. He yanked his weapon back and slashed again and again to inflict one massive wound after another. Dimly, as if from far away, he heard someone screaming.

It seemed to take forever for him to realize that it was him.

CHAPTER TWENTY-TWO

He really shouldn't have been surprised to see what was deep inside the terrifying mutant. What felt like minutes of hacking at the flesh was more satisfying than he would have thought, and it was difficult to stop. He did, though. Sal wasn't too far gone—hopefully.

With a gasped breath, he sucked in the mist and smoke-filled air and it seemed like the purest he'd ever enjoyed, mainly because it felt good to have oxygen in his lungs after his endless screams. Unfortunately, he still felt slightly lightheaded.

What was inside, though, was essentially par for the course when it came to Zoo shit. Most of the other huge monsters in the Zoo had it, and his guess had always been that it was what allowed them to exist and flaunt all the laws of nature and physics. The huge blue sacs of fluid similar to what was pressed out of the Pita flowers bulged and throbbed inside the creature.

At that point, it looked like the beast was dead. The tentacles still moved, shivering and shuddering like they went through their death throes. He didn't want to leave that up to the fates, though, and was only too familiar with how effective the healing powers of the goop were. There was no way in hell he wanted to deal with a creature that could remember him hacking into it.

He gagged again at the terrifyingly foul smell the corpse emitted and tugged a couple of the sacs from where they were connected to the monster. With deft motions, he severed the veins that drew the goop from the sacs—or perhaps filled them, or maybe both. He would run tests later. For now, though, it was time to kill a tentacle monster—or make sure it was thoroughly dead.

Once he'd set the sacs aside at what he judged was a safe distance, he returned and retrieved two grenades from his pouch, yanked the pins, lobbed them into the holes he'd cut into the creature, and retreated hastily. The muted thuds of the explosives as they detonated were almost a disappointment, but this was quickly alleviated when the mutant turned inside out and its guts spilled onto the base's damaged street.

It was disgusting, but Sal could see an effect similar to that of pulling a Pita plant out by the roots. Simply put, they had a few seconds before the entire Zoo descended on them in a murderous rage that would make their last attack seem like it was conducted by angry children.

Sal whirled and raced to where Madigan still held her ground. The dino was dead but the other animals showed signs of aggressive agitation and began to attack in larger numbers.

He drew his sword again and sliced through a couple of creatures that resembled rats mixed with centipedes.

Dozens of feet scrabbled and churned the asphalt as they stalked toward Madigan and barely noticed his approach before they were slashed in half.

"Let's get out of here," he yelled as he hastily stored the goop sacs in sealed containers and shoved them in his pack. She nodded and tossed a couple of grenades to clear the way to the Hammerheads. He could even see the trees beginning to move, the motion crumbling and rending the buildings that were still in place on the base.

"Something tells me that if we don't get clear of this place, we might have to walk all the way home," she said as she fell in beside him in a determined sprint toward the vehicles.

"Is that your common sense?" he asked. "Or maybe your inner Captain Obvious?"

"It's weird how you think it's a good idea to tease a woman who has all kinds of ways to tear you at least fifteen new ones," she pointed out. He merely grinned, secure in the knowledge that she wouldn't waste any bullets on him. They already faced real problems of bullet rationing if they were forced to remain there any longer.

Sal was quick to slash the tentacles that were still wound onto the wheels of the Hammerhead. Unlike before, they were now thoroughly dead although they'd locked into place, and others didn't replace those he removed. While the gross visual display of the creature's end was enough to satisfy him, he rather liked this additional indication that it was dead.

"We need to get out of here now!" he yelled at the team as he severed the last of the vines with relative ease. None of them argued since it appeared the trees had begun to ease in to cut off their escape. He wasn't sure if it was merely his eyes playing tricks on him or if the massive trunks really did move, but now wasn't the time to pause and watch what they were doing.

While the team scrambled into their vehicles, beaten and battered, he vaulted onto the roof of the one that lacked defensive capabilities. He guided two of his arms to lock onto the sides and hold him in place, much like he activated the magnets on his boots for the same purpose.

He handed the assault rifle to one of the arms and held his sword in the other so he could both hack and fire at any of the mutants that came close enough. Connie—or whatever had transferred from her before all comms with the outside went down—maintained an ongoing assault and cleared their adversaries from the way ahead as they made a hard drive to the outside of the base.

One last push was all they needed. Sal couldn't help the thundering of his heart as hundreds of animals attacked them from all sides, including above and below. Sweat beaded on the inside of his suit and his muscles burned as he struggled to focus on the fight. He was exhausted—like he'd been there for days and they could only now consider the idea that they might make it out of this alive.

He wasn't even sure how many people they still had to count on. A couple of teammates leaned out of their vehicles and joined the fight. Gregor clambered onto the roof of the lead Hammerhead. He fired consistently and managed to keep the path open ahead of them despite the trees that had begun to close in on the last stretch.

When they pulled out into the bright sunlight, Sal couldn't resist the urge to drag in a deep breath. He sucked in air that was clear of the green mist, which had begun to dissipate with the death of the tentacle monster. They moved away from the base and the last trails of fog and the beasts gradually abandoned their attack. By the time the beaten and battered Hammerheads crested the first dune, there were no more mutants to deal with.

"Holy fuck," Sal gasped and leaned back on the arms that propped him securely on top of the vehicle. He tried to brace for the shuddering and shaky ride that lay ahead and keyed the comms system with his chin. It was still active, and Anja responded quickly.

"Sal, is that you?" the Russian woman asked.

"You're damn right it's me." He laughed. "We're out."

"All out," Madigan added with a whoop. "No casualties. We're headed home, baby."

"I'll see you when you get here," the hacker said and leaned back in her seat, loving the low creak that came from her chair. The weirdness of Madigan calling her "baby" over the comms—or maybe she had called Sal that, although she'd never actually heard the name exchanged between the two before—was overwhelmed by the sensation of relief that washed over her. The team was out. The survivors were out, safe, and heading home. A quick check on the satellite imaging told her they were, in fact, completely in the clear.

"Something's wrong with the connection I left in the Hammerheads," Connie pointed out. "There is corrupted data in there which makes it a problem to bring it back into the mothership."

"I'm sure you'll find a way," Anja said and closed her eyes. It had been a stressful day. So far, of course. It was only midday and who knew what lay ahead? The team would need to return to the base to clean off the green residue she was sure they were covered in, which meant they would be busy for the next couple of hours in decontamination. That wasn't a terrible thing, to be honest. She couldn't shake the feeling that she had forgotten something she needed to get done before they reached the US base.

Oh, right.

She keyed into the secure commlink she'd set up a couple of days before when they negotiated with the Russians for Heavy Metal's intervention.

"I'm here to report that your people are alive and out of the base," she said in her native language as another feed came online. She masked her voice, although there was no way to hide who it was on either side of the line. They were professionals like that.

"I have to admit, I am pleasantly surprised to hear that," her contact replied through a voice modulator. "Although we really shouldn't forget about the second half of our arrangement."

"Don't worry," Anja grumbled. "The pieces are already falling into place for that to work itself out."

"Oh, I don't worry." A menacing chuckle punctuated the calm statement. "I have people for that. I look forward to concluding our business together soon. Until then, I must bid you farewell."

"Asshat," she muttered in English as she disconnected

the line. Instead of turning the commlink off, though, she passed it to one of the lines she kept open in Philadelphia and called Anderson. The man's GPS said he was already home. No, wait…still home. Time zones were a bitch.

"Anja," he said and sounded like he'd just woken up. "How can I help you?"

"I wanted to let you know that things are wrapping up satisfactorily here in the Zoo and… Well, we're still waiting for Savage to check in from Brussels, but it looks like he'll accomplish his part of the plan," she said cheerfully while she tried to calculate what time it was in Philadelphia.

It couldn't be that early, right? Oh, maybe it was the weekend and he was having a sleep in. She felt a little bad for calling him. "It's funny. Savage is something of a celebrity there right now. How are things going with you guys?"

"Everything's peaceful around here, considering," Anderson said. He called up some video footage of the security cameras that had been installed in the apartment they were still using, which displayed Ivy and Sam having a chat over coffee in the living room while Terry and Damon played a video game.

"Well, isn't that the best kind of change of pace?" she chuckled. "I'll let you know about any changes to the situation. And make sure to let Sam and Terry know they have been missed."

"And let their egos get too big to handle?" The former colonel laughed. "I don't think so. You have a good one, Anja."

"Yeah," she said as the line went dead. "A good one."

CHAPTER TWENTY-THREE

"Stop moving, you big baby." Savage growled and made no effort to hide his impatience.

"You have the tact of a...something known for lacking in tact, I guess," Molina snapped in return and winced when he bandaged her injuries once he'd cleaned them thoroughly. Between making their escape from both the Russian safe house and the cops, it had taken them a while to reach their safe house where they could finally lick their wounds and recover.

The operative looked battered and bruised, but the armor had absorbed the brunt of the damage. It would need repairs but he would be all right for the most part. He would be aching and stiff for a while, though. Molina, on the other hand, had a variety of cuts and scrapes that could easily become infected, given the time it had taken for them to eventually get them cleaned and treated. From the looks of it, there didn't seem to be any telltale signs of infection. It didn't help that the woman flinched every time he touched her, though.

"Very witty," he replied, tried to ignore the distraction of the blue veins, and dabbed rubbing alcohol over the tweezers he used to pluck tiny slivers of glass from her wounds. "You need to stay still. Otherwise, we could start the bleeding again."

"Be a little gentler," she complained, and he sighed and drew a deep breath. He did want to add a scathing retort, but the fact that she was dressed in nothing but her underwear was a little distracting.

"I'm being as gentle as I can," he said and kept his voice low as he leaned in and used the sterilized tweezers to pluck the last few shards out of her wound before he wiped it with a damp cotton swab. After donning a pair of surgical gloves that had been in the bathroom, he applied antibiotic cream over the last of the wounds in need of care and completed the treatment with a bandage of gauze affixed with paper tape.

"Well, I can see why you became a soldier and not a doctor," she grumbled and inspected the bandages.

"I've had some training in first aid as special forces usually do," he said, removed the gloves, and tossed them in the trash can he'd brought over and used to discard the various other items needed to attend to her wounds. "You never know when you'll need to treat yourself or one of your team when you're too far away from medical help. You can be thankful you didn't need any stitches. I've had to do wounds of my own, and while it was effective, it wasn't pretty."

She chuckled and rolled her shoulders to ease the inevitable stiffness that would most likely have begun to sneak in. "Well, I guess we should consider ourselves lucky that I heal quickly, then. Otherwise, I might have had to try your hand at stitching. As it is, I don't think any of these will even leave a scar."

With skin like hers, having something like a scar would be tantamount to a crime, but he had no inclination to admit that out loud and simply pushed up from his seat without a response. He was minus his shirt since the ice pack pressed against his shoulder needed space and moved to the mirror in the room to trace his fingers over the bruises that had begun to appear on his torso. It had been a tough fight with Solodkov, as evidenced by the fact that the bruises were still dark and puffy and spread painfully across his skin.

"I kind of wish you would agree to take some of the blue stuff," Molina said as she stepped behind him to remove the ice pack from the strap that held it in place. She turned to move away to return it to the freezer, but not before she trailed her fingers lightly over the numbed skin. "That way, you would have been half the way to healed from this ugliness already."

Savage nodded. Normally, he would have disagreed with her on principle, but as it stood, he needed rest. They'd been up for most of the evening due to their somewhat circuitous route back and there was no energy in him to maintain the feud with the woman. He could resume once they'd both had some rest and a bite to eat.

She returned from the freezer with another ice pack and slid it gently into place, showing the tact she'd complained he lacked as she adjusted the strap on his shoulder. Once again, she ran her fingers lightly over his bare skin and lingered longer than she needed to.

He caught her hand by the wrist as it trailed down his back to his hip, just shy of going too low, and turned quickly to face her.

"Don't," he warned simply but found himself unable to pull away from her. She sensed his hesitation and eased closer. He was taller than she was, which forced her to look up at him as the hand he hadn't caught traversed his bare chest, gently enough to leave a tingling sensation rushing from his skin and down his spine. "Just...don't."

"Why?" she asked, and he realized it was a good question and lacked an answer he could provide quickly. "Hate me all you like, Savage, but you do know I'm attracted to you. I've made no secret of it, and despite your dislike of me, I sense some attraction from you too."

Savage wished that he could say something to the contrary, but she was right. He still hated her guts but he wasn't too puritanical to say that he couldn't also be physically attracted to her at the same time. There was a weird connection, but it was there.

"So, what say you?" she whispered and leaned in close enough to let him feel her hot breath on his skin. "Do you feel like satisfying these carnal urges that come to us after we've been through tough times together?"

She made another good point and at that moment, he lost the inclination to listen to her. He didn't feel like talking either and he moved his hands up her sides. The decision had been made and all he could do was go with the flow. He touched her carefully and avoided her bandages as she tilted her head to look at him. When he stooped to catch her lips in a hungry kiss, a soft moan turned to a growl and he put his bruised muscles through more work to lift her by the hips and hold her in place. Her legs twined around his waist and he walked them to the bed while she returned the kiss enthusiastically and raked her nails over his bare skin.

Yeah, maybe not the best decision you ever made.

But also not the worst, he decided with a chuckle while he enjoyed the lukewarm stream of the shower he'd stepped into afterward. She'd taken a shower first, even though she'd extended an invitation for them to clean up together. Despite the hopeful look in her eye, he had declined and preferred to spend time on his own after what had happened.

He didn't intend to justify it with any emotional connection or even berate himself for it. What had transpired between them could not be changed and honestly, it felt like they'd both needed it. Considerable tension had to be worked through, and while it wasn't all gone by any stretch of the imagination, the interlude would provide them something of a respite for a while.

They had both needed to get it out in the open. Besides, while he had been far from his best, it was still a satisfying experience. He was tempted to find out if there was any sexual advantage to taking blue stuff since it had reached the point where he had almost literally held on for dear life.

If nothing else, it begged further investigation, he thought, stepped out of the shower, and dried himself quickly before he headed into the room with the towel draped around his waist.

Molina was still nude, draped across the bed and propped against the headboard while she toyed lightly with the newly applied bandages. She smiled when she saw him leave the bathroom, tilted her head, and patted the bed beside her. He shrugged and joined her, letting the woman lay her head on his chest and trace her fingers idly over his skin.

"It's probably not the most pressing issue right now," he said and broke the silence between them, which prompted her to angle her head to look him in the eye. "But why are we watching the news?"

"I was alerted by my people in Prague to something breaking on the news circuit that might interest us," she replied and increased the volume using the remote. It didn't help since he still couldn't speak French, but the images displayed on the flat screen were telling enough and yes, he had to admit, it was interesting. They played what looked like dashcam footage from the police cruiser that had pulled them over, along with a couple of other perspectives—traffic cameras and the like. Savage wondered if Anja had been a little too busy covering their tracks with the Russians to be able to do her regular work of making sure any footage out there was quickly expunged.

The video showed him knocking the cops around—the first with the door, the second with his pistol, and the third dragged out of the car and punched into unconsciousness. The first man was handled quickly as well when he tried to recover, and Savage helped Molina out of the car before they hurried out of view.

"Will people around here be looking for us now?" he asked. "Do we need to lay low?"

"The newscasters say that there was no clear view of either of our faces," she replied, her head still resting on his chest. "The cops are still in the hospital, so they haven't been able to give an accurate description of your face. But you're not wrong and we should get out of here as quickly as possible before the police and the Russians locate our trail."

"Agreed." He nodded and leaned back. His muscles immediately began to relax and the need to sleep threatened to overcome him. They could make good their escape once they'd had some rest, right? There was no need to rush into things.

There was one thing that did tick him off a little, though, and he narrowed his eyes at the TV. "I could be wrong, but it sounds like they're calling me by name, over and over again. Do they have my name?"

"No." She laughed. "It's a happy coincidence. They started calling the attacks savage—or *sauvage*—and they decided to roll with it. They now use it as a nickname for you—like a superhero moniker, or maybe a supervillain, in this case. It means savage, in French. The adjective, not the noun."

"Yeah, I got that." He snorted and shook his head as he allowed himself to relax once more and his eyelids began to droop and drag him into a much-needed sleep. The issue was one he'd need to discuss with Anja. He wasn't sure what the woman could do about images that were already transmitted across the national news, but he wouldn't doubt her abilities now.

Then again, there was the possibility that this was all her fault, he thought. It did seem like her kind of a joke.

But there would be time for that later. For now, he assumed Molina's first choice for their location to run away to would be the Zoo. She would no doubt insist on going there to collect the data he had helped Anja to transmit. The woman was likely still pissed that he'd undermined her efforts like that, and she would simply have no choice but to head out there to claim it. That notwithstanding, she had to understand that he had merely followed orders. Not hers, but orders nonetheless.

Maybe that would be enough to piss her off, he thought and stroked her hair absently as he drifted off. It would be a long couple of days, and there wasn't any point in dwelling on what would happen later on.

Besides, this whole him turning viral on the news had to be some kind of message from Anja. It felt intentional, and he simply wasn't sure what she was trying to tell him.

He'd have to ask when they reached the Zoo.

CHAPTER TWENTY-FOUR

Returning to the compound took far longer than expected and most of the day was spent getting those who needed medical attention to the hospital. This was delayed even more by the fact that they all needed to go through the quarantine procedures to clean the residue from their armor and the Hammerheads they'd used. They needed extensive scouring and given that the battered vehicles had barely managed to reach the US base, it would be a long time before they were battle-ready.

It would be a while before they were ready for even regular, day-to-day driving, which meant they needed to rent some of the vehicles at the base. No one was happy about that, honestly. That said, those who didn't stay behind for proper medical attention were more than willing to use the underdeveloped vehicles as long as they made it to the compound in the shortest possible time.

Sal was one of those who wanted to head back, although the fact that he had survived the mist intact complicated things. He fielded the inevitable curiosity with vague responses and considerable acting skill to convey the impression that he was too shaken and exhausted to even think about it.

Not that he could blame anyone. All the others who had encountered it without armor to protect them had their skin effectively melted off, after all. He did have a few theories regarding that. Most involved the fact that he had been taking the blue stuff himself, which might have rendered him immune like the Zoo monsters had been, but Courtney would run a couple of tests when they got back.

The plan was to return to the compound to start running those tests, and he would be subjected to a few that focused on the residue they had collected. Others would investigate the sacs of fluid that had been harvested from the hopefully still dead tentacle monster.

They needed to decide on a better name for the creature. Unfortunately, he hadn't been able to collect any new data on it since his HUD had been thoroughly destroyed when he'd landed head-first in a nearby building. They would have to work off the data they'd collected in Chernobyl as well as whatever he could recall of the inner workings of the critter he'd hacked into. In all fairness, he didn't remember much since he had been rather...enthusiastic at the time and that had swamped his scientific interest.

Simply arriving home was enough to make him think about putting all tests and studies off until they'd all had some rest. Anja was there to greet them with a hug, even those she didn't know. The Russians, including Gregor and Alexei, had remained with their fellow countrymen.

"Are you sure you don't want a ride to the base?"

JUSTICE COMES DUE

Madigan asked as they headed toward the kitchen in their little compound. "Might you want to hang out with your people and make sure they're all okay?"

"Well, given that my people tried to kill me for the simple act of trying to uncover the shit the FSB has been doing and releasing it on the Internet, I think I'm good here." The hacker chuckled and poured coffee for herself as the team settled in the common area. "Don't get me wrong, I'm glad they're alive and sad that so many of them didn't make it. But at the same time, I think it's fair to want to keep my distance."

"Totally fair," Sal agreed with a soft chuckle. "They needed medical attention, although most of them only needed it to treat the effects of oxygen deprivation and malnutrition during the time they were stuck under-ground. Only a few of them sustained wounds during the fighting and none were exposed to the green mist stuff, which—again—we still need to find something to counteract."

"Given that it didn't affect you, shouldn't we synthesize something from your skin or blood?" Madigan asked.

"I think it's a little more complex than that," he said but scowled when he saw Courtney enter the room from one of the labs, toting the tools she needed to collect the necessary samples.

"Well, we need to start somewhere, anyway," she said with a grin and brandished the equipment menacingly under his nose. "I'll need samples from you."

"The kind that need a cup and a dirty magazine?" Anja asked with mock innocence.

"Well, I don't think he'd need a magazine with me around." Courtney grinned and bit her bottom lip.

"Ew, and gross." The hacker shuddered. "I think that's my cue to leave. I have shit to work out with what's coming here tomorrow—which might include Savage and Elena Molina, so there's considerable work to do. You guys...uh, do whatever you have to do. You are all nasty is what I'm saying."

Sal shook his head as the Russian headed to the safety of her server room. There was a ton of work to deal with before tomorrow came. If Savage and Molina were coming, they had any number of things to arrange first.

Which meant a long night of sleep would probably have to be relegated to the distant future somewhere. He was already starting to miss the vacation period.

"Oh, and Sal?" Anja called over the intercom. "You have a transmission from the commandant waiting for you. Do you want me to tell him you're not around?"

"He knows I'm here by now," he said with a sigh. "Put him through."

"I'm starting to feel like your secretary," she growled disgustedly as his commlink came alive with the call. It reminded him that he needed to make repairs to his suit once it was cleared from the quarantine.

"Dr. Jacobs," the commandant said and sounded less than pleased, although he still tried to keep a civil tone. "It's good to hear you and your team are back and doing good work. I'm trying to confirm the reason why I'm suddenly looking at the papers for the treatment of a group of Russians who were supposed to have been written off as dead—by their own government, no less."

"Oh, yeah," he said and rubbed the bridge of his nose. "As it turns out, their deaths were greatly exaggerated. You can probably expect a call from the Russian authorities to thank you for your efforts in saving their people any minute now."

"Huh, really?" The man grunted, a sound that could have been either irritation or anticipation. "Well...I suppose... Would they be calling now?"

"Well, on the off chance that they are, I wouldn't want to keep you on the line and make them wait," he said. His thinly veiled attempt to manipulate his caller into hanging up succeeded and, after a few more seconds of bluster about someplace where he needed to be and people he needed to see first, he hung up.

It hadn't been a lie. The official story would be that the American base had mounted the rescue operation. It was a part of their deal with the Russians, which wasn't a terrible thing. Heavy Metal would be mentioned and included in the mission reports, but the story would be that it was a mission that was jointly approved by the Russian and American militaries, which allowed them to make a show of working together.

Sal shook his head as Courtney returned to the lab, apparently thinking she could get her samples another time, which meant that maybe he would have the chance to grab a nap. He moved away from the common room and all but ran up the half-flight of stairs to his bedroom.

He yanked his shirt off and tossed it into the corner of the room he'd reserved for dirty laundry since he'd appropriated the space, then dropped on his bed as Madigan entered to join him.

She came over to the queen-sized bed and lay down beside him, wound her arms around his shoulders, and drew him closer to her. He popped one eye open. "Are you sure you don't want to go back to your room? You keep telling me you have trouble snoozing with someone in the bed with you. Unless you're exhausted, or...boned dry, I think was the term you used at one point."

She chuckled. "Well, I'm exhausted right now but I wanted to check on you and see how you were holding up."

"Surprisingly well, considering," he said, leaned into her embrace, and played idly with her dark hair as she shifted slightly to nuzzle his neck. "We have some very interesting new additions to our collection from the Zoo, what with the new data on the tentacle monster, plus new pita flowers, and a couple of huger than usual sacs of blue fluid we need to study before we send them off to be sold for what I can only assume will be an impressive commission."

"Why aren't you working on that now then?" she asked. She propped herself on her elbow and traced her fingers lightly over his chest as if to outline nonsensical symbols on his skin. Or maybe she was merely practicing signing her name. He couldn't tell. She had terrible handwriting skills.

"Well, given that none of us had that much sleep last night and with a stressful day like today under our belts, I'm too tired," he said. "I don't do good work when I'm tired, so I don't think there's any harm in getting rest before I dive into it."

"Right." She grunted and tilted her head to look at him. "But that's not the only thing that's bothering you."

Sal shrugged and smiled when her wandering fingers

began to tickle. Unlike most other folks, he liked being tickled. That probably came with not being particularly ticklish.

"Well, I think you know I haven't...licked Madie for a while," he explained. "Not since Chernobyl, anyway."

"I seem to recall you using your tongue on me quite a few times since then," she joked and leaned in to place a light kiss on his stomach. "The last time being not that long ago, as I recall."

He grinned. "Well, yes, true, but come on. I'm being serious here."

"Sorry." She apologized quickly. "Carry on."

"Anyway, I haven't exposed myself to the blue stuff for a while and I guess the biggest surprise is the...lack of a reaction," he continued and scowled at the ceiling. "There's been no sign of withdrawal and no indication that my body has even tried to go back to the condition it was in before I started self-medicating."

"Given that it probably saved you from having your face melted off, I think we can thank our lucky stars for that," she pointed out. "I think Davis might want to be in your shoes in that case."

"True enough," he conceded. "But you remember what happened in Chernobyl. The way the monster was able to communicate with me and connect with my mind like that."

"Do you remember anything about what it tried to say?" Madigan asked curiously.

"Not really." He tried to concentrate and recall the details. "It's a weird thing—like my senses were over-whelmed by the sudden influx of data. It seemed like the bridge between us went both ways, but I didn't understand most of what I received, and my mind therefore simply discarded everything except for a couple of snippets of memories. I'm convinced those belonged to the humans who were already fully under its control.

"Anyway, that's not the point. The point is...well, we managed to avoid a repeat of that by giving the monster a fire shower before I jumped in this time around, but there's no guarantee that I'll be able to do that again. It might catch us by surprise the next time we run into one of them, and I'll be rendered helpless again. That's not an experience I look forward to repeating."

She nodded. "I get that, believe me. I remember watching you go limp in that lab, and it might have been the most terrified I've ever been. I'm used to seeing you able to handle yourself. For the most part, anyway. You still need me out there, watching your ass and making sure your curiosity doesn't get you killed. But...yeah, seeing that happen... I felt helpless in there, and I don't want you to ever go through something like that again."

Sal nodded, looked at her, and clasped her hand in his. "I appreciate that. I hope you know how much I appreciate it."

"Of course, Sal," she whispered but avoided his gaze. "I care about you and your health. And while I admit that I'm...ahem, appreciative of the changes, I don't want them to continue if they're detrimental to your health."

He nodded and took a deep breath as he tangled his fingers with hers. Spending time with her like this was more relaxing than a nap would have been.

"Besides," she continued after a brief pause, "we have

what Savage collected from the Russians. With Anja going through that, we might be able to find some way to reverse the process of what happened to your body. Eventually."

"Yeah, I guess. She probably has bigger problems than that right now, but I'll talk to her later and see what was collected by the Russians. It was all the result of human testing and will forever be tainted by that, but—"

"You're going to say something about how the results are there and if we simply toss them out of the window, that would waste the lives of the people who died?" Madigan challenged and raised an eyebrow when his voice trailed off.

"Yeah," he admitted. "Am I a bad person?"

"Maybe on some level, but that's not the point here." She laughed. "Using the data doesn't necessarily make you a bad person, in my opinion. But I do tend to be more… utilitarian than moralistic about this kind of shit. I'm the kind of person who thinks that if you're dying of hunger, how painful the animal's death was doesn't matter. Am I a bad person?"

"Yeah, but that's not the point here." Sal grinned and broke away when he heard the door open. Courtney entered and closed it behind her, lacking the scientific tools she'd been toting before.

And clothes, he realized.

"Is this a good time to get those samples from you, Sal?" she asked, undid her bra, and tossed it onto his pile of clothes.

"It's as good a time as any." Madigan grinned as the other woman joined them on the bed.

CHAPTER TWENTY-FIVE

"You know, I never thought I would ever set foot anywhere near the Zoo," Molina commented, her gaze fixed on the desert they currently flew over. "Honestly, I've spent my whole life avoiding dangerous places like these and simply sent others—people like you—to do and die for what I have to admit is a massive amount of money. When you know you won't have to pay out on half the claims, you can put the citations through the roof."

"I have the feeling you expect some kind of reaction from me," Savage replied. He sat across from her and sipped the coffee that had been provided to them with their breakfast in the air.

"I feel like I've earned some kind of reaction," she admitted as she added a small bottle of whiskey to her coffee before drinking it. "Something like...being impressed with my business acumen, or maybe you're a little disgusted by how little effort I put into saving the lives of the people in my employ. I seem to recall that being something of a sensitive issue—for Anderson and Monroe, anyway, as well as the other people who fight with them. Heavy Metal and those types. Although, of course, I am well aware of the fact that you aren't the kind of person they are, so I'm not sure what the reaction will be. I do still expect one, though."

He shrugged carelessly. "I've come to expect shit like this from people like you. I've come to expect some kind of reaction like being aghast as to your failings as a human being from the folks at Heavy Metal, with some icy fury from Anderson and Monroe. For myself, though…I have to say I've seen the best and the worst of humans. I've traipsed along the edges of good and evil for long enough that your pragmatism simply no longer shocks me. People die, shit happens, and when you get right down to it, deaths are only a statistic and life goes on."

She tilted her head and narrowed her eyes at him. "If that is the case, then why do you hate me so much? If all I'm doing is pragmatic and therefore not shocking to you as you claim."

"Because you targeted my family." He scowled, and his entire demeanor changed.

"I never—" she started to say, but he was quick to cut her off.

"Or you enabled those who did, same difference," he interrupted. "When it comes right down to it, I understand the why of it all, but simply because I understand doesn't mean I condone it. And when there are so few things in the world you care about, you tend to get a little tetchy when someone tries to fuck with them. Shoot, kill, and torture me. That'll never be something personal. Go after my wife and kid, and I will hate you with the passion of a thousand suns."

"Ex-wife," she reminded him.

"Ex...wife, yeah," Savage conceded. "The hatred still stands."

"Careful, you don't want to make me jealous, Savage," she said and sounded like she was only half-kidding.

"Try me," he snapped in a similar tone as the plane began its descent toward the landing strip of the American base. It was a quick and smooth landing, although it did appear that there were numerous others landing at around the same time. He had never been to this particular base and, as he began to disembark, he could tell it was nothing like the others in which he had spent most of his time while in the armed forces.

Because, for starters, it looked like most of the landing craft sported Russian markings.

"What the fuck is going on here?" Savage asked and studied the amount of decidedly non-American activity that took place openly in what was supposed to be an American facility. He held his hand instinctively on the weapon he carried inside his coat. He'd had to send his half-suit to Philly for repairs as Bev and Amanda were still there on vacation. While it had been appreciated and he looked forward to using it again, he also didn't want to damage it beyond repair, which would leave him without the suit for possibly months.

For now, Amanda had said that maybe a couple of days of work would get it back into fighting condition. While he would be without it for this particular mission, the chances were good that it would be ready again when he returned to Philly.

If he returned to Philly. Savage's gaze was drawn inexorably toward the mass of green on the horizon that lurked in a sliver above the partially built wall. It looked like a premonition of bad things to come and he couldn't help wondering who had thought it was a good idea to build a base so fucking close to the jungle in the first place.

No, wait. When they'd first built the facility, it was far enough away to seem safe and the jungle had merely continued to grow, which explained the walls they were erecting to contain it. These loomed in the distance to either side like silent sentinels, even taller at the section where the base proper was located.

They had to think about moving the base farther away from the wall, though, he decided—maybe even beyond Wall Three if they ever got around to building it. No one would feel safe in a place that was as close to a hundred kinds of death and mayhem as the Zoo was reported to be, Savage not the least of them.

As they began to walk away from the plane, which would refuel quickly and immediately leave, a couple of Hammerheads churned slowly toward them. He recognized the design of the vehicles, although they hadn't been the ones he usually used back in the day. Even so, they were enough to elicit a slight sense of nostalgia in him as both came to a halt not ten yards away from where the duo waited.

Courtney stepped out of one, dressed in jeans, boots, and a t-shirt that was a little too big for her. Her blonde hair was swept into a messy bun and she wore a pair of thick glasses. She looked like she didn't anticipate any kind of trouble and was simply there to pick them up and take them to the compound Savage had learned they owned. It made sense, if they were starting out on their own, not to have to depend on the less than reliable military powers in the area, especially when they didn't look like they knew how to build a damn base right. Where were the defenses?

If Monroe didn't expect any trouble there, someone else—Savage was willing to bet on Molina—expected nothing but. The group of eight or so that exited the second Hammerhead appeared to be ready for a trip into the Zoo themselves. They wore full combat armor, complete with assault rifles and grenade launchers, and one of them even had a miniature Gatling gun mounted on his shoulder.

Monroe looked surprised at the arrival of the group and raised an eyebrow as she looked at the newcomers.

"I'm...here to drive you two out to the compound?" she said and finished her statement with emphasis on the unspoken question—*who the fuck are these guys?*

"Well, I hope you don't take it the wrong way, but I had my people reach out to a handful of mercenaries here on base," Molina explained and moved in to lightly shake the hand of the apparent leader of the group. "It's not that I don't trust you but...yes, I don't trust you. Savage has, on more than one occasion, acted on someone else's orders, not my own, and that leaves me with no other choice than to ensure that my investment pays off."

Monroe shrugged in an off-hand way. "Whatever helps you sleep at night. Will you ride with them or with me?"

"With them," the other woman answered.

"Fantastic." Her response carried an undisguised edge of sarcasm and she shook her head. "Savage, get in with me. You guys can follow me to the compound. Make sure to keep up, though, since I drive fast and I won't wait for anyone."

"Understood." The merc leader nodded and gestured for his team to mount up again, with Molina following them. Savage joined Monroe in the shotgun seat and breathed a sigh of relief as the air-conditioning turned on quickly. The vehicles in his day didn't have such luxuries, but he supposed they could be afforded when you were as rich as Monroe was.

"Her bringing mercs into the equation," he said after they'd driven for a few minutes in silence and were now clear of the base. "Do you think that changes anything?" They followed a two-lane road that stretched on into the desert and away from the Zoo, thankfully.

"We had word that she'd put feelers out for guns to have on her side last night," his companion explained. She hadn't been kidding about driving fast and not waiting for anyone. He could see she had initially left the other vehicle in the dust, although they eventually increased speed and began to catch up. "Anja suspected it would happen, and she left feelers out. Her suspicions were correct. On top of that, Molina's 'people'"—she implied the quotes since both her hands were busy holding the speeding Hammerhead on the road—"made sure it was clear to anyone who wanted to join the mission that they should expect trouble. Based on that, I assume it's safe to say they'll not simply be there for intimidation purposes. We might be looking at her trying to kill us even if things are resolved peacefully."

"And...that doesn't change anything?" Savage reiterated his question. He'd been with or near the woman ever since they'd escaped the Russian safehouse together, which begged the question of when she had managed to get these orders out. Sure, she had her people, but... Then he recalled that he'd been in the shower, she'd mentioned to him after that they had told her about his inclusion in the news. A window of opportunity, he realized.

"Oh, it changes everything." Monroe nodded. "Thanks to Anja's efforts and forward-thinking, though, we've had time during the night and early hours of the morning to implement those changes, so everything should be ready to welcome Molina into the Heavy Metal compound."

"Fun times." He grunted, leaned back in his seat, and allowed himself to relax a little. It had been a stressful few days, but when had things not been stressful while in Monroe and Anderson's employ? The hacker had filled him in on the details surrounding his family, both those he was related to and those he wasn't.

His ex and their daughter were still having their home surveilled by the police and also by Anja. Sam and Terry were in Philly, still recovering while keeping an eye on Anderson and his family. With Molina as busy as she was running around Europe with Savage, it appeared that she wouldn't give them much trouble in the near future.

The drive lasted about forty-five minutes, with little conversation shared between Savage and Monroe. The two knew each other well enough that the silence wasn't uncomfortable, at least on his part. Besides, he was too busy reaching into the cold, dark part inside himself and pulling it into the forefront of his mind. His soft and gooey side had been out in the open for far too long, and it was time for that other part to have its day in the blazing Sahara sun.

Once they drew into the compound, they dismounted from the Hammerhead and he scrutinized the surroundings carefully. The Heavy Metal enclave looked better defended than the American base they'd left behind. It was considerably smaller, of course, but he could see a group of towers rising from the prefab walls that formed the perimeter. These looked strong enough to have someone on top of them, but they were mostly there for the detection devices—motion sensors and the like—and each boasted weaponry that could repel an attack. They must have some kind of AI running the defenses, he assumed.

While it was smaller than the base they had left behind, it somehow felt a good deal safer.

The second Hammerhead moved through the gates and into the open area in front of what looked like the main building. As it came to a halt, the top of the vehicle opened to allow the merc who wore the Gatling suit Savage had noticed before to emerge and drag a heavy machine gun with him. He mounted it to the top and positioned himself in the gunner's position. The men had come prepared for a fight, all right.

That particular weapon was more than capable of transforming any combat suit into a Swiss cheese impersonator.

The other mercs dismounted quickly and fanned out around the vehicle to assume defensive formations. Elena was the last to emerge. She still didn't have any weapons of her own but her combat prowess, even without a suit, was enough to ensure that she couldn't be discounted.

The first indication that the Heavy Metal team had prepared for something like this was when the machine guns mounted on the defensive towers—which were supposed to aim out at any potential attackers—suddenly activated and swiveled to aim inside the perimeter.

"The shit's about to go down." Savage growled and immediately drew the needle gun in his holster and primed it. The doors of what looked like a cross between a garage and a warehouse were pulled open and what he imagined was the full Heavy Metal team stepped out, also ready for a fight in full combat armor and armed to the teeth.

It was an impressive sight to see Madigan stride forward in the tank of a suit she was known to wear. Courtney walked over to them and gestured for Savage to follow as Sal stepped through the team in a six-armed hybrid suit, a sword in one hand and an assault rifle in the other. He handed the rifle to Courtney, who quickly adjusted for the weight of the weapon and checked to make sure she was ready for a fight too.

A handful of others made seven armed and armored Heavy Metal fighters ranged against Molina's mercs, along with Savage, Courtney, and whoever controlled the weapons in the towers.

The newcomers were suddenly very aware that they were outnumbered and outgunned, which was only made worse when a man stepped out of the main building. He chewed on an apple and lacked any combat gear. Solodkov was very much alive and while he did look a little the worse for wear, he most definitely was not dead.

Savage knew as much, of course, having pretended to knock him out of the fight in Brussels with a concussive round that was designed to destroy the facemask but nothing more. Still, he was surprised to see the man was already in the trenches again. He would have assumed he would be laid out in a hospital bed for a while.

It was a blow to his ego, as he'd thought he'd done a little better in the fight against the man in the safehouse, but it didn't matter.

Molina looked shocked to see the Russian alive and well for about a second, but she processed the new information quickly and sent Savage a sour look before she retreated behind her hired guns. "What's going on here, Solodkov?"

"Well, I would have thought it was fairly obvious," the Russian said and remained well away from where the fighting looked imminent. "I made a deal with Heavy Metal to work with them exclusively in the Zoo in exchange for killing you, among other conditions on both sides. Many negotiations were involved, and Heavy Metal does drive a hard bargain, but I think it will be profitable for all parties concerned."

"Why?" Molina asked and sounded like she might be stalling for time. "Why not simply kill me in Europe?"

"Killing a billionaire philanthropist like you requires that some hoops be jumped through," Solodkov explained and moved casually toward the building. "As desperate as you were for the data in our servers, you were willing to move away from a continent where your death would have resulted in a hundred different investigations. This way, you willingly entered an area known for unexpected deaths. Here, we can deal with you and blame it on the Zoo."

Molina turned to look at Savage, who already aimed the needle weapon at her. "This was your idea, I take it?"

"Interestingly enough, no." He chuckled. "I'm only along for the ride."

CHAPTER TWENTY-SIX

Savage was the first to move. His gaze had caught a hint of motion from the guns on the towers. He liked his pistol, but he was painfully aware that he had the least armor and firepower of the group that had assembled. Solodkov, the only one who had less, was already disappearing inside the main building from where he would have the benefit of cover to work with. He, unfortunately, had nothing, unless he counted his teammates' suits. While he could use them as meat shields, that would be a dick move on his part.

Besides, what did they expect him to do in this fight, anyway?

The guns on the towers were the first to fire and erupted in a coordinated burst that eliminated the merc who manned the turret on top of their Hammerhead. The shooting was a little too accurate to be the work of a human. Only AIs could shoot that accurately these days, and it had taken the man's head apart to the point where there was only the top of his suit left.

Interestingly enough, something happened with the

313

suit that turned the machine gun it still held to aim at the group positioned around the vehicle. He guessed it was one of Anja's tricks, maybe, or perhaps it was merely dumb luck. A volley from the machine gun punched through the armor of a couple of the Molina team and killed them almost instantly.

The Heavy Metal team opened fire as one and used the initial moment of distraction to launch a barrage at the mercs, who bolted away from the vehicle and tried to discern why they were under fire from all sides.

Savage wondered if Molina wouldn't have been better off recruiting the higher caliber men and women around the area. Then again, it seemed that Heavy Metal were the ones that attracted the best and brightest and left the dregs for the less successful ventures or newcomers like her.

It certainly explained her difficulties when she'd targeted them in the past.

He had been the first on the draw and had managed to fire his needles with the soft whine of his pistol the only sound that could be heard. Seconds later, it was easily drowned out in the cacophony that escalated within seconds. He flung himself to the side to avoid the vicious exchange of bullets, remained low, and crawled slowly away from the battle, although he paused now and then to add a couple of shots of his own.

He stopped abruptly when a booted foot collided with his ribs, hard enough that he was forced into a fetal position. Another kick landed on the side of his head and stars drifted across his vision as he tried to roll away to avoid another kick. He was only partially successful, and the third strike caught his shoulder.

It was obvious who it was. If he'd been kicked by one of the mercs in combat suits, most of his bones would have already broken. He'd be laid up in the hospital for months.

As it was, Molina merely tried to exact some kind of revenge before she faced her inevitable demise. He was still alive, thankfully, and also in a reasonable fighting condition.

He continued his roll and shoved onto his hands and knees barely in time to block a powerful knee aimed at his nose. While he managed to catch it with his hands, the impact jarred all the way to his elbows and launched him upward to thump painfully on his back.

"Do you think you can cross me like this and merely walk away?" Molina shrieked as she tried to straddle his midsection and was hastily kicked away. The woman was strong—too strong and unnaturally so. It could only be the blue stuff she was taking. He'd talked to Sal about something like that before.

"Honestly, yeah," Savage said and looked around as she gathered her strength for another attack. The first kick had knocked his pistol out of his hands, but it couldn't have gone far. Sure enough, it hadn't and was only a few feet away from him. Molina surged forward again, screaming something in what sounded like French as she shoved his legs aside and landed a punch to his chin, powerful enough to spawn a myriad of tiny little lights in his vision.

He amended his initial summation. The bitch was impossibly strong.

Instinct clicked in and he jerked his head out of the path of the next strike. A sharp crack preceded a scream when her fist connected with the hard ground. If he ever had a chance, it was now.

His legs, still unencumbered, moved quickly to twine around her body like an anaconda as he rotated his body upward and pushed himself into the lock. He grasped her injured hand and twisted it savagely as his legs wrapped around her shoulders to complete the triangle armbar. She writhed and grunted with the effort to free herself, but he held her in place with one hand as the other stretched to grasp his pistol.

He wouldn't be able to hold her for too long but thankfully, he didn't have to. She stopped her struggling when the steel barrel of his weapon pressed against her temple.

"So, do you think I'll get away with it?" Savage asked and grinned while he panted for breath. "Did you ever think I would forgive and forget what you've done and what you're responsible for?"

She rolled her eyes and offered a token effort to escape the armbar. "Shoot me and spare me your moralistic bullcrap."

"I won't kill you, bitch." He snarled dismissively, released his hold on her, and shoved her onto her stomach as he held his weapon trained on her.

"Not yet, anyway," he added.

"Jacobs!" Molina shouted and glared at him from where she had made no effort to push off her stomach. Jacobs, Kennedy, and Monroe moved to where Molina was now captive. "What did you find? Did you...find something that could help us with our unique problem? You have to tell me."

"Sorry, Elena," he replied and inspected his sword casually before he slid it into its sheath. "But telling you anything about that would break some fairly binding deals I made with Mr. Solodkov."

Savage looked into his eyes, and he could swear that there was a hint of a gleam when he said that.

"Are you not telling me because you plan to keep me alive?" she asked with the tiniest trace of hope in her voice.

"Sorry." Kennedy growled in protest as she stepped forward. "But you're too dangerous to be left alive. You'd merely abuse the use of any treatment that came your way and endanger the lives of the people around you."

"Like he does?" the other woman asked with a meaningful glance at Sal.

"Maybe," the man replied with a nod. "But at least I have things and people I care about enough to pull myself back from the edge when I get too close."

"You're goddamn right." Monroe grinned and patted him on the shoulder.

Molina glowered at them. Her mercs had been disabled with ruthless efficiency. Those who weren't dead had already surrendered and were on their knees and their weapons cast aside. The Heavy Metal fighters were already disarming their suits but suddenly stepped aside with an alacrity that made the Heavy Metal team stiffen and look for potential danger. The weapon on top of the attacker's Hammerhead swung and immediately opened fire on the prisoners.

"Connie!" Anja yelled. "What the fuck?"

"It was necessary," the AI responded calmly.

"Godammit. You can't fucking shoot people after

they've surrendered. You should have at least asked. Jeez, you stupid fucking—"

"This is exactly the reason why I didn't ask. I am tasked with protecting this compound and all those in it. Those meat bags cannot be trusted. They are what you call bottom-feeders, and would inevitably have mouthed off about what happened here."

"Yes, but—"

"I can understand why you'd be upset," Connie said soothingly. "I, fortunately, do not have the moral dilemmas humans struggle with. I identified a valid threat and took the necessary steps to eliminate it."

"Jesus fucking Christ." Madigan looked absolutely livid. "I suppose we should at least be grateful that you warned our team to get the fuck out of the way." She rubbed a hand over her face. "Shit. Next time, you stupid, cold-blooded bitch, you talk to us first."

"Yeah, Connie," Sal said firmly. He was shaken but saw the need to step in. "We work as a team here. You are part of that. Don't ever do something like that again."

"Well, if you feel that strongly—"

"I do, Connie. Fuck. Enough already."

The three of them turned to walk away but Savage remained where he was, the needle gun pressed to the back of Molina's head, and waited for the order. He was an attack dog, sure, but he was a well-trained one.

"Finish her!" Monroe called over her shoulder. He didn't think twice. It had been the only reason he'd agreed to this whole mission, after all. He pulled the trigger once, twice, and three times to make sure the woman would not get up. They couldn't take any chances, not with someone like her who had taken that much goop.

He rubbed his ribs as he walked away from the body and looked up as Solodkov walked over to him, two beers in hand. He gave him one and the operative popped the cap. They clinked the glass bottles together and raised them to celebrate the death of Elena Molina.

"It has been a pleasure working with you again, my friend," the Russian said after they'd given the woman her due moment of silence. "Although I have to say, I am surprised they call you Savage, now. Isn't that the nickname we had for you when you trained with us in Siberia?"

"Oh, right." He smirked. "I'd completely forgotten about that."

"Sure, you did." Solodkov chuckled and downed the beer, of which only half was left since it appeared he'd been drinking during the fight. He turned to face the Heavy Metal leaders. "I have to say, I look forward to working with the three of you in the coming months, but if you will excuse me, I have to deal with the arrival of a large force sent to retake our base. You don't mind dealing with the bodies, do you?"

"Would it matter if we did?" Kennedy grumbled.

"Not really." He grinned and strolled to the Hammerhead he'd used to get to the compound. *"Dasvidaniya!"*

CHAPTER TWENTY-SEVEN

It would be a long flight over the Atlantic to Philly but thankfully, they didn't have to do it in the cargo hold of a military aircraft. Monroe had pulled her magic strings to secure them a private jet—probably the last one they would see for a while—that would take them all the way.

Of course, the flight wasn't meant for him. They merely took advantage of the fact that Amanda and Bev needed a return flight to the Zoo and Davis needed one to Philly. The fact that Savage needed a flight too was merely a happy coincidence. He certainly didn't complain.

The plane had landed and was refueling, and the two women had already disembarked. Both looked like they had enjoyed their time away from the death jungle. He could only sympathize. He'd been there for a couple of days, recovering and hanging out with Anja for the most part, and the ever-looming danger of having the Zoo this close was stressful. It was no secret that he would be happy to return to the land where people were free to shoot him as long as he was free to shoot them too. That particular scenario was far more relaxing.

"Amanda," Monroe said and greeted the woman with a warm hug. "It's nice to have you back, girl! How was Philly?"

"Cold as a *puta's* tits," the armorer admitted with a chuckle. "Which honestly makes it a nice change of pace from this fucking place. Still, I'm glad to be back where I don't have to wear three layers of clothing to go outside."

"That'll change in a while, I promise you." Monroe grinned. "I don't want to swamp you this early, but we do need work done on the Hammerheads after what happened, and you're the only one I trust to handle them."

"You're a wise woman," Amanda replied and smirked. "But I won't work on them at the compound. I don't think I can handle more of Connie's bullshit."

"Well, the fact that she might have transferred some of her programming into the Hammerheads might be a downside to that," the other woman confessed as the two of them turned to walk to where Savage stood beside Davis' wheelchair. "It's a corrupted version, though, so maybe she'll be a little nicer."

"Yeah, keep dreaming." The woman rolled her eyes. She had already taken the job and was merely bitching to be able to up her contract price. While she was friends with Courtney, she still had a business to run. She extended her fist to Savage, bumped his, and the two of them wrapped one another in a quick hug.

"I did some work on your suit and it should be ready for a fitting when you get back to the warehouse," she said.

"And I made improvements to the design. I don't want to spoil the surprise, but I think you'll like it, *cabrón*."

"I'm sure I will," he said and grinned broadly. He would miss having the woman around.

"Later, gang," Amanda called. Bev was already negotiating a ride to take them to the French base.

"I'll talk to you soon, Jer," Anja said and hugged Savage before he headed to the plane.

"Sooner than you think," he replied. "I still need your help to find out how to access that money I made at the casino."

"We made," she corrected him. "We split those profits fifty-fifty, and don't you forget it."

"I won't." He laughed and ruffled her short, dark hair. "Take care, you crazy Russian. Just because they've let you and Gregor off the hook doesn't mean folk won't still come after you."

"I pity the fool that tries," Gregor said and placed a hand on his arm. "Have a safe flight."

Savage nodded, and he and Davis moved toward the plane.

"Do you need help getting on board?" he asked when they reached the steps leading to the cabin.

The ex-soldier scowled at him. "You're fucking joking, right? Do I look like Bo-fucking-Jangles to you?"

"I only asked because, last I checked, the crew is very accommodating about helping the lesser abled up those steps." He grinned and punched the man in the shoulder. Davis couldn't help a smirk, knowing it was all in good fun, and they began the process of boarding.

Sal, Courtney, Madigan, Gregor, and Anja watched as the jet took off from the tarmac.

"I like that Savage fellow," Gregor said and nodded firmly. "He has spunk and fire, and he can kill people in the blink of an eye. I like that in a man."

"Are you…" Courtney started to ask and looked at the Russian, who was now a fairly permanent member of the Heavy Metal team.

"Gay?" Gregor finished her question. "Yes, I am. My wife, of course, doesn't know, but she has the credit card to keep her happy."

"Oh, boy, do I have the match for you," she replied with a gleam in her eye. "My assistant Robinson is coming back from vacation in a while, and he'll love you. He's married, though, come to think of it. Huh. Still, it's a good thought."

CHAPTER TWENTY-EIGHT

The Zoo was acting up again. What the fuck else was new?

Helicopters headed in and returned with reports of the animals attacking the walls and the construction crews as well, obviously with intent to delay the process. Too many people were involved with the construction, which meant they had to fly missions every time the civilians saw a little locust peek out from the bush to see what the hell they were doing.

That wasn't to say they wouldn't eventually end up being called for some serious interference thrown at them by the Zoo. Honestly, the bigger situations had already become more and more common these days.

"Those motherfuckers had better be dying on the walls," Bevis, the gunner, grumbled. They had been drinking the night before and were all hungover.

Still, some things simply weren't funny.

"Not even as a joke, man." Dave, the pilot, shook his head and held the helicopter steady as the group flew in formation. "Not even as a joke. They are people out there. I don't care how much your head is killing you. It's not a reason to joke about people dying."

"Who—"

"We the fuck is who cares," one of the other gunners growled. "Game faces, people. We're approaching the wall."

The choppers swept in with the coordinated efficiency that had been drilled into the teams and it was immediately apparent that the area was alive with action. They had been dispatched to support a group that had been tasked to clear the Zoo away from the walls as it had begun to expand a little too close for comfort. It had been done dozens of times before, but it looked like the Zoo had reacted rather poorly to it this time.

They continued the direct approach and a couple of the men cursed when the team noticed the trees begin to shake. It looked like a massive attack. The pilot lit up one of the locations where he could see a larger concentration of the animals. It was a little early, but they hadn't made his callsign Killer Dave for nothing. They needed to distract and entice the creatures away from the wall and the relentless attacks they attempted to maintain.

Rockets flared from the sides of the helicopter, launched into the trees, and ignited a series of explosions across the vegetation. The shockwaves rocked the massive trunks where the missiles were delivered.

"Are we shooting?" Bevis asked and looked around. "I want to shoot if we are."

"Let's do it," Dave said and grinned as the other aircraft in the formation followed his example and opened fire on the monsters that harried the group of men on the ground in massive numbers. A line of explosives traced between the wall and the jungle and the gunners tried to keep the area clear so the folks on the walls would be able to work with some peace of mind. It would also allow them to erect defenses so choppers didn't need to constantly be called in whenever someone grew twitchy about what they saw in the trees.

It wouldn't be the first time they wished they had done this much earlier. Dave honestly doubted it would be last, either. Until they bombed this whole fucking jungle to kingdom come, it would simply return for more until the creatures eventually managed to break through.

A couple of other chopper formations bunched where the animals attacked in the largest numbers to rain all kinds of ordnance on the creatures. Bodies already piled high as their group formed up around their assigned area. It was a cooperative effort between the various bases and countries, although he couldn't see any Russians at all. He didn't blame them, of course. They had their problems with the Zoo's expansion to deal with.

Something moved deeper in the jungle, and Dave narrowed his eyes to focus the HUD on his canopy. What looked like a massive gorilla covered in thick white fur with a massive horn on its head careened from the trees, leapt over the groups of soldiers on the ground, and attacked the helicopters directly. They managed to annihilate him, but it wasn't long before dozens more followed. The mutants used the towering trunks as leverage to reach the aircraft, and before they were able to pull up and out of reach, three of their choppers were pounded by the massive fists and spiraled to plummet earthward, out of control. Explosions and thick black smoke obscured the wreckages for the moment.

"Oh, we're fucked!" Bevis yelled. Thankfully, the man had the presence of mind to keep his cursing off the comms. You never knew when the brass would listen in, and they didn't appreciate that kind of language in the mission reports.

Which didn't mean he was wrong, of course. The ape creatures had them all out of formation and in disarray and forced them closer to the wall.

Two of the monsters launched from the trees and their enormous frames seemed to move both in slow motion and yet impossibly fast. Worse, they somehow found the ability to defy gravity and covered the distance between the jungle and the choppers with apparent ease.

They would ultimately latch onto the aircraft and drag them down, and God only knew what would happen when they were grounded. Things were seriously bleak when the best you could hope for was that your body was lost in the explosion and fire so the animals wouldn't be able to reach your remains.

Seconds before the creatures reached grasping range, the air around them exploded into an impossible spray of blood and white when two missiles collided with the monsters and all but obliterated them. Dave gaped in shock as a formation of Russian MI-24s swooped in to save the day. There were enough of them to annihilate the gorillas almost effortlessly and they raked the jungle in a swathe of flame to ensure the beasts couldn't continue to use the trees for their airborne attacks.

Dave, still in shock, wondered why they hadn't thought of that.

"Explosives are set," one of the engineers on the ground called to them. "Thanks for the assist guys. Over and out."

"Roger that," he replied and eased the helicopter way the hell up and away from the jungle as the others turned to return to the base. The Russians, however, banked and set a course toward the east.

"I guess they have to deal with what happened to their base there," Bevis commented, still off the mission comms.

"I wish them all the best," Dave replied and saluted the MI-24s as they shrank in the distance, barely in view.

———

Solodkov wished they hadn't asked him to come. He was the one in charge of this whole operation—a position he could thank and curse Savage for, in equal amounts. The brass whose careers and reputations depended on the operation being a success wanted someone they trusted and relied on to have boots on the ground and relay the information to them over their secure channels.

Still, all that politicking notwithstanding, it sucked. He and Savage had needed to sell that fight in Brussels to keep Molina in the dark, and the man had landed more than his fair share of blows that had left him in pain for what felt like weeks after.

To their credit, they had sold the act and would now actually reap the benefits of it, but that didn't mean he wouldn't have to suffer the effects of that damned operative's new half-suit for a long time. He was too old for this shit. There had been a good reason why he'd retired from active duty, after all.

He turned to look at the rest of the team, all decked out in the best combat armor the Russians had available for their military. They worked with a team of Spetsnaz, who were specialists in the use of the heavy armor.

"It's time to send this jungle a fucking message," he stated belligerently. Their group of attack helicopters, in impressive formation, descended on the base and unleashed a wave of hell on the jungle. There was no sign of the green mist they had been told to look out for, but they'd also been told that it came and went, so they couldn't be too careful.

The ground shuddered violently as payload after payload of explosives were launched into the jungle-infested base to carpet-bomb the entire area. With what they now did, not a single building would be left standing and they would have to rebuild the entire facility from the ground up.

Honestly, they would probably have had to do that anyway. This was merely cutting to the chase and doing what should have been done to this fucking jungle at the beginning but hadn't for some reason.

More helos approached. Some would be attack heli-copters like the ones that now leveled everything in a ten-kilometer radius. Others would bring the troops who had been temporarily stationed at the American base until this whole operation had been approved. There were soldiers and scientists galore, and the crazy kind too. They had to be since they had been told about what happened to the people who had populated the base before them and decided to come anyway.

Then again, they would need the new architects too, Solodkov thought. The flames built and the aircraft moved toward the outer edges of what had been their base—and what would hopefully be their base again.

The architects would come too but only tomorrow, along with the crews and materials needed to build the damn place again, practically from scratch.

Hours passed as the destruction continued, cleansing the area with fire and wave after wave of explosions until it looked like the memory itself had been obliterated from the earth. The choppers would work well into the night to burn the Zoo back to its original borders from before it had decided to swallow the human outpost for no particular reason.

Or maybe there was a reason and it was merely classified. Despite his level of clearance, Solodkov was under no impression that he was in the know about everything that happened, even in his own branch.

They moved into the smoldering remains and there appeared to be a couple of animals that had survived the onslaught. Teams had already headed in to place explosives in central locations. It was wise to be extra thorough with the cleansing of the area.

Again, he wondered why nobody had thought to level it for good when this whole Zoo situation started in the first place.

Well, the reason was probably because the whole operation had been run by Americans. It was nothing new to see that they lacked the guts to bomb the crap out of their own personal Frankenstein monster.

Solodkov chuckled. There was nothing better than being able to gloat with the pride that came from nationalism.

As the team pushed deeper into the base and avoided the places that were earmarked for more thorough cleansing, he couldn't help but admire the way the Zoo had resisted the leveling it had been subjected to. Even now, while most of the other plants still burned and crumbled to ash, he noticed a small plant that had survived the bombardment. It looked like a Pita plant, but it had red and blue petals instead of only blue.

"Huh." One of the other men with him grunted. "That's interesting. I've only ever seen those fucking plants with the blue petals. Do you think one of our scientists would like to take a look at that?"

"I don't doubt that they would." Solodkov chuckled, shook his head as he raised his boot over the tiny plant still clinging to life after the bombing, and crushed it underfoot. "But I'm afraid doing so would step on the toes of the agreement that was made to get those few survivors who were stuck in this miserable base out before we could legally bomb the crap out of it. I'm afraid my hands are tied."

He looked across the designated area that so many Russians had called home. It was a pile of ashes now but he could see the potential of what was to come—a base that he would be in command of.

Now that was worth exchanging blows with someone like Savage for, he thought with a chuckle.

AUTHOR NOTES -
MICHAEL ANDERLE

AUGUST 21, 2019

THANK YOU for not only reading this story but these *Author Notes* as well.

(I think I've been good with always opening with "thank you." If not, I need to edit the other *Author Notes!*)

RANDOM (*sometimes*) THOUGHTS?

So, I have had some fantastic ideas for these *Author Notes* for the last couple of days. Except, I forgot them. Figures.

OH! Here is something new! I saw the play *Kinky Boots* in Dublin with my wife, Judith, and Lynne and Marc Stiegler (thank you for treating us, Lynne!). (*Editor's note: So welcome! That was a blast and a half! Great dinner you and Judith cooked* ;) For the most part, I don't like plays. It could be that (in general) it just isn't my favorite form of entertainment except for two (2).

One is *Hamilton*. I was predisposed to enjoy that musical because Jacob and Joseph listened to the soundtrack for MONTHS, and I practically could sing many of the songs. The fact that it was good was just icing on the cake.

Although that ending! Because of the ending, I will (most likely) not see the musical again.

The OTHER of the two is *Kinky Boots* and I would absolutely be happy to go see it again. Why? Because it doesn't dawdle on the negative scenes. Even the pseudo-negative scenes are handled with care, and I enjoyed the singing. There were enough UP (happy) moments that I would look forward to watching it again.

I've never seen the movie or read the book. Lynne's husband Marc mentioned that since I've seen the musical, he doubts I could watch the movie and enjoy it without the singing.

He might be right.

(*Editor's note: For those of you who hate musicals, try the 2005 movie. It is excellent!*)

AROUND THE WORLD IN 80 DAYS

One of the interesting (at least to me) aspects of my life is the ability to work from anywhere and at any time. In the future, I hope to re-read my own *Author Notes* and remember my life as a diary entry.

Beijing, China (International Publishers meeting and Beijing Book Fair.)

So, it took about three planes, three airports, two layovers and twenty-four hours to get to Beijing for the book fair this week. My plan, once I crashed on the couch upon arrival, was to sleep.

You see, my job in the company is the English side of the products, and we are in China. Definitely not English.

(Ok, you could make an argument I had responsibility but did you see the comment about twenty-four hours? I was TIRED.)

Judith mentions that there is the International Publishers meeting downstairs and starts reading off a litany of who's who from the speakers list.

I was guilted into going.

(Not really. *Totally really*.)

That many knowledgeable people in one room, the event was just fifteen floors beneath us, and I was going to skip it?

Yeah, didn't happen. A shower later, and we went downstairs.

It was an interesting meeting. Up to, and including, when we got asked to move from the "nowhere" bleacher-type seats in the back up to the second row.

It's interesting. Last year, we had our pictures taken a lot of times (I assumed because we were two non-foreigners at the Fair, and they wanted to prove it was relevant to others to come and check it out.)

This year, it happened again. They have us move to the front, and cameramen start taking shots that make it obvious we are in the video or pictures

Now I know what Kardashians must feel like.

Ok, that's not true. At most we were in fifty shots. Kardashians might be in thousands.

FAN PRICING

$0.99 Saturdays (new LMBPN stuff) and $0.99 Wednesday (both LMBPN books and friends of LMBPN books.) Get great stuff from us and others at tantalizing prices.

Go ahead. I bet you can't read just one

Sign up here: http://lmbpn.com/email/.

HOW TO MARKET FOR BOOKS YOU LOVE

Review them so others have your thoughts, and tell friends and the dogs of your enemies (because who wants to talk to enemies?)... *Enough said ;-)*

Ad Aeternitatem,

Michael Anderle

CONNECT WITH MICHAEL TODD

Want more?

Find us On Facebook

https://www.facebook.com/Protected-by-the-Damned-193345908061855/

OTHER MICHAEL TODD BOOKS

PROTECTED BY THE DAMNED UNIVERSE

PROTECTED BY THE DAMNED*

8 Book series

WAR OF THE DAMNED*

8 Book series

DAMIAN'S CHRONICLES*

4 Book series

WAR OF THE ANGELS*

8 Book series

ZOO UNIVERSE

BIRTH OF HEAVY METAL*

10 Book series

APOCALYPSE PAUSED*

12 Book series

SOLDIER OF FAME AND FORTUNE*

12 Book series

TEAM SAVAGE *

3 Book series

Dungeon Core TV*

6 Book series

Dungeon Rails*

3 Book series

Hellspawned Chronicles*

3 Book series

The Sheva Chronicles*

6 Book series

Unlikely Bountyhunters*

6 Book series

House Drakonnen

The Accord

The Anchor's Inheritance Saga

* DENOTES COMPLETED SERIES

www.ingramcontent.com/pod-product-compliance
Lightning Source LLC
Chambersburg PA
CBHW050513110726
47899CB00005B/1446